I

THE WITCH AND THE COWBOY

Ryen Rowe

Three Dots Publishing LLC

To my parents,
for always making sure I had a horse to ride
and a book to read.

CONTENTS

CHAPTER ONE

Walker

"Loosen up, Walker," Laney begged.

I glanced up from the crackling fire I'd been staring at. It was already on its last leg, though it'd only burned for a couple hours. As per usual, Sawyer's efforts to build it were lackluster. We were lucky the moon was bright and cast the entire mountain in a soft glow. We sat in a grassy field that sprawled an acre in front of my house, next to a woodsy valley. Grass swayed easily in the breeze, and stars blanketed the sky above us. It was no wonder my mother used to call the place her pocket of peace.

Peaceful or not, I couldn't fight the shivers that seized my body.

"I'd be looser if it wasn't so damn cold," I replied.

I glared at Sawyer pointedly. He grinned at me, revealing his single crooked tooth that all the women in town found charming and pulled his girlfriend of the month, Laney, closer. She flashed him a pretty smile, and he ran his callused hand through her bleach-blonde hair.

Being a third wheel sucked.

"I'll go get more firewood," I huffed and walked toward the tree line.

I doubted they heard me over Laney's obnoxious giggles. As my boots crunched across the crisp grass, I cursed Brody for bailing on tonight's plans and leaving me alone with the two of them.

Oh, well.

It was a beautiful night, other than the chill, and it was always a good thing for me to leave the house for something other than work. I approached the forest that banked off into the valley and the river that ran through it. I listened closer and heard its familiar rush. The wind lessened under the protection of the trees, and I was finally warm under my Carhartt jacket. As I walked, the trees grew more abundant, other than where a small creek cut a path through the forest.

I'd walked alongside it, all the way to the river, many times. Partially for some peace and quiet and partially because there was little to do in a town the size of a walnut.

I found an oak tree with a couple fallen limbs nearby and grabbed some of the smaller pieces. I was tempted to forget about the wood and leave the happy couple to themselves, but I'd already told them I would bring it. I tried to make a habit of following through on promises. I sighed, reached down for one more piece, and fell flat on my face.

Might be time to slow down on the beers, I thought. I wasn't a huge drinker, but I didn't know anybody—including Sawyer—who could hang out with Laney sober.

I hauled myself off the ground and nearly fell again. I wasn't *that* drunk. The rattling of rocks drew my attention to the creekbank.

An earthquake with a stronger aftershock? I thought.

A low hum resounded through the forest and filled my ears. I couldn't even hear the river. I scrambled to my feet and searched for the source of the strange noise.

"Hello?" I called, like any dumbass in a horror movie.

I could still see the dim glow of the fire behind me, but instinct drew me deeper into the forest. I knew every creature that lurked in these woods, and none of them *hummed.*

I watched my steps more closely and avoided nearly every stray twig or crunchy leaf. The humming grew louder, until I could make out strange chanting. It was spoken in a harsh language I'd never heard before.

The chattering weaved through the trees and almost

eclipsed my thoughts. If I couldn't see that no one was there, I would've thought someone whispered the chant in my ears. Fear gripped my chest, but I couldn't stop following the sound. Curiosity, strengthened by the pull of the chant, and my own survival instincts warred against each other. I ducked behind the nearest juniper and prayed my broad form would be hidden by shadows.

I needed to get out of here. *Now.* I peeked around the tree and stifled a gasp.

Tree stumps smoldered, as did blackened grass. My gaze didn't linger there, but on the molten rock that encased a woman, all the way up to her knees. Her hands were bound in thick, copper shackles. Inscriptions blazed on the shackles, though they made about as much sense as the chant, which still hummed throughout the forest.

The woman wore a torn, black jumpsuit and a huge gash bled from her thigh. She'd bleed out in minutes with a cut like that, yet she didn't even appear afraid. Her chin was tilted with a touch of defiance, and her fiery hair cascaded freely down her back. She was unnaturally pale, which only made her coppery eyes more frightening.

She stared at someone I couldn't see. Though she barely gripped life, she sneered.

"You're finally able to best me, friend. Too bad you had to get high on the deaths of our kind to do so."

"Oh God," I whispered.

Her eyes met mine.

Run, she mouthed.

I wanted to run—every instinct in my body screamed at me to run, yet I stood as still as a statue, paralyzed by the thought. A different woman's face flashed through my mind. An older, kinder face with laugh lines and my blue eyes. A face that was ruined in the hit and run that killed her.

Though I doubted the woman trapped in the woods was old enough to be a mother, *someone* must be looking for her. Someone's world would tilt off its axis without her, all because I was too scared to help.

I couldn't leave her—I was her last hope.

I pulled my pistol from its holster and raced toward her, though I doubted the weapon would do much against whatever had crafted her trap. I kept it on me for bears and wolves, not bizarre hostage situations. The strange, musical chant grew louder with my every step.

She shook her head frantically, but I reached for a nearby rock and ignored her. I smashed the rocks that trapped her legs to no avail. Pain laced up my arm from the impact, but I hit it again and again. The woman swayed above me, and her leg brushed against my neck. Hot, sticky blood stuck to my skin. Time was running out.

Laughter twinkled behind me. I spun around, but only darkness, looming trees, and fallen pinecones greeted me.

"Silly mortal," a bodiless, feminine voice purred. "Are you going to shoot me?"

"Where are you?" I shouted. "Too scared to show your face?"

My voice was more stable than I felt. My hands shook at my sides, and my heart thundered so loudly, it almost drowned out the chant. I strained my eyes, but I couldn't even discern a silhouette among the trees.

"You're the one that's scared, mortal," the voice crooned. "I can smell it."

Nausea seized my stomach. It was no longer the desire to help that kept me in place, but the weakness of my knees.

"Settle, mortal," the voice continued, "you won't remember this anyway."

*

"Dude," Sawyer said, "where's the firewood?"

For a second, I could only stare at him in confusion, then I glanced at my empty hands. Laney paused assaulting Sawyer's neck with her tongue long enough to offer a concerned look.

"You drink too much?" she asked.

I shook my aching head. "I don't think so. I just-just need

to get home is all. It's late. I should check on Cadence."

Sawyer threw his head back dramatically, and Laney almost fell out of his lap. If I wasn't so overwhelmed by the strong urge to check on my sister, I would've laughed.

"You can't even get the firewood?" he complained.

I grew more impatient with the conversation with every passing breath.

"Get it yourself," I said and turned to walk home.

"Man, I don't get you," he called, "you've been crazy overprotective ever since—"

As I heard what he didn't say, my steps stuttered.

Ever since your mom died.

Well, Mom didn't just die. She was *killed,* and not even maliciously, but by some idiot out there who had the bright idea to drive drunk. Anything could happen to Cady—the world overflowed with idiots. My head ached with worry.

I shut off all thoughts of Sawyer and hurried home to my sister. I kept a pace that left me breathless until I finally swung open the old doors of our house, crept down the dank hall, and slipped into her room.

Moonlight pooled over Cadence's lightly tanned skin. Light brown, ram-rod straight hair fanned across her pillow. Her little face was scrunched up, like she'd eaten a sour lemon. She'd always had vivid dreams.

I sat on the edge of her frilly, pink bed, and stared at her. I couldn't stop myself. I had to assure myself she was safe, though I didn't know why. Maybe I had separation anxiety, like Sawyer said.

I couldn't remember what exactly had triggered the need to see her and every time I tried to pinpoint it, my head throbbed. I'd probably just drank too much and gotten spooked. Alcohol had the tendency to make me uneasy.

After staring at her for a few more moments, I felt like a creep and left her to her dreams. The tiny hall that led to my room needed to be swept, but at least there was minimal dust on the family photos that hung on the walls. Dad's snoring filled the space, despite his closed door. I rolled my eyes and continued to my room, which was farthest down the hall, next to Cadence's.

Unlike Cadence's ridiculously decorated room, mine had four beige walls, adorned only by some shelves and a George Strait poster. I tipped my hat at the country legend, which reminded me of how desperately I needed sleep.

I stood before the mirror on my dresser and studied myself. My features hadn't changed—my brown hair still curled under my hat, and my cheeks were still a touch too chubby to be chiseled—but my blue eyes were hollow. Something on my neck caught my attention.

It was blood. I must've cut myself on a stray branch. I thought back to what had happened in the forest. My headache worsened.

I grabbed the firewood, heard something that frightened me, and headed back to camp, right?

Right?

CHAPTER TWO

Freya

The bone was dry and brittle in my hand. It was a poor remnant of my mother. It matched my cream, lace dress. I toyed with one of the flared sleeves and swallowed. I loathed the color of death.

I'd worn far too much of it lately.

"She's in Summerland now," Josephine reminded me. "She'll return to this plane one day."

But, according to the Elders, she wouldn't return as my mother. She would be some other witch, or a flower, or maybe even a swan, but Sybil Redfern was gone. Forever.

So unfair.

I was only eighteen years old—practically a baby by a witch's standard. I wasn't meant to lose my mother yet.

I scuffed my boot against the smooth, black stone floor of Josephine's apartment. Mom never favored Josephine's more modern style. I studied the white granite countertop, and the various herbs neatly organized in glass cabinets beyond the island.

The rest of the coven enjoyed the apartments Josephine designed. Each one in the building was in use. I always admired my goddessmother's eye for sleek choices, though Mom's cozier aesthetic had always felt like home. Still, I couldn't bring myself to return to our quaint cottage. It was far too quiet without my mother's laughter to fill it.

"I can't see straight with so many clean lines," Mom would

say about Josephine's place. Like many things she said, it made little and lots of sense.

Arion rubbed against my legs in an attempt to comfort me. I petted my loyal familiar, who was currently in the body of a lovely calico. He peered at me with round, amber eyes, only a few shades lighter than my own.

"You need to let go," Josephine said gently. "It's what she would want."

Her face didn't match her words. Her dark brows scrunched over glassy, green eyes, and her usually olive skin was pale. She toyed with one of her many necklaces. Josephine tried to be strong for me, but I knew she loved Mom as much as I did. She was just trying to eat what the Elders fed us so she could feel better.

"She would want me to find who killed her—and all the other witches," I argued. "She would want me to *end* them."

Circe, Luna, Rose, Helena.

Their names rang in my head. As the future leader of our coven, I carried the weight of their deaths on my shoulders. Hecate knew it was up to me to end the deaths, considering the lousy job the Elders had done to stop it. My mother and Josephine had been the only ones to take action, and it had gotten Mom killed. I wouldn't let my goddessmother die next or any other witch.

"It was her dying wish to save us," I continued.

"And you will." Josephine smiled. "Because I found the killer. You *will* have your vengeance, dearest. I'll make sure of it."

*

Walker

Lost in the easy gait of my horse's lope, I nearly forgot about the night before and the invisible eyes I'd felt on my back ever since.

"Whoa," I said and sank into my seat.

Jesse, my horse of six years, came to a halt. Together we overlooked the rolling hills of lush trees, green grass, and trickling creeks. The rain from earlier in the morning made it all smell even fresher. A breeze sighed across the valleys and ruffled the hair under my hat.

"You know, Jess," I said. "Being a cowboy might not pay well, but it sure does have some benefits."

He snorted and shook his big yellow head, as if to say, "Like you could do anything else?"

I considered that I might talk to my horse too much and decided to get back to work. We jogged along the fence line, until I noticed how loose a couple of the wires had become.

When I reached the broken remnants of the wires, I cursed under my breath and climbed off Jesse. Using some tools and spare wire I stored in my saddle bag, I quickly mended the fence. Jesse nibbled grass behind me without a care in the world.

I walked to his side and put my left foot in the stirrup. When I had swung myself halfway on, Jesse shot out from under me and nearly dumped me on my ass.

"Whoa, boy," I ordered and squeezed my reins.

He spun around and turned a wild, blue eye to the fence I'd just fixed. I almost didn't believe my eyes. The same wires were cleanly cut in two pieces.

"What the hell?" I wondered.

After several minutes of calming Jesse down, I climbed off and fixed the wires. Again. My hands shook the entire time, which made the process even longer, much to Jesse's discomfort. I worried about what could cause such a reaction from him. Grumpy and moody were definitely in his wheelhouse, but not skittish.

The next time I climbed on, he stood patiently. I hoped that meant he'd recovered from whatever frightened him and, frankly, me. I thought about what could've caused it, but my mind came up empty. The harder I tried to consider it, the less clear the truth became.

I pushed the thoughts aside and figured I probably just wasn't as good at fixing fences as I liked to believe. The ride back to the main barn was peaceful. The fresh air steadied me, as did the familiar sights of rolling hills and green forestry.

Cows grazed and ambled about their business. The sun peeked through trees and warmed my skin. A gentle breeze tousled my hair but didn't blow violently enough to toss off my brown hat.

As I reached the main barn, I had finally convinced myself that everything was fine—until I noticed the *open* gate that had once held the cows meant to go to the sale tomorrow.

The pen was now empty.

I face-palmed myself and turned Jesse around. I couldn't believe I hadn't noticed the extra fifty cows in the larger pasture. I wasn't one to miss such a big detail, nor had I ever failed to lock a gate. I prayed I could corral the cattle once more before Nathan noticed.

I doubted the old man would fire me. I'd worked for him since I was fourteen years old and made much bigger mistakes in the last five years.

Doesn't mean I'll get out of stall-cleaning duty.

"Walker!" a gruff, familiar voice called. "What the hell is going on here?"

I groaned and turned Jesse around. Nathan charged down the hill so quickly, I worried he might take a tumble. On top of the hill, the barn's metal roof glowed from the slowly setting Sun. Already, the temperatures dropped. If I didn't get those cattle soon, I'd be working in the bitter night's cold and have a hell of a lot harder job on my hands.

When Nathan finally reached me, I got off my horse. His rants were always lengthier if he didn't get the satisfaction of peering down at me when he gave them.

"I just can't find decent help anymore," Nathan grumbled.

He crossed his behemoth arms over his unnaturally broad chest and prattled on about how I was more trouble than I was worth. The lines of his aged face were even harsher than usual from his scowl. We stood in the gateway of the empty cow pen for more than five minutes. I was shocked the old man had enough breath in his body to talk for so long.

"Hey, boss," Sawyer called from up the hill, near the main barn. "Maybe you ought to let him go catch the damned things, then continue? That way, you get two gripe-fests instead of one."

While Nathan grumbled to himself, I mouthed, "thank you" to Sawyer. He winked at me, though I had to squint to see him clearly. The Sun drooped even lower on the horizon. Before Nathan could continue, I hopped on Jesse and took off for the cows. Sawyer climbed on his own horse and followed me.

Just like that, our fight from the other night was forgotten.

"Thanks, man," I said. "You really saved my ass back there."

Our horses jogged alongside each other. Sawyer's mare, Rosy, was a burly thing with a temper, but Sawyer cared for her like most people did their children. I'd always thought that was why girls fell so easily for him—they assumed they'd get treated as well as his horse. They were wrong.

At least he has girlfriends, I thought. It was more than I could say for myself.

"No problem," he said with an easy grin. "That's just the kind of friend I am. Are you all right, though? It isn't like you to do dumb shit."

"Yeah," I replied. "Sorry for stealing *your* thing."

*

Freya

He was the most mundane witch hunter I'd ever seen, not that I'd seen many. I just assumed his day would consist of more than mucking out stalls, fixing fences, and hunting down cattle. Admittedly, I was the cause of two of those problems.

I stood among the trees of the huge pasture and carefully avoided piles of cow dung. The hunter chatted casually with his friend and searched for the cattle I'd released. I finally ended my Invisibility spell. I needed him to find the cattle so his friend would leave. I hadn't expected something like *him* to have friends.

The pair laughed at something I couldn't hear. His ease had to be an act. Surely, he knew I hunted him by now. He must've sensed my magic earlier but wanted to face me without bystanders, like his disgruntled boss and obnoxious friend. Though I wasn't particularly fond of them, and I hated to oblige *his* wishes, I didn't kill innocents, nor did I risk exposure. It was better to let the fear sink into the hunter anyway. It would make his death so much sweeter.

Arion purred at my side. He always enjoyed hunts even more than me, but this time was different. The stakes were higher, and the punishment—the one I would deal—was far greater than ever before.

I eased my mind with three steady breaths. With each one, I focused more on my surroundings and the potential magic I could shape to my will. Crisp, dry air burned my throat, and water gurgled in a nearby stream. Dahlias swayed in the wind, as did the tree branches high above my head.

"Magic is everywhere," Mom used to say. "That's why you must always be observant—know where and how you can get it."

Not all natural magic was my forte, but luckily, I could manipulate air without a second thought and draw power from earth to craft a mean spell. Mom hadn't finished my training in fire or water before she—

Before she was killed.

Josephine, my second greatest mentor, had told me to stop saying that.

"Witches can't be killed," she had reminded me. "They can only be transformed."

But screw that. I wasn't going to sugarcoat reality with the pretty language the Elders crafted.

My mother was dead. Gone. Ripped from me all because some foolish hunter decided to pick up his family's business once again. Josephine had explained it all to me. The Reids had long ago given up their family dynasty of killing witches in a peace treaty with my coven, until their youngest son broke that peace. His jacket, which he wore even now, was stained by my own mother's blood.

I'd been shocked to learn he was responsible. We'd gone to school together since we were young. He was well-liked and well-mannered. He'd always seemed so innocuous, but I knew plenty of monsters who hid behind pretty faces and polite smiles.

His laugh echoed through the valley, and I saw red.

Three deep breaths.

One...two...three.

He would die tonight.

CHAPTER THREE

Walker

Two hours and fifty cattle later, we were done. I triple-checked the gate, then walked Jesse to the barn. When I slid off, my legs were numb stumps. The temperatures had dropped with the Sun, and my breath fogged the air. With Sawyer and his mare beside me, I creaked open the barn's large, wooden doors. The rest of the horses, already tucked into clean stalls, nickered at the cold air that swept in.

"Settle down, you babies," Sawyer called.

I walked Jesse to his stall at the end of the barn and enjoyed the familiar clop of his hooves hitting padding across the matted floors. The barn was my favorite place to be. Lush valleys and breathtaking views were exciting but being surrounded by horses brought me peace. Warm lights glowed gently down the aisle that ran between two rows of five stalls. Sandwiched between stalls were the tack and feed rooms. Each had heaters for colder months.

Some quiet part of me longed for a place like this of my own. It was out of the cards, of course. I couldn't even afford our family home if not for the inheritance money from Mom's parents. Hopefully, I'd be able to hold onto it long enough to get Cadence out of the house and into college. My sister was crazy-smart. She'd secure a scholarship. I was sure of it.

I couldn't be sure of anything else.

When I turned Jesse into his stall, a shadow flickered behind me and disrupted my reverie. I nearly jumped out of my skin. Jesse lurched at my sudden movement. I cursed my jumpiness, but I couldn't place its source.

"Sorry, buddy," I said into his ear. After a few pats on the neck, he settled down.

I took off his bridle and checked that he had plenty of hay and water. I gave him one last pet and walked out of his stall.

"Walker," Sawyer huffed. "Forgetting something?"

I spun around and winced.

I'd left the damn saddle on.

Even Jesse seemed put-out with my never-ending dumb-assery. As I threw a halter on his head and tied him to the metal bars on his stall, he huffed and pinned his ears back.

"What is with you, man?" Sawyer asked and carried his saddle to the tack room.

I had no answer for him. I made quick work of untacking Jesse, wished Sawyer farewell, and headed home. The cluster that was my day was due to an overabundance of stress and not enough sleep.

It had to be, yet the shadows followed me home. I threw my hat on the dashboard and fired up my old, blue Chevy truck. Despite the exhaustion weighing down every muscle in my body, I couldn't relax.

All along the winding road that led to my house, dark figures danced in my truck's windows. They popped up left and right in the shapes of leering faces and violent actions.

One appeared directly in front of me. It was a dark sketch of a woman that I swerved to avoid and nearly careened off the road. Luckily, the shadows dissipated, though it did nothing to calm my thoroughly rattled nerves. I was not used to being so damn afraid.

I gripped the steering wheel with white knuckles and kept my eyes trained on the road. Country music blasted through the speakers, but I barely heard it past the unsteady thrumming of my heart and odd hum in my ears. I wanted to pull out my gun and start firing, but I wasn't sure what I'd shoot at. I shut down the thought of calling the police.

Hi, Sheriff, I'd like to report some shadows that are following me? No, I didn't catch their license plate. Sorry about that.

Finally, the gateway that led to my driveway appeared. Like always, the gate was wide open. This had to be some prank the guys were pulling on me. Sawyer had probably told Brody about what happened at the bonfire, and they wanted to punish me for being such a wuss. I prepared myself to deck them, then have a good laugh about it.

I passed the burned patch of grass where we'd had our bonfire. A strange tingle went down my spine at the memory, and my head throbbed. I focused instead on our quaint farmhouse. Its white paint needed a new coat, but its wraparound porch was still in shape, though it could hardly be seen in the darkness. I couldn't even glimpse my mother's old bench.

The driveway was darker than usual. The moon hung behind thick clouds, and the stars were tiny specks of dust in the sky, but that wasn't the only cause of the darkness.

My porch light was off.

It was never off. Cady *always* left it on for me.

I skirted the truck to a stop. Whatever followed me, I didn't want to face it in the house, where my little sister slept. I took a deep breath and prepared to step out of the truck. My hand lingered on my pistol, until I finally pulled it out of its holster.

Please be Brody and Sawyer, I thought. I kept the safety on in case they were the culprits, though my instincts screamed, *danger.* The shadows calmed, but I knew I wasn't alone. Something still hummed in my ears.

With one last wish for some liquid courage, I hopped out of my truck. My boots hit the gravel driveway with a crunch, but the rest of the forest was quiet. Too quiet. No animals stirred, no water rushed, and even the low hum was silenced. One small gust of wind blew my way. It smelled of honeysuckle and rain and coppery blood. Unable to bear the silence, I called out.

"Who's there?"

Three heartbeats passed.

A huge gust of wind came from the east and blew me into my truck. As I hit the metal frame, I grunted and bit my lower lip. Blood pooled in my mouth and my bones rattled from the force of the crash, but shock numbed the pain. I scrambled to right myself and searched frantically for the source of the wind or shove or whatever the hell just hit me.

"Man up!" I yelled and spat out blood. "Show yourself!"

A dark chuckle drew my eyes to the left.

"Do I look like a man?" a girl asked in a musical voice.

She stood perfectly still, dressed head to toe in black, with one manicured hand on her hip, and the other clutching her chin, as if in deep thought about the question she asked me. She couldn't have been older than me, though the rage in her strange, copper eyes aged her. Her fiery hair was as wild as her expression. Something about her was familiar, though I didn't know what. I'd certainly never seen a girl like her before.

A calico cat coiled around her legs and meowed. She peered down at him and scratched his head.

"Not yet, Arion," she purred. "This one is mine."

Surely this girl, with her small stature, pretty, freckled face, and house cat couldn't be behind my torment. Her copper eyes met mine once more.

"Boo!" she whispered.

Another gust of wind assaulted me, though this time it went for my legs. I slammed to the ground on my face. My nose took the brunt of the fall, and blood spewed from it. I ignored the blood and the throbbing pain, so I could rise to my feet. With one hand, I still clutched my pistol, but I couldn't bring myself to turn the safety off.

This is some twisted joke.

"Who are you?" I asked and winced. Already, my voice had grown nasally from the swelling in my nose. She scoffed at my question.

"As if you don't already know."

"*What* are you?" I questioned.

Her hands squeezed into fists at her sides, and a quiet

chant—familiar, though I didn't know why—fell from her lips. The dancing shadows surrounded me once more. I was wrong to think it was a dark night. *They* were darkness. The female silhouettes swallowed all the starlight.

The shadows drew closer and reached for me with taloned hands. One of them grazed my neck, and coldness like I'd never felt seeped into my skin. I waved my gun at the damned thing, and something giggled in my ear.

"I am your atonement," the girl said. I could barely see her past the shadows that closed in on me.

"For what?" I yelled, "I don't even know you!"

The shadows stuttered, but only for a moment, before they continued their slow descent upon me. More and more of them reached for me. My teeth chattered. I released the safety on my pistol.

"Lying won't save you, hunter," the girl growled. "Nothing will now."

Her words shook, but I didn't know if it was from apprehension or pure menace.

"Please," I begged. "Just don't kill me here."

She laughed humorlessly.

"You want to choose where you get to die?" she asked. *"They* didn't get to pick where you killed them."

"I didn't kill anybody!" I said.

"Then why is my mother's blood on your coat?"

My mind went to last night's fuzzy memories, and the blood that was stuck to my neck. I tried to check my coat for stains, but the shadows crept closer. If darkness could be hungry, her dark minions were. They leached the warmth from my body and the breath from my lungs.

"I-I don't know," I stammered, "but I *didn't* do it."

"Walker?" a small, all-too-familiar voice called. "What's going on?"

My heart lurched.

Cadence.

CHAPTER FOUR

Freya

Nothing made sense.

Josephine had found his blood-stained coat. When she looked for my mother last night, she realized that Mom died on the hunter's property and had a hunch that the Reid family was responsible. They hadn't been active hunters in decades, but it was too convenient for a witch to die on their land. Everyone knew Clyde Reid spent most of his days in the bottle, and the daughter was too young to be guilty.

That left Walker.

But how can a witch hunter be so defenseless?

"Walker?" a small, feminine voice called. "What's going on?"

A young girl—Cadence—stood on the porch of the house at the end of the driveway. Her brown hair was in a clump on top of her head and her pink pajamas were wrinkled. She must've come as soon as she heard the commotion.

The hunter's face crumpled.

Just don't kill me here.

"Go back inside, Cady," Walker ordered gruffly. "Everything's fine."

I dissipated my shadows. The girl was innocent. She didn't deserve to be frightened.

I wasn't even sure that Walker deserved it.

But he has to be guilty, I thought, *or else the real killer is still out there.*

"Who is that?" she asked. Her voice dripped with skepticism.

"Go back inside," he grumbled.

I drew on the life around me and muttered a quick sleeping spell under my breath. Cadence's jaw went slack, and she wandered back inside to her bed. Though it was for her own good, guilt gnawed at me. Her young mind was so easy to command.

"What did you do to her?" the hunter demanded. "What did you *do?*"

He charged me. I summoned my shadows once more, but he walked right through them. His face was pale as a ghost, and he shook from their chill, but he didn't slow down. I muttered a spell to *make* him stop. His steps stuttered, but he kept walking.

It didn't convince me he was a trained killer, but his willpower did impress me.

I could've knocked him back with a gust of wind, but I let him get closer to me, until he stood inches away. His tall frame towered over me. This close, I noticed dark circles under his eyes and stubble on his chin. The faint smell of animals still clung to his clothes.

I waited for him to throw a punch or attempt to use the gun he clenched so tightly, but he did nothing. He flexed his fist, but it stayed at his side.

"I don't know who you are," he said slowly, "but I'm not who you're looking for. I'm not a *killer.*"

I studied the desperate lines of his face, his clenched fist, and the pistol in his hand. He'd use it if I didn't tell him where his sister was, yet he didn't throw a punch now. I'd done nothing but terrorize him, yet he showed me mercy. Even if he did attempt physical force, it only further proved he was no trained witch hunter. My mother wouldn't have died at an amateur's hands.

I believed him.

"Your sister is safe," I assured. "She's just sleeping."

I knew it was what he most wanted to hear because it was what I most wanted to hear when Josephine had returned from her search for my mother.

"But *you* are not safe—that's not a threat," I explained. "You've been deemed a witch killer. Others will come for you."

My words weren't a bluff. The rest of my coven wouldn't give him a chance to explain, nor they would stretch out his death as I had intended to. Even if he were innocent, none of them would shed a tear over a Reid's death. His very blood robbed him of his innocence—I could've killed him and been celebrated for it.

But I was so very sick of death.

"W-witch?" Walker stuttered.

"What do you think I am?" I asked. "A mermaid?"

"Yeah," he huffed and glanced at my hair. "I thought Ariel sent an army of shadows after me."

He ran a hand through his curls and laughed humorlessly.

"This is insane," he breathed. "Witches aren't real."

I tried to be patient with him, but we didn't have much time for processing. I'd exposed my kind. Even if his family had ties to the magical world, Walker hadn't known about us, and I should've kept it that way or killed him.

Our only shot at survival was to find the real killer and clear both our names. Then, Walker's memory of us could be wiped clean, and he could go back to the normal life he clearly belonged in.

Maybe he needed further proof that wouldn't scare him.

I lifted my hands, and fallen leaves beneath our feet mirrored the motion. With a tiny bit of wind, I twirled them around me. Walker's eyes grew as large as saucers, and his jaw went slack.

"We *are* real," I said, "and someone has been killing us. The first remain was found last night."

"It belonged to your mother?" he asked softly.

I wasn't sure if the sympathy on his face made me want to yell or cry, so I kept my response short.

"Yes."

"I'm sorry for your loss," he said.

"Thank you."

I meant what I said. The sentiment felt so much more real than *you'll see her again* or *be grateful she's transcended this life.* I didn't care if it made me a bad witch. I was tired of sugarcoating my grief.

"I know someone who can help us," I said, "but we must go to her quickly. I won't let another witch die."

"Walker?" a familiar, childish voice yelled.

Impossible, I thought. I lowered my hands, and the leaves drifted to the ground.

Cadence walked down the steps of her home and eyed me wearily. Her eyes shouldn't have been open at all. The spell I'd cast was meant to last at least two hours. As she ventured closer, her emerald green eyes caught me off-guard. I'd never seen such a bright color outside of the Moonflower family—a *witch* family.

Maybe the Reids had gotten their hands on some witch magic over the years, and it still protected their descendants. It wouldn't be the first time hunters used our own power—the power they deemed unholy—against us.

Leaves and twigs stuck to the girl's pink pajamas, but it didn't slow her down.

"Cady." Walker sighed. "I'm just talking to a friend. Go back inside."

Cady looked me up and down, then scrunched her nose.

"But she's a girl," she said. "You *never* bring girls over."

"Whatever," Walker mumbled. "I do occasionally. I thought I told you to go back to bed?"

Walker's cheeks reddened, and I bit back a smile. He had no reason to be embarrassed. Surely, no human girls rejected him. Labor had toned his body, and the Sun had bleached pieces of his brown curls. His face was masculine, but held onto youth in his slightly plump cheeks. He was boyish but handsome. Though he wasn't my type, I could certainly see an appeal.

Cady scratched her head.

"Wait," she said. "You did—but not before I saw... something."

"Walker," I interrupted. "Shouldn't we run that errand I talked about?"

"An errand?" Cady questioned. "At eight o'clock?"

She glanced between the two of us.

"Something isn't adding up here," she said.

Cady was too smart for her own good, and I couldn't have her following us.

"We're going on a date," I said.

"You?" she said. "With *him?*"

"Yes," Walker replied. "With me. Is that so hard to believe?"

"Way to shoot out of your league, big brother."

I snorted, and it was my turn to blush. Arion weaved between my legs in efforts to comfort me and himself. He was confused at this turn of events, but he would stay loyal to me, no matter what.

"Oh, I see," she said and studied Arion. He cocked his fluffy head at her. "She brought a cat on your date. It's making more sense now."

I laughed and decided that I liked this little girl.

CHAPTER FIVE

Walker

A witch sat in the passenger seat of my truck.

She'd offered her own "special" form of travel, but I'd declined. I'd had enough special in one night to last a lifetime.

She stared out the window with pursed lips. Her copper eyes studied the trees we blurred past as if she planned on drawing them. Her legs crossed, then straightened, then crossed again. Her fingers drummed against the door. She hadn't commented on the truck's dusty interior or faint smell of cow crap, but the longer we traveled, the more uncomfortable she grew.

"Don't like car rides?" I asked.

"No. Neither does Arion."

Her cat—which I suspected was more than a cat—sat on the console between us. His hackles remained raised, and he glared at me every time I looked at the witch.

"You never told me your name," I said.

She hesitated then sighed.

"I suppose I might as well tell you," she said. "I'm Freya—Freya Redfern, daughter of Coven Mother Sybil Redfern."

"Okay, Freya Redfern," I said. "Where exactly am I taking us?"

"To the only witch I still trust," she answered. "To my goddessmother, and interim Coven Mother, Josephine. Once I convince her of your innocence, she'll know where we need to go next."

"I thought you said the witches were going to shoot first and ask questions later?"

She chewed on her lower lip.

"Josephine won't," she assured me. "At least, I don't think so."

I sighed. "Great."

"Turn left here," she instructed.

I steered away from the winding road that led down mountain and into heart of Hol Creek. The tiny lights of the downtown street twinkled in the darkness, and a few people milled about like ants in the valley. Along the mountainside that overlooked town, we drove past several homes. This was where the business owners and pretty much everyone who wasn't a rancher lived.

The houses all had multiple stories and huge windows and anything else that oozed money. I'd always thought it was a bit ridiculous. The gravel road led upward, and we reached an apartment complex I'd never seen before. I hadn't even known our town *had* apartments.

They perched on a hill above the road. Trees covered most of the black stones they were crafted from, though what showed glinted in the moonlight. Windows peeked through the trees, but I couldn't see what was inside the building.

"How have I never seen this place?" I asked, "or heard about it?"

Freya smiled mischievously.

"How have you never seen me before? I've known you my whole life. Park over here. I don't want you getting in a wreck and blowing this whole operation."

She pointed down the street, but not too close to the apartments. When I shifted the truck into park, a brief hum filled the interior. I searched outside for a threat, then looked at Freya and nearly jumped out of my skin.

It was Freya, but it wasn't.

Her hair was strawberry blonde instead of orange and red, and her copper eyes were muddy brown. Her shoulders slumped, and her arms were thin. Her skin lost its dewy luster, though her freckles remained. I knew I'd seen those freckles before.

"Emily?" I said. "Emily Banks is *you?*"

She laughed, and even that had changed to a flat cough. Her smile was bright. I wondered what it looked like with her real face.

"My mother wanted me to be raised familiar with the human world," she explained. "She said if I were to lead, I needed to know our greatest threat inside and out. So, I've been splitting my time between witchcraft apprenticeship and human public school all my life. I couldn't exactly attend with my normal appearance and not attract attention."

"Didn't want to beat off poor human boys with a stick, huh?"

"I only meant that my features are rare for humans, but I'm glad to know you think I'm beautiful."

"I-I didn't say that!"

Oh, God. Did I really just flirt with a mythical creature who attempted to murder me an hour ago?

She snickered at my frustration, then switched back to her "normal" appearance. One second, she was plain-faced, and the next, she was Freya. Watching it gave me a headache.

"So, you use *magic* to hide this place?" I asked, "and yourself?"

"Magic isn't a swear-word, *Walker*."

Neither is my name, I thought. I turned off the truck and hopped outside. Naturally, I walked around the front of the old thing to open Freya's door, but she'd already gotten out by the time I reached it. She frowned and stepped around me. Arion was hot on her heels. I needed to lay off the chivalry. She was a *witch.* Freya could take care of herself.

"Everyone should be at the gathering in the wood," Freya said. "They're performing a spell for clarity about what happened, but all the others have been fruitless. Whoever's responsible is covering their tracks with some pretty remarkable magic."

"What about the woman—witch—we're here to see?" I asked.

"She's staying by her portal in case I need help tonight. She wanted to come, but I insisted I work alone."

"Yeah," I said. "It would've been horrible if something went wrong while you were trying to kill me."

Freya sighed and stopped. We stood in front of my truck on the paved road that led to the apartments. The moonlight poured down on us.

"I am sorry," Freya said. Her copper eyes stared deeply into mine, and she tucked a stray curl behind her ear. It sprang free immediately. "I thought you killed my mother. I wouldn't have hurt you, had I known the truth. I wouldn't have dragged you into any of this."

Tears welled in her eyes, and I suddenly felt like an ass. The poor girl's mom had just died. I knew how that felt. It was why I kept the pity out of my stare.

That was all anyone could offer me after Mom's death, other than whispers they thought I didn't hear about her "tragic accident." Then came the talk of how poorly my dad handled it. For my last two years of high school, I was reduced to *the kid whose mom died* or *Drunk Clyde's son.* Only Sawyer and Brody didn't treat me differently, and that was the one thing that made it bearable. That, and their understanding when I'd snap for no reason or go days without talking.

If I could've killed the guy responsible, I would've.

"Consider yourself forgiven," I said. "Just don't let it happen again."

"No promises," she said and winked.

I really hoped she was joking.

I followed her up the paved road, which curved to the left and transformed into white cobblestones. The apartments loomed taller than I expected, and a second building stood across the cobblestone street, farther up the mountain. Well-groomed flowerbeds flourished in front of the apartments. A dark, stone fountain trickled in the middle of the cul-de-sac.

Inside it, a statue of three women spat water into the pool. No cars were parked anywhere.

We walked around the statue to reach the entrance to the farthest apartment. One of the women's faces was lined with age, the other's was round with youth, and one was somewhere in between.

"It's the faces of the Goddess," Freya explained, "the Virgin, the Mother, and the Wise Woman."

I nodded. I wasn't sure what else to say. There wasn't a lot of religious diversity in a town with one stoplight. At least, not that I'd been introduced to until now. Up until high school, I hadn't even known anyone believed in anything other than God.

We walked to front of the tall, white doors that led into the apartment building. An awning perched above us, and a golden door knocker gleamed. I reached around Freya and opened the tall door. She stepped into the entryway. A bright, golden chandelier hung from an arched ceiling that was crafted from cedar beams. Our steps echoed on dark stone floors, which were similar to what the complex's walls were built from. We faced a gold-paneled elevator. Hallways branched to our left and right.

Freya snapped her fingers. The elevator dinged and its door slid open. I followed her into the tight space. Freya's hair was extra bright against the elevator's shimmering, white walls. We traveled up four floors before we reached our destination.

"Let me do the talking," Freya instructed and swept into the room.

I stepped out of the elevator. The suite had an open floor plan. A huge kitchen stocked with various herbs was to my right. Beyond that sat an expensive-looking, green velvet couch, a white fur rug, and a couple of black leather chairs that anywhere else, I would've loved to test out. Plants were spread throughout the space in pots of different sizes. They were some of the only pops of color. The white, cleanliness of it made my work jeans and tan Carhartt coat feel especially dirty.

To the right was a separate room, which I assumed was where the witch slept. She probably lurked there now.

"Josephine?" Freya said.

A root slithered from a small tree potted to my right. I jumped out of its reach, but it chased me and wrapped an iron-clad grip around my ankle. Arion hissed at the bedroom door.

"Josephine!" Freya yelled. "Stop! He's innocent!"

The root's grip didn't loosen, but it didn't tighten either.

"Come out, and I'll explain," Freya begged.

The black door of the bedroom creaked open, and a tall, beautiful woman—presumably Josephine—stepped out. She wore a dark, shimmery dress that was oddly formal for someone home alone. The witch's onyx hair was pulled back into a tight ponytail. Her olive-toned skin radiated youth, but a small worry line creased between her bright green eyes—eyes that reminded me so much of Cady's, I nearly gasped.

"How could you bring him here, dearest?" Josephine demanded. "He's a *Reid*."

"I don't know what you've been told," I interjected, "but I'm not from a line of witch hunters. I didn't even know you existed until today!"

"Is that so?" Josephine purred. The root slithered farther up my leg, until it wrapped so tightly around my calf, only pride kept my screams in check. Freya glared at me, and I recalled her order for me not to speak.

Maybe I should let her handle it.

"He couldn't have done it, Goddessmother," Freya argued. "He couldn't hold his own against *me*. Mom could've killed him six times before he even decided to fight back."

Her goal was to defend me, but *damn.* She might as well have proclaimed me neutered.

"But the blood," Josephine argued.

"We'll get to the bottom of it," Freya assured her.

"Child, you better!" Josephine scolded. "His family's history…it's not history to all of us. Some of us remember the Reids before their *retirement*."

Josephine glared daggers at me. Her bright-eyed gaze might have been frightening if I wasn't hung up on what she'd revealed. I blamed my shock for my idiocy.

"How old *are* you?" I asked.

I regretted the words as soon as they spilled out of my mouth.

Stupid, stupid, stupid.

I knew better than to ask any woman that, let alone a witch.

Freya stepped in front of me. "See? He's far too stupid to have killed Sybil."

Considering she was several inches shorter than me, Freya's body shield was comical, but it distracted Josephine. The older witch shook her head and sighed. When she spoke to Freya, her voice shook.

"You know I can't protect you if the coven discovers what you've done, dearest. You've risked Debasement."

"Debasement?" I asked. "What's that?"

If Josephine had spat on me, it would've felt more respectful than her answering glare.

"Exile," Josephine answered. "Or worse, an undignified death—one that ends in torment."

CHAPTER SIX

Freya

I was tempted to strangle my goddessmother.

"You knew this?" Walker asked, "when you…"

I'd never intended for Walker to discover exactly what I risked by sparing him. Already, he thought he owed me, which he didn't—it was written clearly across his face, but I saved him as much for myself as I had for him.

It was what Mom would've done.

"Yes," I snapped. "Don't make me regret it by getting all sappy."

He slammed his slack jaw shut. His jawline became a hard ridge, and his gaze was laser-focused on a fern across the suite.

At least he's not looking at me like I'm a hero. It was ridiculous—he was grateful simply because I hadn't killed him.

"Do you have any advice for where to start?" I asked Josephine.

She glanced between Walker and me several times. She sighed, then uncrossed her arms.

"We still haven't heard from the wolves. I've been meaning to send someone to investigate."

"I could leave without the rest of the coven wondering why," I mused. Walker could disappear too, and none of them would think to go looking for him in wolf territory. One quick spell could conceal his location, so no one could track him magically.

"Wait." Walker paused his brooding. "*Werewolves?*"

"Yes," Josephine said. "Keep up."

Walker rolled his eyes and ran his hands over his tired face.

"And we can get closer to discovering who's really responsible," I continued. "This is a good idea."

"Dearest," Josephine assured with her usual grandeur. "I only have good ideas."

I smiled at her. It was the first thing she'd said in days that sounded like her normal self, and not some automated message crafted by the Elders.

"I can't leave Cady defenseless," Walker interjected.

"Our coven won't hurt her," I promised.

"I'll protect her myself," Josephine vowed. "You must help Freya clean up this mess, unless you want to bring the danger right to your sister's doorstep."

He considered this and slowly nodded. He was probably less worried about the coven and more worried about his father, but we both knew she was better off with him than wherever in the Goddess's name this investigation took us.

"We'll set off as soon as the next sun rises," I declared. "Ready for your first hunt, Walker?"

*

I slept in the bed of my enemy. Well, my enemy as of a few hours ago. I wouldn't call us friends now, but at least I wasn't trying to kill him.

Walker snored from his place on the floor, in front of the bed. I'd offered to sleep there, but he insisted he could sleep comfortably anywhere. From the power of his snores, I believed him. Truthfully, I would have been fine sharing a bed with him, but Walker was determined not to make me uncomfortable, and I didn't mind the extra space.

His room was what I expected—simple but clean, and above all, functional. A fan whirred on a bedside table to my left, and crickets chirped outside. I longed for the scent of Mom's garden—jasmine, lavender, and rosemary—and her much softer snores.

I still hadn't returned to our cottage since her passing. Though it would still smell like her and have all her decorations and herbs, she wouldn't be there. I couldn't face the truth yet— that it wasn't a place I missed, but a person and that person was gone.

I was homeless.

My chest ached with grief. I had thought losing Mom had killed my brittle heart, but it still sent hot, slow pain through my body.

Arion curled up against my back. I leaned into his warmth.

Now that I'd exposed witch-kind, I couldn't even attend the Transcending Ceremony for Mom. Everyone else in the coven would get a chance to grieve and celebrate her. They would rely on each other for strength, while I fought to protect us all. This should've made me angry, but I couldn't feel anything beyond the ache in my chest.

Witches aren't meant to be alone.

It was what Mom always told me on days the coven particularly annoyed me.

I stared and stared at Walker's white ceiling. Exhaustion weighed on my body. I'd expended a lot of magic today and needed to recharge, but my mind refused to settle. My chest threatened to burst.

Alone in the dark, I cried.

*

Walker

"Walker!"

I rubbed my eyes and flipped over. Maybe whatever disturbed me would go away if I ignored it.

Cold water splashed across my face. I sat up, gasped, and swung blindly.

"Hey!" Cadence reprimanded. "Watch it! You gave me no choice. I *tried* to wake you nicely."

Cadence stood over me with an empty cup in her hand. She shot daggers at me with her burning gaze, then wagged her little fingers at my bed.

Oh, shit. Freya.

"Why is a *girl* in your bed?" she whisper-yelled.

"It's a long story," I said. One that I couldn't explain to her.

"Mm," she dragged out the syllables, "Hm. I'm *sure*."

Great. Ever since her one day of sex education, Cadence loved innuendos.

"I slept on the floor," I pointed out.

"Or did you hear me coming and move?" she argued.

"Yeah," I said, "because I was so alert."

"Maybe you've taken up acting," she said, then sighed. "Okay. I'll admit—that one was a little far-fetched."

Freya whimpered in her sleep and distracted both of us. I wondered how someone so scary could have nightmares.

"Mom," Freya whispered.

Damn. Even the wicked witch missed her mom. Cadence frowned.

"Is she like us?" she asked. "Is her mom gone too?"

I nodded and shooed her out of the room. With one last sympathetic glance at Freya, she scurried away. I stood and wondered how best to wake the witch. I definitely wasn't stupid enough to try Cadence's trick on her, but I didn't exactly want to get in her space.

I couldn't see her face under her pile of hair. My brown sheets were twisted around her creamy skin. She'd grabbed some pajamas and a change of clothes she kept at Josephine's apartment. It unnerved me to see her in a sweatshirt and shorts. The mundane look didn't match her wild appearance, but I guessed witches slept like everyone else—comfortably.

Freya whimpered again.

I cursed myself for being afraid of a sleeping girl and picked up my pillow. I lightly tapped her legs with it and braced myself. She didn't budge. I tapped her again with a little more force, and she shot up. An invisible force pushed me against the wall, but as soon as her wide-eyed stare met mine, the force released me. The impact knocked the breath from my lungs, but

I didn't think it would leave a bruise.

"Oops," she said and frowned. "Did you hit me with a pillow?"

"Lightly," I answered and rubbed the spot on my back that had collided with the wall. She rolled her eyes at me and stretched like a cat. Her sweatshirt slid up and exposed a strip of her toned stomach. Before she caught me staring, I quickly looked away. Maybe Cadence was right—having a girl in my bed was weird, no matter the circumstance.

I grabbed a few things from my closet and headed into the bathroom to shower and change. I wasn't sure when or if I'd get to do so again. I also wasn't sure how to break the news to Cadence. No version of the truth or lies was believable.

"Breakfast is ready!" Cadence called. "I have some for you too, girl-in-my-brother's-bed!"

Some days, I was grateful my dad was an alcoholic and usually slept past eleven.

I stepped out of the bathroom and bumped into Freya.

"Sorry," we both said at the same time.

She dropped the clothes in her hand, and I picked them up for her without a thought. When I handed them to her, she wore a strange smile.

"Are all human boys this chivalrous?" she asked.

"Only the good ones," I answered. I wished Sawyer had seen it—that was actually pretty smooth.

Shit. I needed to get out more. I was being *smooth* to witches.

While we waited on Freya, Cadence and I enjoyed the breakfast she prepared. It consisted of slightly soggy cereal, a banana, and a glass of orange juice. Simplicity was typical of our kitchen—Cadence learned everything she knew from me.

Freya emerged from the shower in a black leather jacket thrown over a hunter green shirt, and black jeans. Her damp hair already threatened to burst free of the braid she'd woven it into. A few gold necklaces hung around her neck, and each one held a different symbol or trinket. She wore a ring with a decent-sized blue and red stone on her right hand. She noticed my stare.

"It's a bloodstone," Freya explained. "It promotes strength." She pulled out the chair next to me and lifted her banana.

"Walker doesn't believe in crystals," Cadence chimed in, "he says to never trust someone who puts their faith in jewelry." I glared at my oh-so-helpful sister and clenched my jaw.

"Does he, now?" Freya asked.

She smirked and dug into her breakfast without a complaint. I wondered what witches usually ate. My gaze fell on Cadence, and I searched for the right words to tell her I was leaving.

"Walker," Cadence chided, "you're staring."

"Sorry," I mumbled. "I was just thinking—I have to tell you something, Cady. I'm going on a trip."

She blinked at me.

"Where are we going?" she asked.

"No," I corrected her. "I have to go—you have to stay here." She glanced down the hall, toward Dad's room. Guilt gnawed at me.

"What?" she said and rose to her feet. "No—no, I'm coming with you!"

"You can't," I said, "where we're going is too dangerous. You're safer here."

"So *she* gets to go?" Cadence yelled and pointed at Freya. "You're leaving me behind to go on a trip with some girl you met ten seconds ago! Don't tell me about the *danger,* Walker. Enjoy your romantic getaway without me."

She stormed out of the kitchen, but not before I caught a glimpse of the tear that fell down her cheek. Her door slammed shut, and I winced.

"That could've gone better," Freya said.

"Really?" I replied sarcastically. "That was *exactly* the reaction I was looking for."

Freya munched on her banana and took a swig of orange juice.

"At least she doesn't suspect the truth," she said.

She made a fair point. I should've been grateful for my sister's assumptions. They were easier to deal with than her usual tenacious curiosity, but it didn't ease my churning stomach. I was supposed to be Cady's caretaker—someone she could rely on—and I'd let her down. She'd had enough of that already in her short life.

"Hey," Freya said and placed her hand over mine. "You're doing your best. It's all you can do."

Her small hand was warm against mine. Too warm. I pulled away and nodded.

"Thanks."

So much for being smooth, I thought. She jerked her hand away and rose to her feet.

"We better get moving," she said and hurried out the front door.

I placed the abandoned dishes in the sink and washed them. I checked the fridge and freezer—there were enough frozen meals, waters, and milk for them to eat for at least a few days. I prayed I wouldn't be away longer than that.

Dad's snores echoed in my ears.

Why do you have to be so useless?

I couldn't make myself leave with Cadence still in his care. Faced with no other option, I called Mrs. Morris, the mother of Cady's best friend, and left a message when she didn't pick up.

"Sorry for the late notice, but I'm going out of town for a few days, and I really need someone to watch Cady. Please pick her up as soon as you get this."

Arion emerged from my bedroom. He must've really enjoyed my bed, since he'd actually strayed from Freya's side long enough to sleep in. As he prowled into the kitchen, the cat stared at me with keen, amber eyes. If he weren't a cat, I would've thought he looked smug. I guessed I would too, if I were a four-legged creature who kicked a human out of his own bed.

The cat meowed by the door Freya had exited through, but I ignored him and walked toward Cadence's room. I knocked lightly on her door, which needed a fresh coat of paint. I'd meant to apply one soon, but, like many things this week, those plans had gone awry.

"Go away!" she yelled.

"Cady," I pleaded, "I don't want to leave you. Please don't be mad at me right now. At least give me a hug goodbye."

Desperation tangled my insides, and I fought to keep it out of my voice. There was a very real chance I wasn't going to return home. I didn't want to leave with the knowledge that our last interaction had been so ugly, but I couldn't make her suspicious enough to follow me either.

"I don't want to," she huffed.

I flinched.

"Okay," I said, "I love you, Cady-Cat. I'll call when I can."

I waited a few minutes for her to answer, but she kept silent. With one last sigh, I walked away.

CHAPTER SEVEN

Freya

"So," Walker drawled, "werewolves have been living in my backyard this whole time?"

"Yep," I said, "and your neighbors are a coven of witches."

He mulled this over but kept his steady pace. We walked through the thick forest beyond Walker's house. Pines and other trees climbed high in the sky. Wind swayed their branches, as well as the thick grass beneath our feet. The fresh air was revitalizing.

After three hours without more than a five-minute break, my legs ached, and my breath was unsteady. At least we'd make good progress. The valley was only a few hundred feet away. Water trickled in the creek, and I quickened my steps in anticipation. We'd agreed to take a lunchbreak once we reached it. As we journeyed closer, the trees thinned, and the neighboring mountain came into view. It was not as gently sloped as the one we currently traveled down. Jagged rocks layered its sides.

I internally groaned. The only thing worse than hiking downhill was hiking uphill. Arion prowled along beside me without a care in the world. My cat was in better shape than me —maybe it was time to work out a bit more.

"There's no way to reach these wolves by truck or car?" Walker asked, "or just a phone call?"

"Magic-blessed creatures don't put much faith in technology," I explained. "We don't like what we can't control.

That's why we usually use portals or astral projections."

"And why can't we...what was it? Portal? Astral project?"

"Regretting the trip already?" I asked.

He frowned and ran a hand through his hair.

"No," he said. "This is just a lot to take in. I feel like I don't know anything anymore."

That makes two of us, I thought.

"Some witches can summon portals." I hesitated. "It's not exactly my strong suit. I only know how to travel through established ones."

He fought a grin. "Is it really that painful? To admit you don't know how to do something?"

"Yes," I said quietly.

He chuckled, and I lightly swatted his arm. He held up his hands in a 'don't shoot' gesture. "I'm sorry! It's just funny. You can literally create tornados and dancing shadows with magic, but you still think you have something to prove to me. You don't."

I was so busy staring into his earnest gaze, I nearly tripped.

I *never* tripped.

I cleared my throat and continued. "I could use astral projection, but I want an inside look on what's going on with the wolves. We're usually allies, yet they've rejected our requests for in-person strategy meetings since the first witch went missing. Something is amiss."

He pondered my words, and we walked in companionable silence for a few minutes. Though I wasn't known for my patience, I appreciated these quiet moments. It was rare to come across someone who truly thought before they spoke.

"You think they're behind the dead witches?" he finally asked.

"I don't know," I answered honestly. "I hope not."

I thought of Ryder. Surely, he wasn't angry enough over our ended dalliance to let such a thing happen without telling me. Wolves could be possessive creatures, which was exactly why we'd ended our relationship, but Ryder hadn't cared *that* deeply. We'd even remained friends these past months, up until the witches disappeared.

If the werewolves were behind the deaths, we'd have very little help fighting them. I pulled my head away from my worries —there would be plenty of time for them after we discovered just how screwed we were.

"So," Walker drawled and pushed a branch aside. "Josephine said something about being old enough to remember my family when they were still hunters. I hope it's not rude to ask, but what's a witch's life span?"

"Recently?" I said. "Not terribly long."

He grimaced, and I laughed brittlely.

"That was a shitty joke," I admitted, "but to answer your question, anywhere from six hundred to a thousand years. Our connection with magic grants us longer lives than humans."

"How." He cleared his throat. "How old are you?"

I chuckled. "I'm eighteen, Walker. Just a hair younger than you. We went to school together, remember?"

He sighed with visible relief. A flush crept up his neck.

"What is so embarrassing?" I asked.

"Oh nothing," he said and adjusted his hat. "If you were seventy or something, I was just gonna tell you, you look great for your age."

Unexpected laughter burst out of me. It felt so nice, it dawned on me that it'd been a while since I was genuinely amused.

Walker was more comfortable traipsing over fallen limbs and swatting away branches than I thought he would be. He was more comfortable in nature than some witches. He lifted a stick to swat away a huge spider web in his path.

I spoke too soon.

"Wait!" I yelled.

He paused and raised an eyebrow at me.

"You wouldn't want someone to destroy your home," I pointed out, "especially a home so beautiful."

I studied the delicate network of the web. Sunlight reflected off it with a gentle sheen. On the bottom corner of the web, minding her own business, was the home's creator. A sac clung to the wolf spider's body.

"She's a mother," I noted, "and she's not even poisonous. We can walk around her."

Walker's jaw went a little slack at my display, but I ignored him. After a few heartbeats, he fell into step behind me.

"Witches be crazy," he mumbled under his breath.

I sent a small gust of wind at him in retaliation. It lifted the hat off his head, but he hurried to catch it. I fought a smile.

We finally reached the valley. The Sun was high in the sky, among scattered clouds. The warmth, paired with a gentle wind, made me sigh contentedly. Walker brushed past me and crouched before the stream. He splashed water across his face, and I noticed how sweaty he was.

Did I set too fast of a pace? I thought. *He could've asked me to slow down.*

"You okay?" I asked.

"Yeah," he said, "why wouldn't I be?"

I kept my observations to myself and sat on a nearby rock. Sand and rocks shifted beneath my feet. Foliage sprouted sporadically in the poor soil, and a fish splashed in the creek.

I pulled some homemade jerky from my pocket and dug in. Walker grabbed his own jerky and sat near the creek.

"I would've taken you for a vegetarian," he said.

"My coven believes in every facet of nature," I answered. "Hunts—honest hunts with handmade weapons—are a part of that. That's how we get our meat."

"Geez," he said. "You're making me feel bad about my Slim Jim."

We laughed, and my body felt lighter than it had in days. Walker flashed me a smile, and his face became a boy's again— younger and full of joy. It was a nice sight.

"Don't fret, cowboy," I teased, "unless you're secretly a witch—you wouldn't be a very good one."

"You'd certainly know what it is to be a poor excuse for a witch, Redfern."

For Hecate's sake. As I recognized the voice of Mara Morningstar, my skin crawled. I leaped to my feet, and Walker mirrored the movement. His hand rested on the gun strapped to his hip. Arion hissed, and his hackles raised.

"Not yet, boy," I whispered.

"At least I'm not Lucifer's bitch," I called back.

The dark witches—Lucifer's witches—hid from sight, though Mara's voice had come from the mountain we'd just crossed. I sensed no magic, so they had to be hidden among the trees. I cursed myself for not noticing their presence sooner. The dark witches trained in all forms of trickery and sneaking, which made them excellent spies.

As I strained my eyes to catch sight of them, I summoned a shield of wind that surrounded Arion, Walker, and me.

"You're too weak to hold his power," Mara called back. "It's why your coven is getting picked off like prey animals."

Though her words made me want to scream, I refused to give her the reaction she sought.

"If you're so powerful, show yourself!" I demanded.

A stiletto-clad foot stepped out of the shadows of the pines. Slowly, the rest of Mara's body came into view. She wore a fitted black gown that was slit past her hip and revealed a long strip of her porcelain skin.

A ruby hung from a silver chain between her collarbones, and her lips were painted red to match the stone. Her silver, curly hair was cut just below her chin. Her eyes, like all dark witches' eyes, were completely black. There was not a pupil or iris to be seen. Though I couldn't see the rest of her coven, she never traveled alone.

"Like what you see?"

The sultry question was directed at Walker. Open-mouthed, he stared at her with something far from lust. He slammed his jaw shut.

"Devil-worshippers aren't really my thing," he snapped.

"Your devil—our angel," she argued and walked closer. "One who believes in liberty above all else. One who bows to no one and nothing."

"Is that what this is about?" I asked. "Power? We never asked the dark witches to *bow*."

Josephine and I had discussed Mara's coven as suspects, but we never truly thought they'd take it this far. They *had* morals, no matter how flawed they were. Witches didn't kill other witches. Though we had our occasional squabbles, the dark witches usually kept to their mountain, which was miles from ours.

They too often risked exposure by picking off human virgins for sacrifices, but they'd long ago agreed to only two or three of those per decade, and they hunted various neighboring towns, not ours. Despite our different philosophies and general dislike of each other, we lived in peace.

"No," Mara said. "*You* haven't, but your coven bows to the High Witch."

A shiver ran down my spine. My shield wavered.

"You want to challenge the High Witch Cordelia?" I whispered. Just saying the words felt dangerous.

Mara grinned and flashed her jagged teeth.

"I'm challenging the whole damn court," she explained and cackled. "We are witches—we shouldn't cower at the feet of human filth like our ancestors in Salem. It's time for redemption."

My heart thudded erratically, and my vision blurred. This was so much worse than I'd ever imagined. If Mara's efforts caught the attention of the High Witch, or any member of her court, the whole town could be decimated. My coven and I would certainly be guilty by association. If any humans became suspicious, they'd be dead too. If Mara was willing to kill off her own kind, she certainly wouldn't hesitate to share that I'd exposed Walker to the truth.

A darker thought paralyzed me.

Did Mara kill my mother?

As silence stretched, Walker stared at me.

"And you'll kill whoever stands in your way," I added.

"I'll kill whoever it takes," she agreed. "Now, I've had enough of this chatter."

She beckoned at her cohorts and glanced behind her.

"C'mon, sisters!" she called. "It's time to get to work."

CHAPTER EIGHT

Walker

Werewolves—I can handle, but Satanists? This day had become too much. Even Freya was frightened. Though coiled into fists at her sides, her hands still shook, and her eyes searched the forest relentlessly. Clouds polluted the once bright sky and even the breeze had slowed, as if it too were afraid of the monstrous creatures we faced.

The witch—Mara, Freya had called her—was ageless. Her hair was coarse and gray, yet her features remained soft. Her eyes were endless pits. Like witnessing a bad car wreck, I wanted to stare into them and look away all at once. Her shoes were ridiculous.

You'd have to be magical to hike in heels like that, I thought, *or crazy enough to worship Lucifer.*

"I'll kill whoever it takes," Mara said. "Now, I've had enough of this chatter." She spoke as if we'd met up for a friendly lunch.

Freya's forcefield of wind nearly drowned out all the sound outside our bubble, but not quite. A hum filled the air, which I now suspected was a sign of magic. Arion paced and hissed relentlessly.

"C'mon, sisters!" Mara called. "It's time to get to work."

A louder, shriller hum flooded my ears. It filtered past Freya's shield and gave me a splitting headache in no time. I wrenched my gun from its holster and tried to ignore that I pulled it on actual people.

Well, on things that look *like people.*

Freya had tried to prepare me for the dangers of this mission, but judging by her own shakiness, preparing to kill and actually killing were two distinctly different acts.

More witches stepped out of the shadows in the forest. There were at least twelve of them. All of them wore black, skimpy dresses similar to the one Mara wore and the same outrageously tall and narrow shoes.

Their skin tones varied greatly, but none of them appeared to have seen the sun in ages. They squinted against the light. Their ashy skin became even duller under its shine. All their eyes were the same inky black. They surrounded us in a circle and clasped their bony hands together. Though I couldn't discern what they said, their lips moved rapidly.

"I can't shoot with the shield in the way," I told Freya.

"If I let it down," she argued, "they'll have a million assault spells coming right for our heads."

The force field shook. Freya toyed with her necklaces and swallowed loudly.

"It might not matter anyway." She sighed. "Okay, Arion. It's your turn, buddy. I just need to do the liberation spell...a quick protection spell before I set you free."

"Freya," I said, "are you okay?"

She swayed on her feet but nodded and whispered something in a strange, lilting language. Warmth slid over my skin, from head to toe, and the wind-powered forcefield was gone. The shrill hum intensified.

"Godsdammit," Freya muttered and rubbed at her eyes. "They're draining me...I-I can't..."

Freya's eyes rolled back in her head, and her body went slack. I barely caught her before her head hit the ground.

"Freya!" I yelled, but my voice was lost to the incessant hum of magic.

Arion foamed at the mouth, like he had rabies, and meowed wildly. It did nothing to wake Freya up. She was out cold.

"Scared, mortal?" Mara crooned. "Your little girlfriend can't save you now. And with her out of the picture, there will be no one powerful enough to retaliate against us. The Great Betrayer will be pleased. We might even get a taste of your sister now that you'll both be dead."

Rage and fear sharpened my voice.

"My sister has nothing to do with this," I argued.

My fingers wrapped tighter around the gun. It had never felt so slippery in my hands. Facing off Freya, a part of me had known I wouldn't actually shoot her. That part of me was quiet now.

"Your sister has *everything* to do with this," Mara sneered, then licked her lips. "And she'll taste so delicious."

Mara looked at Freya with dark, hungry eyes, as if she forgot I were even there. There was no time to wonder what the hell the witches wanted with my sister. There was only time to stop them.

No one to retaliate against us...

The heartless witch cleared her throat. Her followers watched her with fervor. They giggled and drew closer, then clasped hands. I'd never witnessed such glee for death.

And we would die—Freya, me, Cadence.

Freya had told me a mortal gun was powerless against a bunch of trained witches, and maybe it was, if said witches thought to defend themselves—if they thought I would actually have the gall to strike back.

I raised the gun and fired.

Boom!

The shot reverberated down my arms, to my very bones. Ringing, louder than ever before, deafened my ears.

Mara clutched her stomach, where black, thick blood poured out. She bared her sharp teeth in anger and shock. The rest of the witches rushed to her, but she held up a hand to stop them and barked orders I couldn't hear.

Freya stirred beneath me then gasped.

Her eyes fluttered open, and she shot to her feet. She

paused for one heartbeat at the sight of the gun in my hand and the hole in Mara's stomach. A heartbeat later, Freya mumbled lilting words.

Arion meowed shrilly, then the sound grew deeper. He transformed—his jaw became as wide as his body, until his body expanded nearly as wide as a horse's barrel. His calico fur shed and was replaced by a spotted, orange coat that gleamed under the Sun. He shook his new coat, and the ground reverberated under the weight of his huge paws. Talons protruded from them, and fangs extended from his white maw.

"Kill them!" Mara screeched.

Arion lunged for the nearest witch. The woman's black eyes became even wider, and she scrambled away, but not fast enough. Arion caught her ghostly pale leg, then flung her body into the trees. Something hot splashed against my face. I wiped it away hastily and looked at my palm.

It was blood.

Dark, thick blood.

"Walker!" Freya snapped.

Arion chased the others away, deeper into the forest behind us. Mara hobbled across the creek with the support of two witches, but five witches still launched spells at Freya. She stood inside her crumbling shield of wind. Their magic flooded the air with something akin to an electric current. Goose bumps covered my arms under my jacket, and the hairs on the back of my neck rose.

The witches drew knives from sheaths under their dresses and raised the knives to their own forearms. Together, they cut made horizontal cuts without a single wince or whimper. Midnight blood trickled down their arms and chants poured from their lips.

Whatever freaky ritual they performed, it worked. The air grew colder and colder.

Unsure of what else to do, I fired my gun at them. The bullet hit an invisible force field and hovered there, completely intact.

The witch I'd fired at craned her head to peer at me. Not a single crimson red curl was knocked out of place. She flashed a blinding white smile and flicked her bracelet-clad wrist at me. The bullet sailed back in my direction.

I dove behind a nearby rock.

Splash!

The bullet hit the creek, which was only inches from my face.

I scrambled to my feet, but it was too late to retreat. The witch snarled like a rabid animal.

"Stupid mortal," she spat. "You dare hurt the Mother and now *this?*"

She broke away from her cohorts and took a step closer to me. She licked her red lips.

"It's been so long since I've tasted something as divine as you," she mused. "Your soul is pure—it would please Lucifer for me to consume it."

Shit. Shit. Shit.

"I can tell you about who's killing the witches," I lied. "Surely that's of some interest to you."

She laughed.

"Oh, how your ignorance amuses me." She tittered. "Lucifer has blessed me with this—a tasty, defenseless hunter."

"Shouldn't you help your friends?" I asked. I cleared my throat and spoke louder. "They don't seem to be faring too well without you."

The witches hesitated in their assault on Freya, and Freya seized the moment. Crying out a spell, she slipped past their defenses and sent two of the witches flying back, across the river and into the trees. Their bodies thudded against the pines, and they didn't get up. A short but vicious-looking blonde witch broke away from the group.

"You think we're weak?" the blonde witch asked and muttered a spell.

A stream of water rose in the air and turned into ice. The witch bared her sharpened teeth and flicked her wrist. The ice spear shot at me, and I dove again. Again and again, the witches launched rocks, sticks, and ice at me. A few of the rocks landed. Every one of them undoubtedly left bruises. Adrenaline kept my body in motion, but a shard of ice stabbed my calf, and I crumpled.

Rocks dug into my face and stung my skin. The tiny pains were dull echoes of what radiated from my calf in hot waves. Blood flowed from the wound and from my nose. With bruised arms, I raised my upper body. When I tried to stand, my calf refused. More blood surged out of it, and my head swam. I fell back on my ass. Never in my life had I felt more helpless. The dark witches each wore smug grins, but it was the short one who spoke.

"Who's weak now, hunter?"

She raised her hands, summoned a huge spear of ice, and pointed it directly at me. The other witches chanted, and the air around me got even colder. My ragged breath fogged before me.

"I may be weak," I admitted, "but at least I'm not damned."

"Stop this!" Freya screamed. She rushed them but bounced off an invisible shield. "He's got nothing to do with this and you all know it!"

"Okay," the blonde witch crooned. She pointed at Freya, and the ice rushed her.

"No!" I gasped.

Despite the blood gushing from my leg, I forced myself to stand.

The spear changed at the last second. The ice shifted into thick shackles that wrapped around Freya's wrists, ankles, and neck. Her body sagged beneath their weight, but she quickly righted her posture and bared her teeth.

"The Betrayer will be pleased," the red-haired witch purred.

"Wait," the other dark witch said. She pointed her long, pale finger to the woods. "Do you hear that?"

For a second, I heard nothing but the erratic beat of my heart. Howls pierced the silence.

Freya chuckled.

"You guys are screwed."

Those are some big-ass dogs.

Darkness tunneled my vision, and I fought to hold onto consciousness. The six wolves were almost as big as Arion and looked just as mean. They charged down the mountain and leaped with uncanny grace across the creek. As they lunged for the dark witches, their huge claws dug into the earth. One wolf, who was as black as night and had bright yellow eyes, tore into the evil redheaded witch.

I looked away from the gruesome scene. The witches had nearly killed us, but it was still too much to watch. *Everything* had become too much. Dizziness blurred my vision and muddled my thoughts. I stared at the rocks. Blood spattered them, both black and crimson. I reached out to touch it and lost my balance.

I barely felt my body thud against the ground. The rocks had softened. I wanted to sink into them and rest for days. Sleep was something I often longed for, but, this time, I allowed myself to drift away.

CHAPTER NINE

Freya

Walker wouldn't stop bleeding.

The remaining dark witches fled or were decimated, so the magic binding me in my shackles finally evaporated. I didn't understand why the dark witches had wanted to take me hostage rather than kill me outright, but there was no time to ponder it. Arion stormed through the woods and rushed to my side. Black blood stained his maw, and he bared his teeth at the wolves who surrounded us. He'd never been a fan of theirs.

"Hey, friend. I was starting to get worried about you. Thanks for your help." I scratched him behind his ears. "I need your help finding a few herbs."

I listed the various things I needed to heal Walker—lavender, sage, and tarragon—and instructed him to search for them.

The wolves came to a halt around me. Their synchronized movements had always freaked me out. Covens were close, but packs were something else. It was as if they shared a single brain.

"Shift," I instructed the nearest wolf, Ryder. I'd recognize his dark coat and dayglow yellow eyes anywhere.

Ryder did as I asked. He ran a hand through his shaggy, black hair. Sunlight gleamed against his light brown skin and rippling muscles, which were on full display. Werewolves weren't known for modesty.

When they look like this, why should they be?

A loose string had fallen to his ankles. Attached to it was a small bag of clothes. They'd clearly meant to encounter others if they'd bothered packing a bag. I wondered if I was the one they were tracking.

"I need you to use that nose of yours and search for the herbs—Walker is bleeding too quickly."

He opened his mouth to argue, but I headed for Walker's prone body. When werewolves spoke, walking away from an Alpha—or an Alpha's son—was a huge form of disrespect, but I didn't have time for diplomacy or fragile male egos.

I took off my jacket and placed it under Walker's pale face, then grabbed the bottom of my shirt. I found a sharp rock and used it to tear off the strip. I wrapped it around Walker's leg to cut off blood flow. The bleeding persisted, but at least it slowed.

I hoped Walker had passed out more from the shock of bloodshed than from his own blood loss. Watching witches die—even deceitful, covenant-breaking ones—had been hard. Death by werewolf was certainly not the way I wanted to go.

At least they're on your side, I thought, *for now.*

"What the hell, Freya?" Ryder snapped and stormed over to me. He'd finally thrown on some sweatpants. The other wolves scattered, hopefully to search for what I needed.

"I thought I asked you to do something," I said and checked Walker's pulse. For now, it was steady. I tried to send magical feelers across the woods for the herbs, but healing magic wasn't intuitive for me, and I was drained from the fight.

"That's an interesting way to say thank you," he huffed.

I sighed. "I'm sorry. It's been a taxing few days."

He gave me a hard stare, like he wanted to ask what I meant but was also hesitant to hear the answer. I wondered if he'd heard about my mom.

I prayed he had nothing to do with it.

Arion returned with the lavender and tarragon in his mouth. He spat it in my hand, already ground up from his sharp teeth.

"We still need one more thing," I said.

Ryder's gaze hardened, and he gritted his teeth.

"Just leave him," he implored. "He's going to get you killed anyways. I can't believe you told a fucking human."

One of the nearby wolves growled in agreement.

It would've been the smarter thing to do. I could've left him here and righted my wrong with the witches, but the idiot —albeit the *brave* idiot—had nearly died because of me. I just hoped I could heal him.

"No," I snapped. "Help me find the sage. It's the last thing I need."

"You're wasting our time," Ryder argued. "The dark witches could be back with reinforcements at any moment. We need to get into wolf territory—they wouldn't dare follow us into my father's jurisdiction. Besides, are you even sure this will work? Your healing magic is shit."

My nerves coiled like snakes in my stomach. Damn him, but Ryder was right. I'd never had the patience to be any good at healing, but his reminder wasn't helpful.

"Either help me or get lost," I barked. "And I'll have you know I've been working on it. I've gotten quite good."

The lie rolled easily off my tongue. My mother had taught me there was nothing more valuable than false confidence in a crisis.

"Darling," she said to me after a particularly grueling and humiliating training session. *"No one ever feels like they know what they're doing, but any half-competent witch doesn't let anyone see those doubts except for the Goddess herself."*

Though it was far from my favorite subject, Mom made sure I had some rudimentary healing skills. She could've made sure there was no scar, but I wasn't concerned about the cowboy's skin. I just wanted him to live.

He had a sister to go home to.

I grew impatient waiting for the sage. I'd wanted to monitor Walker, but I needed that ingredient *now.* Determined to find it, I prepared myself to cross the creek. The sage was probably on the dryer side of the valley. Ryder was hot on my heels, until a wolf howled to my left.

"He found it," Ryder told me.

The wolf ran toward me and dumped the mushy sage in my palm. As I raced back to Walker, I mixed the ingredients on my arm.

"Hang in there, cowboy," I whispered, then spoke the incantation to activate the ingredients of the salve. My muscles protested. I'd already pushed the boundaries of how much magic I could weave without being overwhelmed by exhaustion. Faced with no other option, I didn't stop.

Black spots danced in my vision, but the spell hummed with energy. With a silent prayer, I rubbed the salve into the wound.

Thank the Goddess.

The bleeding finally stopped.

Until the tightness in my chest eased, I hadn't realized how worried I'd been that it wouldn't stop. Walker groaned and attempted to rise, but I gently pressed him down.

"You can't break the clot," I told Walker. "Ryder will help you flip over."

"Like hell," Walker mumbled, but he made no further attempts to move.

Ryder rolled his eyes but did as I asked. I was grateful he complied without argument, though his bedside manner left something to be desired. As Ryder roughly flipped the cowboy over, I grimaced at the scrapes and bruises that covered Walker's face and hands.

"Here," I scooped some of the salve out my palm and held it to his lips. "Eat this. It'll make you sleepy, but it will heal you."

I forced Walker to eat some of the salve. He gagged but forced it down.

"Thanks," he whispered in a hoarse voice.

"My mom made me eat this when I broke my arm," I said and smiled. "I thought my tongue would fall off from the taste, but it worked."

Walker's eyes fluttered closed. His chest rose and fell in a steady rhythm.

"Someone will need to carry him," I said to Ryder. "The salve will keep him out for at least an hour."

Ryder and the other wolves groaned, but I paid them no mind.

Walker would live. I was sure of it.

With a grunt, Ryder hefted Walker over his shoulder then slung him over the back of a nearby, brown wolf.

"You and I will travel on two feet," Ryder said. "It'll give us a chance to catch up."

"All right then," I said with a sigh and looked at Arion. He wouldn't get to shift into his third form today—my favorite form, albeit his most unruly. Mother had advised me only to call upon it in the most extreme of circumstances. Arion rubbed his huge head against my back and purred.

"You were excellent today, friend," I crooned.

Ryder gestured toward the creek and bowed.

"Ladies first."

Arion walked by my side across the stream, and I subtly leaned on him for support. I needed rest after the magic I'd just exerted, but I wouldn't show weakness in front of Ryder. That was probably why he insisted on traveling on two feet anyway. I'd made him look weak in front of his pack and now he wanted to level the playing field.

Still an ass. I wouldn't let him win.

We crossed the river and hiked uphill. My legs burned, and my head ached from exhaustion, but I pushed past the pain and focused on Ryder. If he was trying to distract me by urging me to walk, then I probably wasn't going to like what he had to say. I took a deep breath of fresh air and let nature strengthen me. Arion sent a bit of his magic to me as well, and I smiled at him. It warmed my veins and gave me the strength I needed to continue.

The rest of the wolves walked in a diamond shape, with Ryder, me, and the wolf who carried Walker in the center. At the top of this mountain, we'd reach wolf territory. Hope lightened my steps a fraction.

"So," I said and pushed a branch out of my way. "Since you're so eager to chat, why don't we discuss why several of my requests for an in-person meeting have been ignored?" Ryder sighed.

"I meant 'catch up' on more of a personal level, Frey." He rubbed his nose. "The rest you'll have to ask my dad."

"You always fidget when you're nervous," I said.

His steps stuttered, and I smiled.

"Glad to know some things don't change."

"You're right," he agreed. "They don't. You're still a total and complete pain in my ass."

I grinned.

Our hike grew steeper. Ryder scaled a short, rocky cliff then reached to help me up. I ignored the gesture and climbed, despite how every one of my muscles protested. He barely held in a laugh at my needless suffering. The other wolves scaled it easily in their four-legged forms.

As I crested the cliff, Walker gasped, and I echoed it. That concoction should've kept him asleep for another half-hour at least. Walker frantically tried to push himself up on the wolf's back. His fingers had a death grip on the wolf's brown fur. The wolf growled and snapped his teeth in response.

"Walker!" I yelled. "Be still!"

I hurried to him and checked his wound. Where the stab wound had been, there was now only a puffy, pentagram-shaped red scab and some remnants of the salve. I shuddered at the dark witches' mark.

"Freya." Walker huffed. "Why am I on a damn wolf?"

I checked his face. Most of the dried blood had flaked off and the bruises were gone.

"It worked," I whispered.

The last remnants of panic released their death-grip on my heart. Walker studied my face with the same intensity I had studied his. Unable to hold his intense stare, I looked away.

"Ryder, help him down, would you? I'd like to see if he can walk on it."

"Of course," Ryder grumbled, "what else am I here for?"

The brown wolf slowly sat, and before Walker hit the ground, Ryder caught the cowboy by his torso. Walker hurried to free himself from Ryder's grasp. When he placed weight on his injured leg, he winced, but his pained expression quickly changed to shock.

"It barely even hurts," he said. He took a step toward me, then another, until he wrapped me in a hug. "Thank you."

For a second, I was too shocked to move. His much taller, warm body seared heat into mine. His embrace enveloped me and made me feel small in a...*pleasant* way. I awkwardly patted his back, and Walker pulled away. I didn't understand.

He looked at me like I was his savior, though he'd gotten hurt because of *me.* I couldn't bear it. I was the heir to my coven. I should've noticed the dark witches before they gained the upper hand.

"You're lucky, you know," I said, "to have survived such recklessness. You challenged *dark witches,* Walker! What is wrong with you?"

He threw his hands up.

"What else was I supposed to do?" he demanded.

"You could've ran!" I suggested.

"I bought us our only chance and you know it," he said. "You would've already been hauled away, and I would be dead if I hadn't. You just don't want to admit that you actually needed my help."

He was right, but I'd never let him know that.

"Whatever," I said. "Try not to bring yourself to death's door again. I might not bother saving you next time."

Lie, lie, lie.

At least he wasn't acting like I was a hero anymore.

"No one needs your help, human," Ryder added. "You should listen to Frey."

"Ryder," I said, "shut up."

CHAPTER TEN

Walker

"We should set up camp soon," Ryder declared. His freaky eyes studied me. "Your charge isn't looking too good, Freya."

I glared at the werewolf. He was a real piece of work. For the last three hours, he'd heckled me about something I never imagined getting bullied for—my humanity.

"You know, fleabag," I said, "you can just say you're tired. No need to blame it on me."

He growled. I was too tired to be frightened by it. Freya was right—I should stop challenging supernatural creatures. It wasn't an easy habit to kick when we'd hiked for three hours uphill. My aching legs and tired muscles wore down my patience. I nearly slipped on another stray rock.

Plants were sparser on this mountain, where the sun barely shined. The hike was less forgiving than the last. The slope was steeper, and the ground was so hard, every step jarred my tired bones. At least I wasn't dead.

Yet.

The sky was purple, and any second, the sun would dip behind the horizon. Already, the temperatures dropped. Ryder was right. He might have fur to keep him warm, but I would need a fire.

Freya's skin was so pale, if she had black eyes, I would've thought she was a dark witch. Despite the cold air, sweat shined on her face. Her steps were sluggish, and her usually perfect posture was wilted. I wanted to ask if she was okay, but not after her fit earlier. Anything I said could set her off.

Witches really do be tripping.

Though she made it clear she only kept me alive for morality's sake, I couldn't help but worry about her. She'd saved my life, whether she wanted to admit it or not.

"It's a good idea," she said. "We're on the outskirts of wolf territory. We'll be safe."

Of course she agrees with him.

For the past three hours, I'd been forced to listen to their endless banter. I had no idea how she got along with the guy. Maybe she bought into his supernatural superiority complex. Maybe she just liked the smile he kept flashing her.

"Don't worry, Frey," he said. "I'll keep you safe."

Gag me.

We found a small cave, just big enough for two or three people to sleep in. While Ryder and I grabbed firewood, Freya shooed the spiders and snakes out of it. She was like a warped Disney princess—always talking to animals or wreaking havoc on those who wronged her.

The other wolves kept watch. If they weren't so huge, I would've forgotten they were there. Every step was silent and stealthy. I wandered farther from camp and enjoyed the silence. I was more than ready for a good night's sleep, even if my bed was a rock.

"Ah-choo!"

I dropped the firewood in my hands and searched for the source of the sneeze.

"Freya?" I called. In the distance, she thanked the creatures of the woods for lending us their home. It wouldn't have been her who sneezed anyway. I doubted witches had allergies.

"Who's there?" I asked.

Only silence answered.

Something moved in the thick brush, and my heart rate skyrocketed. Twigs snapped under racing footsteps. I chased the sound deeper into the woods. My legs shook from exhaustion, but whoever I followed tripped with a gasp. I was ready to pounce. I shoved a low-hanging tree limb out of the way, then skidded to a stop.

"Walker!"

Impossible.

My sister had fallen over a thick tree root. Her puffy pink coat was covered in dirt and grass stains. Her stringy hair was littered with leaves, and her green eyes were wide.

"Cadence." I practically growled. "What are you doing here?"

My mind raced with what all she could've witnessed—the dark witches' violent ways and the violence that met them in return. My brush with death. And, to top it all off, *werewolves* had arrived. I wasn't sure if I was angrier or more relieved to see her.

"I followed you."

No dip, Sherlock.

"All the way across *two* mountains?" I reached out a hand to help her up. Her fingers were cold in my grasp. "*Why?* I told you it wasn't safe!"

She tried and failed to wipe the dirt off her face. Dark circles hung under her eyes.

"Your story didn't add up," she said. "I had to know what you were up to. Why didn't you tell me she was a *witch?* It makes much better sense than you gallivanting off with a lady-friend."

I couldn't hold back my laughter. Even covered in mud, my sister could give me crap.

"Remind me to stop buying you so many books," I said. "I'm only making your burns stronger."

Cadence giggled, but her expression grew serious. "I didn't follow you just because I was curious...I got scared."

"What do you mean?" I asked and threw my arm around her.

"Something," she said, "was watching me."

I fought a shiver. Cadence had probably just gotten scared without me. Since mom died, I'd never left her for longer than a few hours. Still, her words unsettled me.

"Walker," Cadence asked quietly. "Are you okay?" She pointed to my leg.

"Yeah, Cady," I assured her. "Clearly, Freya healed me just fine—I was able to keep up with you, wasn't I?"

Her face lit with a mischievous smile.

Together, we grabbed some more firewood and headed for the others. The cave was cleared out. Wolves milled around our impromptu campsite, except for Ryder. He remained in his human form, glued to Freya's side right outside the cave.

Freya's jaw dropped at the sight of my sister.

Ryder scoffed.

"Another one?" he asked.

I stepped in front of Cadence.

"Watch how you talk to her," I warned.

"Shush, brother," Cady said. She walked past me and dropped the firewood in front of the cave. "I've never been much of a dog person anyway."

Freya snorted.

"I'm glad to see you're alive," she said to Cadence. "You must be one quiet hiker to have evaded my ears and the dark witches'."

My stomach squirmed at the thought of little Cadence anywhere near those awful things. She shrugged, as if she weren't frightened at all.

"I've always been good at sneaking."

Freya nodded, but her pensive expression did not agree with the motion.

I helped Cadence set up the fire but couldn't stop noticing how Freya stared at her. She clearly thought the explanation was more complex than childish bravery and excellent sneaking skills.

I wondered what other explanation existed.

*

Freya

Walker wasn't the only reckless sibling in his family, but I suspected he might be the only human.

I stared at Cadence. She lay on the cave floor with her back pressed against Walker's side. She was so close in the tiny cave that I could reach out and touch her. Walker snored peacefully and drool trailed out of his mouth. Cadence's eyes fluttered behind her eyelids.

I envied their peaceful sleep. I hadn't known it in since my mother went missing, though the loss of her wasn't the only thing that kept me up tonight.

Witches—well-trained ones, at least—didn't amble through the woods without a care in the world. We were tuned to the movements of the forest, from wind-blown leaves, to crawling insects and pouncing predators. The dark witches had concealed themselves with carefully crafted, powerful magic.

How did Cadence do it?

She was more than the little girl her brother thought she was.

I couldn't tell him that yet, though. Not when his world had already been flipped upside down. He needed something steady to hold onto, and there was nothing steadier than a family's love.

A tear slipped down my cheek.

I missed my mom, but I missed my coven too. I wanted to hear Josephine chide me for not mixing a potion *just* right or see the Elders perform a Saturday ceremony that would manifest a bountiful week for the coven. I wanted to smell the old books in the apartment complex's library and grow flowers in the garden.

I wanted, I wanted, I wanted.

So, I closed my eyes and pretended I was home. I heard my friend Thea's laughter, I saw Josephine's rare, but nonetheless dazzling smile, and I felt my mother's hug after a long day. I envisioned it so clearly, the ache in my chest became hollowness filled by self-fed lies.

But my dreams did not.

Silently, I watched my mother scream for help. She stood in front of the Goddess's statue, in between our coven's homes. Her eyes were black, as if she belonged to Lucifer. No one heard her. Elders, acolytes, and other witches milled by without even a glance in her direction. I tried to run to her, but I was frozen in place. I looked down to see what trapped my feet, only to find that I had no feet at all. I was a wisp of wind, forced to watch and nothing else.

An elder, Mabel Lightheart, stopped.

Finally, I thought, *someone is going to help her.*

The Elder tossed her long, white hair over her shoulder and scoffed.

"What is this?" she asked the crowd.

Witches now gathered to sneer at my mother. Hatred burned in each of their eyes.

"A traitor! Sybil Redfern is a traitor!"

"No!" I yelled, but no one heard.

My coven—my *sisters*—clasped hands and chanted a deadly incantation. The Goddess fountain's water turned crimson. Blood poured from her different forms' lips. No one heard my sobs and screams. Silent and alone, I watched my mother die.

*

Walker

Screams woke me up.

I lurched upright and nearly hit the top of the cave. Cadence thrashed and screamed beside me. Her pale face was scrunched, as if she were in pain. Wolves gathered at the mouth of the cave.

Tears poured down Freya's reddened face. Her hands were white-knuckled, and her nails drew blood on her palms. Endlessly, she screamed. Cadence echoed her. Birds fled from the blood curdling sound.

I maneuvered around Cadence to get between the two of them. Physical harm wasn't what hurt them. The remnants of my anger with Freya dissipated. No one suffering like this said mean things they actually meant.

"Wake up, Cady," I urged my sister. Lightly, I shook her arm. "C'mon, Cady-Cat. Get up."

She whimpered but didn't wake.

"Freya." I brushed a curl away from her clammy forehead. "You're safe, Freya. You need to wake up."

"Don't wake them," Ryder urged me.

I hadn't heard him approach. I glanced his way. He crouched in the mouth of the cave. He hadn't found a shirt during the night.

"You'll get blasted into next week when they're this volatile."

"I've woken Freya before," I countered, "and what do you mean by *they*? Cadence is human."

"Really?" Ryder rolled his eyes. "Then how are they dream-sharing?"

"You think they're dreaming the same thing?" I asked.

"No, dipshit," Ryder corrected, "I think your sister is broadcasting her dream to Freya. She's a witch."

I nearly choked.

"That's impossible."

He sighed. "Haven't you learned to stop using that word?"

Simultaneously, Freya and Cadence shot up. Freya clutched my arm to steady herself, and Cadence just stared ahead with glassy, vacant eyes. Their faces were puffy and red from the force of their tears. Slowly, Freya looked at Cadence.

"You saw it too?" she asked my sister.

Cadence nodded.

"What?" Ryder urged. "What did you see?"

"We need to get to your territory," Cadence ordered. "Let's move out now."

She got to her feet and walked out of the cave without another word. I did my best to mask my shock and ignore Ryder's smug expression. Even in a time like this, he found in joy in being right.

What an asshat, I thought. *This proves nothing.*

Freya offered me a pitiful smile.

"She's right," Freya said. "We better get moving. Walker, I don't know how, but I think she might be—"

"Don't say it," I begged and held my hands up. "Nothing against witches—when you guys aren't trying to kill me—but I just can't hear it right now. My baby sister is still my baby sister."

Freya nodded.

"She is," she said, "regardless of anything."

CHAPTER ELEVEN

Walker

Freya magically suffocated the fire, and we were on our way. My body ached from yesterday's travel and my night on the hard ground, but at least the remnants of pain had left my calf. Only a star-shaped scar remained. It might've been a pentagram, but I refused to acknowledge it.

Just too creepy.

All of us were quieter than before. Only the rustling of animals, chirping crickets, and never-ending wind filled the woods. I worried about Cady. Whatever she'd seen, it had left her rattled. She never went more than three seconds without talking. About two hours into our walk, she broke her silence.

"I'm hungry," she announced.

The familiar statement calmed some of my fears. Cady was *always* hungry.

"We'll be there in about twenty minutes," Freya assured her.

"And we'll have plenty of food," Ryder added. "Us werewolves like to eat."

The werewolf had been nicer to my sister since the incident in the cave. Despite his prejudiced reasons, I was grateful. It made him *slightly* more bearable to be around. I wondered if the other wolves shared his warped views of humans. As we walked right into their den, I hoped not.

We crested a hill, and a huge field came into view. In the center of the swaying grasses and sparse trees was a giant log cabin. It stretched three stories high and was nearly as wide as it was tall. Thick cedar columns surrounded the rectangular structure, which was embellished with green windowpanes.

Several people lounged on its wraparound porch. I could barely see their tan silhouettes in the distance, but I noticed they wore little clothes in the brisk weather. It must've been a werewolf thing.

Maybe they always feel the warmth of their fur, even when they aren't wearing it.

As we walked closer, the giant doors of the cabin swung open. An equally giant man barged through them. He had Ryder's freaky yellow eyes and tan complexion, but he was probably in his mid-forties. Smile lines surrounded his eyes, and his black hair was graying. He wore a plaid shirt that was unbuttoned to reveal his hairy chest and jeans, but he wore no shoes. Somehow, he made the look dignified.

I gulped but refused to take the step back that my body craved.

The worst thing to do to a predator was to let it know you feared it.

Cadence stood beside me with a friendly smile across her face. She clearly was unbothered by whatever macho energy this guy radiated. The wolves who had traveled with us walked to our sides and bowed their giant heads at the man.

Ryder did too, in his human form.

The man nodded at them, and they rose, then ran off to the other side of the cabin. The werewolves who'd been lounging on the porch jumped into the woods and shifted midair to join them. One second, they were people. The next, they were wolves.

"Cool," Cadence muttered.

The huge man quirked his head at her, and I braced myself for him to be offended somehow. Instead, he laughed. The deep timbre of it echoed across the field.

"It is, isn't it?" he said to her. He walked down the steps, right in front of my sister, and reached out his hand. "I'm Kai. I'm the Alpha of this pack, and that's my son, Ryder. He didn't bother you too much, did he?"

Cadence took his hand and gave it a hearty shake.

"He's all right," she said. "I don't think he likes my brother too much though."

Really, Cady? Throw me under the bus, why don't you?

Cadence gestured for him to move closer, and he leaned down so she could whisper something in his ear. I couldn't hear it, but the werewolves did and so did Freya. The few who remained on the porch laughed, while Ryder growled.

Is Freya...blushing?

For the first time, I wished I had some supernatural power of my own so I could know what on earth Cadence said.

"I like you, kid," Kai said to my sister and chuckled. "And Freya! It's been too long."

Freya schooled her face into a smile and hugged the Alpha. It was strange to watch such an imposing figure transition into a welcoming teddy bear. He fixed his frightening gaze on me.

Maybe he's still intimidating.

"And you are?" he asked.

I cleared my throat.

"He's the reason I wasn't captured by the dark witches," Freya interjected.

Kai lifted a bushy eyebrow.

"*He* can't speak for himself?" he asked.

"My name's Walker," I said. I refused to break his stare. "And I guess I'm a witch hunter." Kai laughed.

"Interesting company you keep, hunter." He gestured toward the house. "Come. You must be starved. Let's discuss the purpose of your visit over a hot meal." He winked at Freya. "I assume this meeting has a purpose—it's not like you come for social calls ever since my son screwed things up with you."

That explained Ryder's friendliness.

I followed Kai into his cabin, and Cady skipped alongside me. The entryway was grand but simply decorated by a few coffee tables, industrial light fixtures, and a mud-stained oriental rug. The hardwood floors were damaged here and there by claw marks. Two huge staircases led to the upper floors. Beyond them, on the ground floor, were two sets of doors. We quickly walked through one of them and entered a huge dining hall.

Iron chandeliers hung over long, wooden tables with leather-upholstered seats. One table was laden with a huge turkey, various trays of vegetables, and a freshly baked chocolate cake. I was just relieved none of it was raw. My stomach was so empty, though, I wasn't sure that would've been enough to deter me.

I took a seat between Freya and Cadence, nearest to Kai, who sat at the head of the table. Ryder cut into the turkey, and the platters were passed from person to person, just like any family meal.

"Alpha," Freya said. "Why have you denied our invitations for in-person conversations?"

He chuckled.

"I've missed your blunt words, witch," he said, "but we've denied nothing! My messenger met with yours and never returned. I haven't been eager to send another."

He stared at us with eyes that gleamed like a predator's.

"I've only been so welcoming because it's you," Kai continued, "though I do wonder where your mother is and why she wouldn't risk coming herself. She knows about my soft spot for you."

Freya flinched.

"Her mother is dead," I snapped. "Freya only risked so much and traveled so far to get answers."

Kai's jaw dropped in shock.

"Freya," he said, "I had no idea."

As she stared at him, her face was a blank page. I regretted my quick response. Hearing someone easily acknowledge your mother's death was almost worse than having to say it yourself. I busied myself with digging into the turkey, which tasted as great as it smelled.

"It's true," she finally said. "I came here because I have

nowhere else to turn. Witches keep disappearing and the elders have done *nothing.* My mother died trying to stop it. I have to step up now that she's gone."

I felt like an ass for being pissy over her snappiness. Grief and anger were hell on polite conversation. I knew that better than most.

Kai took a swig of water and spoke.

"The dark witches are obviously involved, but they're in no way powerful enough to be causing such damage."

Freya nodded, and Cadence continued to munch happily on her food.

"Yeah," Ryder agreed. "Within a few minutes, we wiped the floor with them."

"You know who I suspect," Kai said.

Freya sighed. "The vampires."

I choked on my food, and even Cadence paused her eating spree.

"Vampires?" I said, then muttered, "of course those exist. Why wouldn't they?"

Kai tossed his head back and laughed. Ryder rolled his eyes. I wondered how the apple fell so terribly far from the tree.

"Like actual bloodsuckers?" Cadence asked.

"Yes," Kai answered with no small amount of disgust. "They're horrible things created only to take life."

"And they'll do anything for power," Freya added. "Including kill a few witches. I asked the Elders to investigate them, and they said they were clean."

"They're never clean," Ryder snapped.

Freya rolled her eyes at him. I mulled over what they'd discussed.

"They wanted to start a fight between you," I looked at Freya, "and the werewolves, then take down both of you when you're weakened."

"Exactly," Freya agreed. She smiled. "You're picking up on supernatural politics pretty quickly, cowboy."

"Thanks, witch."

CHAPTER TWELVE

Freya

As we considered all the problems we faced, the air grew heavier. I'd known someone had attacked my coven, but I hadn't considered that it could've been to incite a war. Such a thing would draw the attention of not only the High Witch, but *all* the supernatural Leaders. Their attention was something we tried to avoid. They were law and law meant blood. We would all pay for letting such chaos brew, regardless of whose side we were on.

"If the vampires are bold enough to stir such trouble," I mused, "they could be bold enough to free the Bloodblade."

Ryder's fork paused on its way to his mouth, and his gaze met mine across the table.

"It only ever leaves a single bone," I said. Tears pricked my eyes. "That's—that's all that was left of her."

"But such a thing would've left a huge echo," Ryder argued.

"Not if its wielder was powerful enough to erase it," I said. "A siphon could've done it."

"Does anyone in your coven have that sort of power?" Kai asked.

"Not that I know of," I admitted, "but my coven has given me reason to doubt the truth."

Walker held up his hand. If we hadn't been discussing a potential war, I would've laughed. We weren't in high school.

"What's a Bloodblade?" he asked.

"Something you never want to encounter," I answered.

Cadence scoffed. "Well, that's vague."

I smirked at her blunt honesty, but I was quickly sobered by the answer to her implied question.

"The Bloodblade is a powerful weapon that decimates its enemies. It's unstoppable—fatal."

It made me sick to think someone could've used it against my mother. No witch should die by such a cowardly weapon. Kai spoke and pulled me from my thoughts.

"If a siphon covered the Bloodbade's tracks, there's no way to know if it's actually in use or if the vampires are involved at all."

"Unless we look for ourselves," I said. A plan brewed in my head. "If it's missing, we would know they're involved."

"Freya," Ryder snapped. "It's kept in the vaults of their castle! That's way too risky. You know we can't follow you there."

Still overprotective and telling me what I can't do.

"He's right," Kai said. "We can't afford to break our treaty, especially without proof of foul play. A vampire hasn't stepped foot on our territory in centuries and vice versa."

"I'll go with her," Walker offered.

Ryder scoffed.

"How are you even involved again?" he asked.

"The murders were pinned on me," Walker explained. "I need to clear my name to survive. I have just as much stake in this as any of you."

Cadence stared at her brother in horror. Walker noticed and blanched.

Stupid Ryder.

There'd been no need to frighten the little girl with the full truth.

"It's a very brave offer," Kai said to Walker, "but how much help can you provide? I know you haven't been trained, hunter. Without that, you're just a human."

Walker touched his holster. It wasn't a threatening gesture, but a display of memory. I doubted he'd ever shot anyone. What he'd done would stick with him.

"I nearly killed the head of the dark witches," Walker said.

"I might be good for something. If nothing else, I make a great human shield."

His lack of survival instincts continued to astound me, but Kai looked at him with reluctant admiration. Even Ryder had no quick-witted retort.

"Well then," Kai said. "It's decided. You two will travel into the heart of the bloodsuckers' lair."

Cadence laughed and waved a finger.

"Two?" she questioned. "I believe there are three of us here. Sir."

"Cady," Walker said. "It won't be safe."

"And leaving me with a bunch of werewolves will be?" she pushed. "Or better yet, leaving me to undoubtedly escape said-werewolves, travel through the woods alone, *again,* and then face a bunch of vampires will be? I'm going with you."

Walker chewed on his lower lip. I didn't envy the decision he had to make. Not only did Cadence's speech hold merit, but her eyes were wide with desperation. Now that she knew the danger her brother faced, she wanted to cling to him even more.

"I'll think about it," he finally said.

Kai threw his green napkin over his plate and rose. He looked at each of us then spoke to Walker.

"Whatever you decide, you should know we would protect your sister with our lives, were she to stay here."

Walker swallowed and nodded. "Thank you."

"For now," Kai continued, "you all should rest. You've had difficult travel, and something tells me it's not going to get much easier. Enjoy this reprieve while it's here."

Part of me didn't want to stop to rest. I *needed* to get to the bottom of things, and that would only happen if I kept moving. Unfortunately, even witches needed sleep.

My sleep just hadn't been very restful lately.

I shivered at the memory of the vision from the previous night but quickly shut it down and rose to my feet. They ached and protested the action.

Please be on the first floor.

"Ryder," Kai instructed, "show them to the guest rooms."

Ryder nodded obediently and led us to the stairs. I barely held in my sigh. No one hurried up the multiple steps. I distracted myself from my aches and pains by admiring the familiar cabin's beauty.

Portraits of ancient alphas hung on the wood-paneled walls. The hallway that led to the first floor of suites was lit by similar light fixtures. Bookshelves held countless werewolf historical literature. The first treaty of all supernatural beings, the coronation of the first Alpha of this pack, and the werewolves' triumph over a long-ago war with the vampires were a few of them. Interspersed between the artwork and books were doors that led to the suites.

"Any of these are available," Ryder said. "Have your pick."

He stared pointedly at me.

"Let me know if you need anything, Frey."

I rolled my eyes, and he grinned, then walked away.

"Good night, Freya!" Cadence called before shutting herself in the first suite to the left.

"Good night," I answered half-heartedly.

"I wonder if she's going to let me stay in there with her," Walker said and laughed.

"I don't know," I said. "She's quite independent, but she won't want you sneaking off to the vampires without her, so she'll probably be willing to negotiate."

Walker shook his head. "What eleven-year-old is so determined to face vampires?" he asked.

I chuckled and flipped my hair over my shoulder. "I was at that age."

"Yeah, but you're crazy."

"Says the one who *shot* a coven leader."

"You practically begged for help!" he argued. Genuine fear lined his face. "You were out cold."

I shrugged. "I had it handled."

Walker rolled his eyes. "Yeah," he agreed. "You were doing a great job of getting captured."

I laughed again. It was *nice* to speak to someone so openly. As the daughter of the Mother of our coven, I'd always had to watch my words around my fellow witches and even other supernatural creatures, like the wolves. Until Sybil's passing, I could never complain too loudly about the Elders or speak freely about my peers and risk stirring up drama. From childhood, I'd always put the coven first.

With Walker, I could exist without judgment.

"Thank you," I said, "for saving me."

He shrugged, like he saved people's lives all the time.

"Every second you don't kill me is a risk for you," he said. He lifted his hat, ran a hand through his hair, and sighed.

"Walker," I said. "Please tell me you don't feel guilty because I didn't murder you."

He chuckled.

"I don't," he promised. "I'm just not used to owing anyone anything."

"Neither am I," I assured him. I stepped closer to him. "Can we make a deal?"

"When a witch asks that, I feel like I should say no."

He grinned, and, when I slapped his arm, he merely laughed.

"I'm serious. Let's vow to forget about any debts between us. They cancel each other out—it's algebra."

"Eighth-grade-math," he agreed.

I smiled at him, but the moment was interrupted by Arion's loud meows. He scratched impatiently at my door.

"I guess this is good night," he said and winked. "Frey."

I rolled my eyes and, before he could walk away, I caught him by his sleeve.

"My name is Frey-*uh,*" I corrected. "That idiot is just too lazy to add the extra syllable."

"Hmm," Walker mused. We stood only half a foot apart. "You sure smiled pretty at him when he said it."

"You think I have a pretty smile?" I crooned. He flushed but didn't break my stare.

"So what if I do?" he challenged.

"What are you going to do about it?" I shot back.

I couldn't believe the words escaped my mouth and neither could Walker, judging by his dropped jaw. He noticed where my gaze had fallen and quickly snapped his mouth shut.

"You're very annoying," he quipped.

I scoffed and fought to hide the odd sense of disappointment that bloomed in my chest.

"Says you."

"Very mature."

"You're the one who started the insults," I reminded him. "Now, I'm not in much of a mood to be insulted."

I turned to leave.

Walker sighed. "Freya, wait."

He grabbed my arm at the same time that I spun to face him, and, for once, I was the one knocked off-balance. I stumbled forward, and Walker caught me. His arms, which I'd never noticed were quite impressive, cradled me. Our chests brushed, and our eyes locked. As Walker's gaze drifted to my lips, heat flooded my body.

Words left me and Walker too, because, the next moment, he kissed me.

His hands cradled my head, and I grabbed his arms. It wasn't gentle, but it wasn't the out-of-control kisses Ryder offered either. His lips explored mine slowly but passionately, like he wanted to get to know me from just one kiss.

I wanted to know him too.

He pressed into me, until my back was against the wall, and the front line of his body pressed against mine. I tugged his warmth, his utter solidness, closer. Butterflies fluttered through my core, and I couldn't recall ever feeling quite so *girly.* This wasn't some sexual transaction—it was a claiming. It was a desire deeper than the heat of his hands as they traveled down my body. It was more overwhelming than our ragged breaths in the quiet hall. It was more intense than his grip on my hips.

"Freya," he whispered between kisses.

His voice was lower and huskier than I'd ever heard it. My body grew hotter and hotter. I reached behind me to open the door to my room. My fingers brushed the handle.

"I brought some extra towels in case–"

At the sound of Ryder's voice, I jerked out of Walker's grasp, but not quickly enough. Towels fell with a thump at Ryder's feet, and I met his shocked gaze. With a growl, he snapped his open mouth shut and stormed away, leaving me alone with the cowboy yet again.

Both of us stared at each other with flushed cheeks, swollen lips, and no shortage of mortification. With more force than I intended, I shoved Walker away and bid him good night. When I slammed my door shut, he stood staring at where I had once been.

I tugged off my clothes and jumped into a cool shower with the hopes of washing away all the heat and shame still mingling on my skin. I couldn't believe myself. A witch killer was on the loose, and, here I was, jeopardizing an alliance with the son of a powerful Alpha to make out with a human. A *hunter.*

I scolded myself again and again, but, when I closed my eyes to sleep, it was Walker's crestfallen face that haunted me.

CHAPTER THIRTEEN

Walker

I leaned against the door inside my suite and wondered when I'd become such an idiot.

I had kissed her.

I had kissed Freya.

What the hell is wrong with me?

Before Cadence could see me so out of sorts, I hurried into the bathroom. A stack of clean clothes had been left for me on a shelf above the toilet. The werewolves were intimidating, but clearly generous.

I climbed into the simple, white-tiled shower and cranked the water as cold as it would go. It wasn't cold enough to erase the heat of Freya's body pressed against mine. The pouring water didn't drown out her soft gasp that echoed in my ears. I ran my thumb across my lips and cursed myself. I turned my face into the stream of cold water.

Maybe I can freeze out the memory.

I doubted it.

I'd never so impulsively kissed someone, not that I had much kissing experience anyway. I'd hooked up with some girls here and there. It had been fun, no doubt, but it hadn't lit a candle to kissing Freya. *Touching* Freya. Two of those times, I'd been heavily intoxicated, and the peck in seventh grade barely counted. I wondered if the werewolves had slipped something in my drink but quickly shut down the thought. They wouldn't need me to be drugged to harm me, and I doubted they had grand plans for humiliating me.

Ryder might.

It hadn't seemed like an embarrassing thing to do in the moment. Her eyes, her proximity, and all we'd been through together in the last few days had converged all at once. It had felt like the only thing to do. I had been so sure *she* wanted it just as badly as I did.

I was almost certain I'd seen her fingers reach for the door of her room. She had pulled me even closer, connecting me to all the soft curves of her body. She was so strong that I hadn't expected her to be so soft. And warm. And pliant.

Stop thinking about it, you idiot.

I couldn't imagine the kiss without reliving the aftermath. When she ripped herself away from me, downright horror had marred Freya's face. She'd been *disgusted,* yet she'd kissed me back. She probably felt that way *because* she kissed me back.

I was just a human after all.

I stayed in the shower for way longer than I ever did at home. Luckily, by the time I emerged from the bathroom, Cadence was fast asleep. Only her dark head of hair was visible under the fluffy, olive-green comforter. A matching bed with a wooden bedframe sat beside it. A little table with a lamp was sandwiched between them. A TV hung to my left, above a huge chest of drawers.

I clicked off the lamp between the beds and climbed under the covers. The clock ticked beside me, but hours passed before I quieted my mind long enough to fall asleep.

*

Walker

"You're extra grouchy today," Cadence so helpfully remarked.

We stood in line for breakfast in the dining hall. Werewolves surrounded us, and, boy, they could eat. Every plate that left the buffet line was piled high with eggs, ham, bacon, sausage, eggs, toast, and anything else you'd ever want for breakfast.

Cadence stacked hers as much as anyone around us, and, though I lacked an appetite, I did the same. In the cowboy business, you always accepted food when it was offered. You never knew when you'd get another break to eat.

When it came to journeying to a vampire castle, I figured the same principle applied.

Freya finally entered the dining hall with Arion hot on her heels. She must've stalled getting ready as long as possible. She wasn't exactly the type to be late. It was absurd for both of us to dread awkward interactions more than vampires.

"Good morning, Walker," Kai said from behind us. "I see the clothes fit."

I was dressed in a t-shirt, some slightly tight jeans, and my own Carhartt jacket. The jeans weren't Wranglers, but they'd get the job done. They'd given Cadence a similar outfit, which fit surprisingly well. Werewolves kept lots of clothes on hand. Shifting into a wolf did sound like an outfit killer that even a Tide stain stick couldn't fix.

"They do," I replied. "Thanks again for your generosity. Our room was great too."

"It would've been perfect if Walker hadn't snored all night," Cadence added.

I rolled my eyes at her antics. If she hadn't gotten up five times in the night, she never would've heard my snoring. Kai laughed and walked to the table we shared the previous night. I grabbed a hot cup of coffee and followed him. I swore I felt Freya's stare, but I was too much of a coward to meet it.

"Why are we walking so fast?" Cady asked.

I weaved through tables without a pause. "I have a busy day ahead."

The lie was bitter on my tongue. I actually hoped to get through breakfast before Freya even sat down. I'd still have to be alone with her for hours, but at least I'd have no witnesses to what was sure to be endless awkwardness by then.

"*We* have a busy day," my sister corrected. "I meant what I said—I'm not getting left behind again."

I groaned at her stubbornness, but she might have had a point. I'd always been the best at protecting my sister—maybe the safest place for her was with me.

I never thought I'd debate letting werewolves babysit my sister.

I dug into my breakfast, and Cadence did the same. Ryder and his father chatted softly and left us alone to our food. I was surprised the great wolf heir had yet to mock me for what he'd witnessed last night, but I supposed Freya's embarrassment was satisfaction enough. All I had on my plate were some eggs by the time Freya sat down next to Cadence. She wore a black top, her usual leather jacket, and her signature jewelry. Her hair was braided, but rogue curls framed her face.

"Morning, Frey," Ryder greeted her.

I snorted at the memory of her thoughts regarding his less-than-clever nickname. Those around me gave me weird looks, but I ignored them and munched on my breakfast.

"Ryder and his team will escort you out of our territory," Kai explained. "It's the best we can do."

Fuck my life.

There would be witnesses after all.

"Thank you," Freya replied. "That is very generous. I'll update you about our discoveries as soon as I can."

"And you, little one," Kai said to my sister. "Care to stay with us for a little while?"

Cadence looked at me with her big green eyes. No matter how badly I wanted to tuck her away from the world, Cadence would refuse it. Maybe I was crazy, but I seriously doubted that even a bunch of werewolves could contain her.

"She's coming with us," I said.

Ryder scoffed. "Idiot," he muttered under his breath.

He left before his father could chastise him. I squeezed the fork in my hand, then set it down. My appetite had disappeared.

"Let's go, Cady," I said.

For once, she didn't argue.

*

Freya

For two hours, I listened to Walker and Ryder argue. They bickered like an old married couple about anything and everything—the pace we set, the fact that Cadence accompanied us, and how to best get to the edge of werewolf territory.

We wandered through a field that sloped down toward the next valley. Grasses swayed in the soft breeze, and clouds twirled above us. Sunshine warmed my skin. I *should* have felt at peace in the fresh air, surrounded by the Goddess's greatest blessing—nature.

All I felt was irritation.

I tried to tune them out. I turned my ear toward the wandering rabbits, the mountain lion who thought he went unnoticed, and even the little ants working tirelessly on their homes. I talked to Cadence, who was funnier than any child should be, but we were persistently interrupted by the two morons I wasn't sure why I'd let kiss me.

I internally groaned at the memory of last night.

My guilt was the only thing that kept me from snapping at Walker. I knew he was hurt by my rejection, foolish as that reaction may be. He *had* to understand—I'd kissed him back. I had damn near done a lot more than that. I just couldn't take things any further. He shouldn't either, not with his sister to care for and his name to clear. I should've explained all this.

Talking about my feelings just wasn't my strong suit.

"Frey," Ryder begged. "Tell this dumbass he can't possibly know a better route when he's never even traveled it."

"Frey," Walker scoffed. "You're too lazy to even pronounce her full name."

As my self-restraint snapped, I stopped in my tracks.

"Ryder." I summoned a gust of wind that knocked him back a step. "You do walk fast—it's obnoxious. And you have *no* claim on me, so shut up. Stick to caring for your own pack."

I faced Walker. He leaned against a tree casually, but it was clearly in an attempt to not be knocked over by a gust of wind.

Smart cowboy.

But not smart enough.

I used wind to lightly slap his wrist with a tree branch. He didn't even flinch—we both knew I wouldn't actually hurt him, but it certainly made me feel a little better.

"Walker—you *don't* know where you're going, so shut up. Also, the only thing lazier than shortening a two-syllable name is stealing someone else's clever words. You've both driven poor Cadence and I to the brink of madness."

Cady snickered and gave me a high-five. The other wolves followed along with us silently, though some of them huffed in a werewolf's version of laughter. Arion weaved between my legs and purred.

Mom had always said I liked to make a scene.

Some days, she was right.

CHAPTER FOURTEEN

Walker

We finally left the werewolves behind at the edge of a lake that stretched for miles. Across it was vampire territory. I never imagined I'd feel so relieved to step onto the bloodsuckers' doorstep. I also hadn't thought it would be so beautiful.

The lake was clear enough that the copper and brown colors of the rocks beneath it were easily visible. Moss grew over the stones, and fish swam peacefully through the lake. Tall, purple flowers grew on its edges. Fog hovered over the water, and beyond it was a tall, spindly mountain. Snow that should've melted long ago capped its peaks.

"Back in the territory battles," Freya said, "they chose this border because of the lake. Wolfsbane grows on its banks, and a priest blessed the lake, so it's composed entirely of holy water."

She tucked the metal torch Ryder had given her in the waistline of her pants, so it rested against her spine. I assumed it was for nightfall, though that was still hours away.

"So the wolves really couldn't help you," I noted.

"There are ways to get across, but the battle that would ensue would be worse than what we already face. The Leaders would probably decimate all of Hol Creek to put a stop to their rivalry."

I silently prayed that would never happen.

"So," Cady said, "how do *we* get across?"

"There's the slow way and the fast way," Freya said ominously.

"I have a feeling I'm not going to like the fast way," I said.

She grinned, and I *knew* I wasn't going to like it.

"It's something I've been practicing," Freya said. "I'm confident it will work—you just have to trust me."

Arion pawed at Freya's leg. As he stared at her, his amber eyes grew round. She bent down, ran her hands through his fur, and sighed.

"Not yet, friend," she cooed. "It's too risky to unleash that form. You know what it does to you."

Arion hissed and sat back on his haunches.

"My idea," Freya said and stood, "is *slightly* less risky."

I didn't have the time or energy to dig into whatever conversation she'd just had with her cat.

"Freya," I said, "just tell us your plan."

"Just be still and have some trust, all right? It'll be a lot easier if you don't fight me."

"Freya—"

She muttered a spell, and a familiar hum filled the air. She pointed her open palms at my feet, then lifted her hands. Air flowed around me like a whirlwind, then whisked under my feet. It grew so powerful, it lifted me a few feet off the ground. I nearly fell on my face, but another gust of wind kept me upright.

"Squeeze your core, cowboy," Freya instructed. "You need to balance!"

"I did not agree to this!" I shot back.

Even Cadence chewed on her lip in concern.

"You sure about this?" she asked Freya.

"Positive," the witch answered without a moment's hesitation.

If I didn't want to strangle her, I might've been impressed by her ability to lie out of her ass. If she were so sure of this, she would've waited to get my permission.

Freya moved her hands toward the lake, and my body followed. Without another option, I did as she asked and fought to keep my balance. I teetered but didn't fall. When I was pushed over the lake, my stomach dropped.

After that first little push, the air moved much more quickly and whooshed past my ears. I flew over the water and through the fog. I gasped in terror, and a scream hovered in my throat. I barely contained it. If I survived my trip over the lake, I didn't want to be killed by vampires.

The landscape blurred past me, and suddenly, I was dumped on the lake's rocky shore. I landed with an *oomph,* but, other than getting the breath knocked out of me, I was okay. I pushed to my feet and scanned the lake for Cadence and Freya. They were mere specks across the massive body of water, then fog obscured what little view I had of them.

After a few heartbeats of silence, worry tightened my chest. I paced the rocky shore. When I was on the brink of losing my sanity, they appeared over the tranquil waters. Cadence sat in Freya's arms like a child much younger than her age. Arion sat on top of her. Once again, Freya's strength surprised me. There was so much of it wrapped into such a tiny body. They reached me in no time and landed gracefully by my side.

"That was awesome!" Cadence exclaimed.

"Why didn't I get a landing like that?" I asked.

"Maybe because I could barely see you," Freya argued. "Just be grateful I guessed where the shore was correctly."

A smile tugged on the corners of her lips. I rolled my eyes and stormed toward the rocky mountain before us.

And she calls me reckless.

"I hate to interrupt your dramatic exit," Freya called, "but you're going the wrong way. We need to head east."

Cadence giggled like a maniac.

I sighed but turned to the left and followed Freya's lead. Silently, I wondered why I'd ever wanted to kiss her in the first place.

I had grown familiar with the ache in my body from the endless days of hard travel, but the rocky terrain made me miss the soft ground and gentle slopes I'd complained about days ago.

The vampire's mountain was desolate and bleak. Black rock sloped sporadically to the mountain's peak, which was concealed by fog and snow. The sky was gray, and the air was still. Nothing roamed the craggy rocks, and the lack of life was stifling. The temperatures were strangely colder on this mountain.

The ground was loose in places, so I walked directly behind Cadence in case she fell. Luckily, she was a better climber than me.

"Why," Cadence asked and shivered, "is it so cold?"

I helped her up a particularly steep path. My breath added to the fog that surrounded us.

"We're not sure which came first," Freya said. Even her words were stilted from the chilled air. "The cold or the vampires, but this mountain has been lifeless for as long as I've been alive. It suits the vampires—the cold is good for preserving their meals and doesn't affect them. Walking corpses don't need body heat. It also slows anyone who dares traverse into their territory."

Fear twisted my gut, but I didn't let it show on my face. I couldn't let doubt creep into Cadence's mind now. It was far too late to turn back.

"Why didn't we pack more clothes?" I asked.

"Because it wouldn't make a difference," Freya said. "The mountain is enchanted—by the vampires or something else—no matter what you do, those with souls will feel the cold. It's why Arion remains unbothered."

The cat purred to emphasize the point.

"What *is* he anyway?" I asked.

I wasn't sure I really wanted to know, but I would talk about anything to distract myself from the cold climb we faced. I was grateful for Freya's outburst earlier. It had broken the awkwardness between us.

"He's my familiar," she replied. "A demon bound to me on my sixteenth birthday to be my forever companion, protector, and fellow traveler. Those three roles are the reason for his three forms."

"Demon?" I repeated.

I made a mental note to get on better terms with the creature.

Freya shrugged and continued climbing. "Think of him more as a spiritual entity. We can't control what we are, cowboy."

Fair enough. Rocks shifted under my feet, and I decided to focus on the task at hand rather than my possibly evil travel companion.

"Three forms?" Cadence asked. "I've only seen two."

Freya looked back and grinned. "Yes. I don't let his third one out very often."

But you let out the saber-toothed tiger? I thought. I hoped I never met Arion's third form.

We scaled the mountains in silence, other than the sound of our shallow breaths. The higher we climbed, the thinner the air became. My chilled feet felt like the rocks we climbed. Balancing became trickier.

"How far until we reach the castle?" Cadence asked.

"It's at the top of the mountain," Freya answered. I tried to find it, but all I saw were hints of rocks through the fog. "We'll travel to the east and enter from the side. There's an entrance to the dungeon there that few know about, so it's less guarded."

"How do you know about it?" I said.

Freya shook her head, but I caught a glimpse of the smile teasing the corners of her lips.

"My mother once had an affair with a vampire," she said. "It was quite the scandal."

"Have witches and vampires ever been friends?" Cadence asked.

Freya wiped sweat off her brow. It was a testament to our quick pace for *her* to be sweating in the cold.

"Our magic conflicts too much," Freya explained. "While we both gain power from the living, witches create life and vampires destroy it. Many witches believe vampires should be eradicated entirely because of that. Some differences are just too hard to overcome."

We walked for what felt like hours across the mountain.

Freya told us that we couldn't afford to stop. We had to reach the vampires' castle well before nightfall—it would be the best time to look for the Bloodblade.

"They sleep throughout the day in the safety of their castle," Freya said, "then hunt at night."

"Does the sunlight really burn them?" I asked.

With a gasp, Cadence slipped on a rock, but I quickly caught her. I didn't dare look down at the rocky fall she would've suffered. Freya frowned in concern but shook herself and continued to climb.

"No," Freya answered, "but there's some grain of truth to that. Daytime is the only time they can be truly killed, and the only way to keep them from rising again is fire."

I reached into my jacket and sighed in relief. The matches I always kept there were safe and sound.

"That's what the torch is for?" Cadence asked.

Freya nodded.

"Walker will use it. I have some fire magic I've been dying to put into use."

I wanted to tell her to keep the damned torch in case magic failed her, but I knew it would get me nothing but another argument. I wasn't afraid of Freya, but I also wasn't eager to break the peace between us.

"There," Freya said. "Do you see it?"

I turned my head to the right, looked up, and squinted.

Built into the edge of the mountain's peak was a dark, stony castle. When we'd approached it from the lake, I'd mistaken the castle's tower for the peak of the mountain. With its few windows and dark, textured exterior, it blended perfectly into the rocky mountain itself. Towers stretched into the sky, and their roofs were peppered with snow. Its lower levels spread wide across the mountain. No light flickered from within.

Fog kept me from getting a complete visual of the castle or an overall understanding of its structure. I couldn't even decipher an entrance, considering there were no grand gates or torches to light the way.

"Cadence," I said, "this is where you need to keep watch and be ready to run when we come out. Can you please do that for me?"

Cadence stared and stared at the mysterious castle and finally nodded. She knew I wouldn't budge on this. She was already too close to the vampires for my comfort, but if we somehow woke them and needed to escape, I wanted to be able to quickly grab her and go.

"Arion is going to stay with you," Freya told her. "He will guard you with his life and get you out of any trouble that comes your way."

The cat's ears flattened on his head, but he nodded. He clearly didn't want to leave Freya, but he would follow her orders.

Cadence ran her fingers through his hair, and he purred. It didn't hurt that he liked my sister as much as he loathed me. Freya muttered a spell and snapped her fingers. A hum surrounded the cat and didn't dissipate like it usually did after a spell was performed. Its buzz lingered in the air like an unanswered question.

"He's free to change at will now," Freya told me and looked at her familiar. "I advise him to do so *only* when absolutely necessary. No killing sprees, got it? We're not trying to start another battle."

Arion meowed, then laid down and sighed. I could've sworn he rolled his eyes too.

"And *no* running off," Freya added. "I don't care how bored you become."

Arion rolled around on the ground and seemingly ignored her. Suddenly, the single ounce of faith I had in the demon-cat evaporated. Freya noticed my stricken face and shrugged.

"It only happened once, and he didn't kill any innocents. He'll be a good boy, won't you, friend?"

Freya crouched and stretched out her hand to the cat. He licked her fingers and rubbed against her in answer. When we weren't preparing to break into a vampire castle, I'd ask her about whatever it was Arion did. For now, I would have to trust Freya, even if I didn't trust her familiar. She wouldn't leave Cadence in Arion's care if she didn't believe she'd be safe.

Admittedly, safe had become a relative term.

Freya rose to her feet and rubbed her hands together. Against the barren landscape, her hair burned like fire amid smoke. I waited for her to lead the way to the hidden entrance, but she stood as still as a statue.

"Freya?" I asked. "Ready?"

She jumped at the sound of my voice but nodded. She pulled the torch from out of her shirt and handed it to me. Its metal handle was cold and slippery in my hands. I wished I'd brought my work gloves.

"I'll light it for you if we need it," she promised and added quietly, "which I really hope we don't."

Cadence tucked herself behind a rock and obscured herself from view of the castle. Arion crawled into her lap. I took one last look at my sister and promised myself that it wouldn't be my last.

"I love you, Cady-Cat," I said.

"I love you too, Walkie."

I smiled at the nickname she'd had for me as a little girl. I could still remember when she had trouble with her R's. With a sigh, I tucked that memory away and followed Freya into the vampires' castle.

CHAPTER FIFTEEN

Freya

Cold gnawed at my fingers, and fear swirled in my stomach. I wondered how my mother survived the many long-ago battles she'd told me about as a child. I knew the spells she taught me and the fighting techniques I'd been tutored in from a young age, but I didn't know how to handle so many lives in my hands. I couldn't let Walker and Cadence die here—not when I was the one who had dragged them into my mess.

I rubbed my sweaty hands against my jeans and rolled my shoulders. The side entrance was straight ahead, just past a slope of jagged rock. As fog drifted, the small, nearly invisible door shifted in and out of focus. The fog was so dense, the rocks the castle perched on appeared to grow out of misty oblivion.

I slipped on a loose rock but caught myself. A few seconds passed before the rock that slipped struck something solid. Its *thump* was so quiet I nearly missed it.

"You okay?" Walker asked from behind me.

"Yes," I whispered. "Keep your voice down. We don't want them waking."

Vampires had excellent hearing and vision. They were the ultimate predators, designed to do nothing but kill and consume. Unlike witch covens or werewolf packs, they only lived together to amass power. Family meant nothing to them.

Only blood mattered.

Please, Goddess, I prayed, *don't let ours spill.*

The entrance to the castle was less than ten feet away. The

doorway was hardly discernable, even this close, but I kept my focus glued to it. The door was cut with straight edges and made from slightly smoother stone, just like Mom had told me.

Almost there, I thought.

I took a step, but no floor met my foot.

I gasped and braced myself for a freefall, but I was jerked back by strong arms around my waist. I sailed back and collided with Walker's chest. While I scrambled for footing, he barely stayed upright. When we finally caught our balance, we stood in silence for a few heartbeats.

"This is off to a great start," he whispered.

If he hadn't just saved my life, I would've hit him.

Instead, I replied, "Watch your step."

He snorted. Lifting his hat, he ran a hand through his wavy hair. The fog had dampened it, as well as our clothes and my own hair. It only worsened the bones-deep chill that seeped through my body.

I studied the steep drop before us, which was hidden mostly by fog. I sent a small gust of wind through it and revealed a twelve-foot-deep ravine that surrounded the castle's border.

"I guess your mom forgot to mention this?" Walker said.

I sighed. "Maybe they renovated."

There was a small ledge on the hidden doorway, but I didn't trust my own balance to jump and land there successfully. I trusted Walker's even less. I could levitate us with wind again, but the more magic I used, the more likely we'd wake the vampires. Their castle was covered in ancient wards to protect them from daytime attacks. Any magical breaking and entering would raise the alarm. I cursed whatever foolish witch had created the protections. Scaling the ravine would be equally risky.

The Sun drifted lower in the gray sky by the second. We only had a few hours before the moon took over, and absolute darkness blanketed the mountain. We would be in the vampires' castle with no way to kill them.

Think, think, think.

Finally, an epiphany struck. "A blending spell."

"A what?" Walker asked.

My stomach flipped with anxiety, but there was no better option.

"A blending spell," I repeated. "You know how I can alter my appearance?"

He nodded.

"Blending is like that, except you *blend* into the elements. I've done it before." *Once,* I didn't add. "It will get us across without alerting any wards that magic has been used, if I do it right. That's why it's called blending—if you completely join with nature, it won't leave a trace."

Walker rubbed his hands together and chewed on his lower lip.

"It sounds dangerous," he said.

"That's because it is," I answered honestly. "There's a chance that witches can-can lose themselves in blending. Sometimes, the pieces don't all fit back together like they did before. Pieces go missing if you're not careful."

Walker gulped but nodded.

"What about me?" he asked. "Can you...*blend* me?"

I shivered and not from the cold. Blending was dangerous to do to oneself. I couldn't imagine putting Walker at risk in that way.

"No," I said. "When I get across, I'll go in through the cracks of the doorway, then disable any wards cast. Be ready to travel your favorite way—by wind."

He nodded and adjusted his hat. "We don't have much of a choice, do we?"

"We don't," I said.

"Okay," he said and rubbed his hands on his jeans. "Okay. Let's do this."

My breath caught. I hadn't expected him to agree to my plan so easily. Unease churned my stomach upon the realization that Walker trusted me.

You can do this, I told myself, *you have to.*

I closed my eyes and recalled the afternoon Mom had taught me how to blend, only a few months ago.

"Feel the earth around you," she instructed. "Feel the air on your skin, in your lungs, and let it move through you. Let it become you."

We stood in our garden behind the cottage. I focused on the warm breeze against my skin and spread my magic beyond my body and into it. I melded my magic with the air, until I couldn't even feel myself breathe—I felt nothing but the warm breeze.

I opened my eyes and found myself bodiless. A scream tore through the memory of where my throat had been, and suddenly, I snapped back into my skin and flesh and bones. Pinpricks of pain rampaged through my body.

"You can't return so suddenly, Freya!" my mother chided. "That's how witches lose themselves. Isolate the fear of your power—of nature—and try again. You are braver than you know. You can do this—you have to."

"Why?" I snapped. Embarrassment heated my cheeks. "This is way too advanced for where I'm at in my training! Most witches—even Elders—struggle with blending! Why must I do it?"

"You are not most witches," Mom corrected. "You cannot be. Try again."

Mom had known I would need to blend, and she'd probably even known Walker would be there to catch me at the ravine. He trusted me and I trusted him, but, most of all, I trusted my mother. She wouldn't have taught me to do this if I were incapable.

"I can do this," I said aloud.

"You can," Walker agreed, but worry lined his face. "Be careful though. For me."

I smiled brittlely. "Careful's not really in my nature, cowboy."

I closed my eyes and focused on the damp, chilly fog that already fought to take over my body. With a deep breath, I relinquished control to it and sank into the damp air. Walker gasped, and I felt his hot breath rustle the air around me. I tuned it out. The vampires' magic tried to pull me away, but I fought back. With invisible hands, I held myself together, until I was still. Solid, and yet completely free of a body.

Only when I was prepared to see myself as nothing at all did I open my invisible eyes. Walker stared at me in wonder. I pushed myself across the ravine then toward the bottom seal of the doorway. Like frostbite, dark magic coated my presence.

These wards are old, I thought, *and powerful.*

I pushed myself through the cracks and ignored the intense claustrophobia that frazzled my many moving parts. The stone was damp and rough beneath me, yet I felt no scratches against my skin. I tuned out the disorienting sensation.

Slowly but surely, I slipped between the stones and entered a dark, damp hallway. Copper, something horridly sweet, and a sewer-like smell shrank the already cramped place. I listened for any signs of oncoming vampires but heard only water dripping on stones.

I shut out the horrible scents as best as I could and summoned all the moving particles of myself to come back together. I trusted my instincts to arrange them properly and took my time, despite the ticking clock that threatened to overwhelm my thoughts. With one last push, I came back into my body.

My feet landed on the slick stones, and I caught myself against the wall. I squinted to see my hands in the darkness.

At least you have all your fingers.

My head was faint from the exertion of so much magic and focus, but I couldn't let exhaustion win yet. I placed my hands on the doorway and shivered at the cold that seeped into my skin. The vampires' magic was too strong to permanently break, but I could manage a temporary unwinding. I only needed a few seconds to get Walker across the ravine.

I whispered a quick spell and pushed the door open. It creaked and grinded against the stone, and I prayed that it wasn't enough to stir any vampires.

Thank the Goddess the alarm bell isn't ringing.

Walker waited for me across the ravine. Without preamble, I sent a gust of wind that scooped him up and carried him inside the castle. He wobbled in the air but remained upright and didn't make a sound. Once through the door, I dropped him more gently than last time. He helped me pull the door closed, though the chilly wind fought to keep it open. The wards snapped back into place as soon as the door shut.

We panted in the dark for a few heartbeats.

"So," I whispered, "did I get myself put back together properly?"

"Yeah," he answered quietly. "You were a cyclops before, right?"

I gasped, and Walker chuckled quietly.

"Asshole," I muttered and trekked down the hall.

I placed my hands on the slick, stone wall and used it to track our path. Walker followed me and continued to laugh quietly at my expense. I was about to tell him to shut up when he spoke.

"You look as pretty as ever," Walker promised softly. "Don't stress your vain, little heart about it, witch."

"What makes you think I have a heart?" I whispered.

I reached a gap in the stone and gingerly pressed my hands into it.

"Please be a secret door," I muttered to myself.

Clammy fingers gripped my hands, and I yelped. I jumped away from the hand and slammed into Walker. With a gentle grip on my elbows, he helped me right myself.

"Wait!" someone whispered. The voice was too raspy to decipher a gender. "Please, you can't leave me! You're—you're not like them."

Drip, drip, drip.

"Who are you?" Walker asked.

I wanted to light the torch to see the figure, but it was too risky. We already drew too much attention.

"I don't know anymore," the person whispered. "I've been

here for too long."

My heart broke. This must have been one of the vampires' living blood banks. I'd heard they kept their favorite flavors alive sometimes, but I hadn't expected to come face to face with one of their victims.

"We need to keep going," I told Walker. "We can't help."

He didn't move.

"Please," the person pleaded. They sounded young.

"We'll come back," Walker promised.

I cringed. That was not a promise I was sure we could keep. Regardless of what I knew to be true, it took everything I had to walk away from the prisoner.

The captive sighed. "Please."

I vowed to myself we would keep Walker's promise and kept walking.

I held my hands in front of me and hoped it was a straight shot to the next hall. All the while, I fought the fear that threatened to swallow me whole. I'd always known the vampires were rotten, but I'd never had many encounters with them. I'd only met one, and that was when I was a child. I hadn't known the reason for his visit, but I remembered his pale face and pointed fangs.

My hands hit slick stone and I nearly jumped out of my skin.

"Stop!" I whispered.

Walker stopped just short of my back. His body heat radiated in the small space, especially in comparison to the chill of the ward that blocked the entrance.

There's more of them?

My back muscles ached, and my stomach felt hollow— both were signs of using too much magic in too little of time— but I had to get through the wards somehow. If I kept us hidden, I wouldn't need my magic for combat anyway.

I whispered the spell and forced my magic to temporarily unwind the wards. Walker shoved the heavy stone door open, and we entered a wider hall. Dim light filtered through windows

THE WITCH AND THE COWBOY

that were at least twenty feet above us, built into a vaulted ceiling. Unlike the dingy exterior, this part of the castle actually resembled a castle.

The floors were such a bright white, they practically glowed. The walls were crafted from the same slick, black stone that the doors were constructed of. Red, silver, and purple tapestries hung on the walls. Some of them depicted battles and others showed portraits of pale figures. Ornate vases sat upon hand-crafted tables. Crystaline pitchers were filled to the brim with crimson liquid. Sculptures of kings and princes peered at us with vacant, stony gazes.

It was terribly lovely.

"We need to find a staircase that leads down to the vaults," I reminded Walker. "It's in the Master's suite."

His steps stuttered.

"Who's the Master?" he asked.

"The Head Vampire," I explained. "It's important we don't wake him."

"Really?" he whisper-yelled. "You don't want to stop to say hi? You never mentioned this part of the plan, Freya!"

I sighed. "Would it have mattered?"

"No," he said and sighed. "I guess not."

We walked as quietly as possible, but our steps still rang across the cavernous hall. We followed the main hall until it curved to the right, and a new hall branched to the left. It was nearly identical to the one we'd just traveled down, except more doorways lined its walls. This was their sleeping quarters.

My mother had described the place as a maze the one time she'd visited. Now that I thought about all the information she gathered from her vampire beau, I wondered if he'd been a mere tool for her.

Probably.

Witches rarely put much value in their fleeting romances.

We came across a grand set of double doors. It was bordered by glittering obsidian, and a red cross hung upside down above it.

"A little on the nose, don't you think?" Walker whispered.

I agreed but shushed him. Now was not the time to critique the vampires' interior design skills.

I grabbed one of the polished silver handles and sensed another ward to get through.

You can do this, I reminded myself. *You have to.*

CHAPTER SIXTEEN

Walker

Freya grabbed the silver handles of the ostentatiously named Master's suite and whispered a spell. As the words left her mouth, her face grew pale. I wanted to ask if she was alright, but the door clicked open. I couldn't risk waking the vampire, so I simply hurried through the doorway and immediately gagged.

Something sweeter than cheap perfume mingled with the dark scent of decay. I recognized it from the rotting animals I'd found in the woods and cows I'd had to remove from pastures.

Death.

To our left, three naked vampires rested on a huge, silver-framed bed—two women and a man. Most of their pale skin was covered by purple sheets. Their chests did not rise and fall with breath, and they lay as still as corpses.

Half-fascinated and half-repulsed, I averted my gaze. A giant, taxidermized wolf head hung over the bed. Its mouth was fixed in a snarl. I thought of Kai's welcoming smile and grimaced. Paintings of pale, beautiful people from various centuries decorated the black walls. Across from the bed sat a black velvet couch, and next to it was a silver table. A decanter filled with crimson liquid sat on top of it.

My stomach rolled so loudly, it was a miracle the vampires did not wake from it. Freya glowered at me, and I shrugged.

How am I supposed to control my stomach? I thought. *Some people don't have spells for everything.*

I followed Freya to the far corner of the room, where a tall bookshelf stood. I scanned the titles.

Dante's Inferno, Strange Case, The Picture of Dorian Gray...
Dracula.

I barely held in a scoff.

Freya ran her hand over the left side of the bookshelf, then the right. I assumed she was looking for some hidden entrance to a secret passage. I followed her lead and ran my hand over the top of the bookshelf. I felt nothing but a flat surface.

While Freya ran her hands over the shelf, I studied the books again.

All the books were perfectly organized alphabetically by author, except for *Dracula*. It was in the H section instead of the S section. I placed my hand on the top of the book and was surprised by how cold it was. I hadn't thought my hands could *get* colder.

I tugged on the book, and the bookshelf groaned.

"Damn it," Freya muttered. She quickly cast a spell. The shelf continued to swing back, but now, it moved silently.

Someone mumbled something behind me.

Both of us froze. We didn't even breathe. Reluctantly, I glanced at the vampires. One threw an arm over the other, then went still again. My heart beat rampantly, though I begged it to shut up. Regardless, the vampires remained motionless.

Freya crept silently into the dark passage beyond the bookshelf, and I hurried after her. Once we were inside, the bookshelf swung closed on its own.

"Should we be worried about that?" I whispered.

She hesitated. "I'll get us out."

We stood in complete darkness. The temperatures had dropped even more, though the air was drier than any other part of the mountain. It burned my throat and my lungs.

"Should we light the torch?" I asked.

No one answered, and I panicked.

"Freya?"

"Oh," she said. "No."

I nearly laughed. "Did you shake your head?"

"Just take my hand, Walker."

I stuck my hand out in the direction of her voice, and her cold fingers found mine. She led me to straight ahead. The hallway was just wide enough for us to walk side-by-side. I kept my other hand on the hall's wall to keep track of where we went. Freya's nails scraped against the stone so I knew she did the same.

"Why can't we light the torch?" I asked.

"We can't risk setting off any wards yet. Vampires tend to keep track of any fires lit in their castle."

As we traveled deeper into the darkness, shapes danced around us. They weren't the same as those Freya had sent after me. They were just sinister blurs of color. They were clearly conjured from my own imagination, considering Freya showed no reaction to them.

Not that you could really see it if she did.

I squeezed her hand, and she did the same to mine.

"We should come across stairs soon," Freya warned. "It's time to risk a fire."

Hope and fear warred in my chest. The closer we grew to the Bloodblade, the sooner we got the hell out of this place, but taking risks wasn't a number-one priority in a castle full of the living dead.

I pulled the torch from the back of my waistband.

"Wait," Freya said. "I might be able to conceal it if I summon the fire with my own magic. Pairing it with a concealment spell will at least be better than nothing."

She whispered a spell, and a hum filled the hall. While I tucked the torch away, a small flame erupted in the palm of her hand. In the orange glow of the flame, her face was even paler than before. The walls and floor shined—not a cobweb or speck of dust could be found.

We journeyed a few feet farther and came across a steep stairway. It descended into complete darkness, but the first few steps were distinguishable. The stairs were crafted of the same dark stones as the wall but were slicker than I anticipated.

Everything about this place was designed to be difficult.

"Nice call on the light," I said.

"I've already had too many close calls with falling to my death," she replied.

We traveled down two cramped flights of stairs then entered a much larger space. Lights turned on around the perimeter of the room and revealed cases of jewels, crowns, and other riches. It was enough treasures to be easily worth triple my lifetime's salary. For a moment, I couldn't help but be impressed. Another light powered on. It came down from the center of the domed ceiling and shined on a silver platform.

An *empty* silver platform.

The fire in Freya's hand went out like a smothered candle.

"They really did it," Freya said. "They killed my mother."

"Don't be so quick to judge, witch," a man purred from behind us.

I jolted in panic and tried to face the newcomer, but my feet were stuck to the floor. No matter how desperately I begged my legs to move, they remained trapped in place. The most I could manage was to bend my knees.

"It's a trap," Freya whispered.

I tried to pull my feet free from my boots, but they also refused to budge. It was as if they'd grown into the floor, and I no longer had any control over them.

"Of course it's a trap," the same man crooned. "And I'm offended you thought sneaking into my home would be so easy."

Footsteps echoed across the room, and the pale man from the suite—the Master—stood before us. Like some twisted, male Snow White, his hair was raven black, and his skin was so pale, it was practically translucent. His eyes were such a dark brown they were almost black. I fought not to squirm under his gaze.

The Master grinned and revealed his yellow, pointed fangs.

"You brought a snack." He clasped his hands together. "That *does* lessen the insult."

"You traitorous bastard," Freya sneered. "My mother never

harmed a vampire—even when others pressured her to do so—yet you *killed* her!"

"Remember where you are," the Master warned.

Several more vampires crept out from the dark shadows of the room. Their stares were hungry, and their footsteps were silent. As they passed under the various lights, their skin shone like moons.

"I don't care where I am," Freya growled. "You will pay for what you did."

She shook with rage, and my chest ached. I had to ask her to do the impossible—control herself when faced with her mother's killer.

"Freya," I warned.

The Master chuckled. "You should listen to your human."

A tear slid down Freya's cheek.

"You'll pay for this," she vowed.

She raised her palms and yelled a spell. For a moment, I thought her pain might actually be powerful enough to save us, but no hum filled the air.

No flames sparked in her palm.

We were officially a vampire's dinner.

CHAPTER SEVENTEEN

Freya

I couldn't stop shaking.

The Bloodblade was gone and so was my magic.

I could still feel the brittle, light bone in my hand. The only remnant of my mother.

I should've known the vampires had done it from that single speck of evidence, yet I hadn't wanted to believe she'd died at the hands of such awful creatures and their pathetic weapon. Their *only* weapon that could have killed a witch as powerful as she.

"Did you sneak up on her?" I asked. "When you killed her, did you give her the chance to fight back? Or did you sweep in with one fatal, spineless blow?"

At least if she'd died at a witch's hands, she would've died in an honest battle. She would've died at the hands of something *living*. A cold, pale face was the last one she'd seen.

Godsdammit, I need to stop crying.

"Your mother was in the way, so she was removed," the Master snapped. "There's no need to make it more complicated than that."

My breaths couldn't come fast enough. My back ached, and my heartbeat rattled in my ears. The vampires crept closer, though I could barely discern them from each other. My vision swam with exhaustion and tears.

Something wasn't right. I'd performed quite a few spells, but nothing that should've pushed me this far.

Walker stared at me in concern. His hand twitched, like he was tempted to reach out and hold mine like he had in the hall. I was glad he did not. Even now, I wouldn't admit to weakness in front of my mother's killers. They wouldn't take that last shred of pride from me.

"Feeling unwell?" the Master asked. He smiled with sick glee. "A little birdie might've told us you were coming. We prepared accordingly."

"What did you do to her?" Walker asked in a low voice—the one he usually preserved for defending his sister.

The other vampires hissed and crept even closer. Their pale faces were contorted by bloodlust. The Master held up his hand, and they came to a swaying stop.

Or maybe I'm the one who's swaying.

Smugness laced the Master's every word. "She's been under a draining spell since she stepped foot on my mountain."

"The dark witches," I whispered.

They were the only ones underhanded enough to pull off such a thing. I'd felt magic clinging to my skin on the journey through the hellish, rocky terrain, but I'd assumed it came with the territory.

Stupid, stupid, stupid.

The Master swept his arms wide and looked at each of his followers.

"Remember, darlings," he said, "we can't kill the witch just yet, but the boy is fair game—just remember to share. We all deserve a little hunter blood."

*

Walker

This is where I finally die.

Vampires closed in all around us. They wore ragged clothes from varying decades, and their blood-stained fangs dripped with drool. Fear and revulsion churned my stomach.

I almost wished Freya had done away with me days ago.

Freya swayed beside me. Her skin was nearly as pale as the undead creatures who leered at us, but she grimaced like she always did when she searched for an impossible solution. I floundered for one too. I couldn't accept death now, not with Cadence waiting outside for me.

I shifted nervously, and metal pinched my back.

The torch.

The vampires were only a few feet away. They were clearly stretching out our deaths for their own enjoyment, which meant they were confident we had no escape route. They might have been right, but I *did* work better as an underdog. Still, the moment they noticed the torch, it would be ripped out of my hands.

I nudged Freya, and she glared at me for breaking her concentration. I quickly glanced at my back and prayed she'd understand my silent message. She hesitated. I looked around at the encroaching vampires, dipped my chin toward her, then glanced behind me again.

"Wait!" Freya yelled.

Perfect.

She grabbed all the vampires' attention. Slowly, I reached for the matches in my jacket-pocket.

"I'm the heir to the coven of Hecate," she said.

I wrapped my hands around the matches.

"You want power?" Freya demanded. "I can offer it to you."

I kept one hand in my pocket and slowly moved the other up.

"Can you, little witch?" the Master questioned. "You don't even know the power we hold."

One of the vampires finally glanced at me, and I scratched the back of my head. She smiled at the nervous gesture and licked her fangs. I gulped, and my fear enticed her more. She twirled a strand of greasy brown hair around her finger and stepped closer.

"Claire!" the Master snapped. "Contain yourself."

Claire stopped in her tracks and averted her eyes. The

smallest ounce of relief warmed my chest.

"We both know my coven could decimate the dark witches with one spell," Freya said.

The Master cackled.

"You think I risked unleashing the Bloodblade because of some promises made by those zealots?" The Master sneered. "That's the problem with you witches—you've underestimated us for centuries—you've thought us hungry fools. That's what your mother thought. We proved her wrong, and we'll prove you wrong too."

Freya shook with rage, and the vampires drew closer to her.

I didn't allow myself even a breath to doubt my plan.

I drew the torch from behind my shirt and struck the match. I connected the lit match to the torch in the next second and waved it in front of Freya. With one last cry of anger, she sent a gust of wind into the flames, sending them in an arc before us.

Six vampires caught fire and fell to the ground. The fire spread from the inside of their bodies to the outside. Flames burned through their eyes and their opened, screaming mouths. Their skin blackened into unrecognizable husks. In mere seconds, they were ash.

Freya raced for the stairs, and I followed her with the lit torch still in my hand. Though she stumbled here and there, her feet did not fail her.

"Get them!" the Master roared.

With one hand, I waved the torch wildly behind us. After seeing their friends burned to the ground, the vampires hissed, but kept their distance. I used my other hand to keep my balance. We practically flew up the steep stairs—now was not the time to be clumsy.

When we reached the top of the stairs, one of the vampires was bold enough to swipe for my torch. His ice-cold skin grazed mine, but instead of panicking, like he'd undoubtedly hoped I would, I tilted the torch and set him ablaze. One thing horses had taught me was to keep my effing calm. The vamp's friends jerked away from the scene.

"Here," Freya said.

I followed her, and we reached the hidden door.

The *closed* hidden door.

"I have an idea," Freya whispered, "but you'll have to give me the torch."

We had only a few seconds before the remaining vampires caught up to us. I handed her the torch, and Freya hurried backward a few steps. Her back pressed against the wall, so she wasn't in the way of the hidden door.

"You can have the human!" Freya yelled. "Just let us talk things over in peace once you're done with him."

She held the flame closer to her face.

"Stay there," she whispered.

Surely, Freya wouldn't actually betray me to work with her mother's murderers? Right?

I had no more time to ponder the question because the vampires arrived.

And they were hungry.

*

Freya

Please don't fail me again, I thought.

The vampires raced down the hall. Their hands were out, ready to grab Walker. Their fangs were fully extended and prepared to tear into his throat.

Luckily, Arion was close enough that I'd been able to siphon some of his power and counteract the draining spell. It was something I rarely did—Arion's power was volatile and difficult to convert, and it always felt like a violation, regardless of how willingly he offered it.

Desperate times call for desperate spells.

The vampires were only a few feet from Walker. Though his fists shook at his sides, he stood stoically before them.

Just a couple steps closer, I thought.

Now.

With the last drops of magic that I'd taken from Arion, I wrapped wind around Walker and pulled him to me. His landing on the floor next to me was far from soft, but at least he wasn't someone's meal. The vampires moved too fast to follow him and collided into the doorway.

Under the force of five racing vampires, the door flew open.

I helped Walker to his feet. Before the door could close again, we hurried through it. While the vampires were still disoriented from their crash, I ended them with the torch. We were out of the dark hallway before their screams diminished, and they were nothing but ashes.

Walker and I raced past the Master's empty bed and into the endless grand hall. The light from the windows had dimmed even more—the sun would set soon. Together, we raced down the hall. I recalled the path we'd taken before—we turned right, then left. I wouldn't be trapped in this maze of a castle. Still, as we neared the main hall, I couldn't shake the feeling that something was wrong.

More vampires than we'd encountered lived here, and the Master wouldn't let us go so easily. I wouldn't make the mistake of underestimating him again. As we made the final turn, my fears were made reality.

More than twenty vampires awaited us.

They filled the hall, which had once seemed so wide but now felt cramped. Each of their pale faces were twisted into hungry sneers.

Someone laughed behind us, and we spun to face them.

The Master grinned.

"Once again," he crooned, "the witch is bested by the lowly vampire."

My heart sank.

The vampires surrounded us but kept just out of reach of the torch. I pushed our only saving grace into Walker's hands and moved until we were back-to-back. I didn't give him the chance to protest. For whatever reason, the vampires would keep me alive, but they had no reservations about killing him. If there was any way he could escape, maybe he could send help.

The hope was fickle.

Who would even try to rescue me?

Josephine, I thought. My goddessmother would not betray me.

The vampires crept closer, and Walker waved his torch wildly.

One of the vampires swiped at me, but I batted him away. Thanks to Mom's training, combat was second nature, but no one could fight twenty assailants, especially without magic. I didn't even have the energy to siphon more magic from Arion.

The vampires knew. They grinned and took turns reaching for us. All of them were careful to avoid Walker's flame. One cut his arm open, and the vampires hissed in anticipation.

This was it—the end.

I weaved my fingers through Walker's and squeezed.

"I'm sorry," I whispered to him.

"Enough toying, children," the Master declared. I couldn't see him past the swarms of pale, ravenous faces. "It's time to feed!"

CHAPTER EIGHTEEN

Walker

At least Arion will get Cadence out of here.

I squeezed Freya's hand and prepared myself for the onslaught of vampires. If I would die, I would take as many of them out with me. The Master commanded them to attack. I raised my torch a little higher and fought the urge to close my eyes.

Boom!

Past the herd of vampires, stone exploded across the hall. Amid the dust and stone appeared a huge saber-toothed tiger with a wild-eyed girl on his back.

Cadence.

My stomach fell to the floor.

As she released a war-cry, my baby sister didn't even look afraid. While Cadence pelted the vampires with rocks, Arion attacked them with his own fangs.

"Move!" Freya snapped.

More motivated than ever to escape, I used the distraction to my advantage and attacked as many vampires as I could with my torch. With every one that turned to ash, I was one step closer to the hall that Arion and Cadence had busted through.

One step closer to escape.

Freya fought ruthlessly beside me. She punched, kicked and elbowed vampires then shoved them into my line of fire. We gained a rhythm in the chaos—if a vampire attacked her, I would attack it and vice versa.

Ash rained in the hall.

The putrid scent of death and smoke burned my nostrils. I didn't have time to risk a glance at Cadence, but rocks zoomed past me, so I trusted she was still alive and fighting.

Crazy kid.

I couldn't say I didn't love her all the more for it.

Finally, we neared the dungeons—our avenue for escape. Only ten or so vampires stood between us and the exit, but more of them were pouring into the hall from behind us. It was now or never. We had to get out of here.

With a roar that shook the walls, Arion ran right into vampires in front of the dungeons and knocked them to the side. He charged down the hall, and Cadence ducked on his back so she wouldn't get smashed by the ceiling. It was a tight squeeze for the overgrown cat.

"You fools!" the Master hissed. "I'll get them myself!"

Freya and I wasted no time—we raced after Arion. Dim light shone at the end of the tunnel, past the cacophony of angry vampires. I could almost feel it against my skin.

A figure moved to my right.

"Please," a small voice croaked. "Please don't leave me."

I stopped.

"Walker!" Freya begged. Her hand tugged my sleeve. "Walker, we have to go! There's no time!"

I waved my torch in front of the cell and nearly vomited.

Blood—new and old—was spilled across the cramped cell. A rotting carcass sat off to the side. It had probably once been a girl, though I only knew that from the ribbon in her hair. Her face and body had long ago rotted beyond recognition and flies feasted on her remains.

Before me—and alive by some definition of the word—was a boy not much older than Cadence. Blood stained his once white shirt and khaki pants. Grease and dirt were matted in his hair, and his bruised face was sunken from starvation. His breath fogged the air between us, though he didn't notice the cold. His hands wrapped around the metal bars between us without hesitation.

"Please," he whispered.

I searched for an entrance into the cell, and Freya cursed beside me.

"It's here," she said and pointed at to my left. "And it's locked."

Cadence and Arion waited for us at the end of the hall. He didn't have enough room to turn around. I wanted more than anything to escape with them, but I'd made a promise. I made a habit of keeping them.

"Go," I told Freya. "This is my mess. I'll deal with it."

She scoffed. "You're a fool, Walker Reid."

"Well," the Master crooned. "Isn't this cute? A lover's quarrel."

I spotted a stray rock and handed the torch to Freya so I could reach for it.

"Stay back," she warned the Master.

I grabbed the rock and beat it against the rusty lock. It should've been replaced years ago, but clearly, bloodsuckers kept their wards far more up to date than their mundane precautions.

"I'd be careful with that torch if I were you," the Master said to Freya. His voice dripped with sarcasm. "Killing a Master would surely get the attention of the Leaders." He giggled.

The rock clanged against the lock, and its resistance reverberated up my arm. On my third swing, it finally snapped.

I took the boy's filthy hand and pulled him out of the cell.

"Walker!" Cadence yelled. "No!"

The boy smiled and revealed his fangs.

Shit.

"My hero," the vampire before me purred.

He lunged for my throat, and I yanked wildly against his hold. His grip was iron-clad. When he was only an inch from my jugular, flames struck his head. I wrenched myself free from his hand right before fire devoured it.

Freya crouched in front of me with the torch lit in her hands. She searched my throat for wounds. Behind her, the

Master lunged. I reached for the torch, but it was too late. He moved faster than anything I'd ever seen and threw our only weapon to the ground. The damp floor easily snuffed the flame.

The Master grabbed Freya by her waist and hoisted her over his shoulder. She screamed and kicked, but the Master only grinned.

I reached for Freya, but the Master was too fast. He raced down the dungeon hall with blinding speed.

"Freya!" I screamed.

Arion roared behind me. The other vampires awaited their master from the entrance to the main hall.

My heart lurched upon the most horrifying realization of my life.

I can't save her.

"Finish them," the Master told his followers.

With fang-bearing grins, the vampires encroached farther.

"Go!" Freya shouted. Tears ran down her cheeks. "Go, now!"

I kept running.

She hadn't left me.

I wouldn't leave her.

Footsteps pounded down the hall behind me. I turned my head and nearly fell to the ground in shock. Cadence raced after me with unnatural speed. Her little arms pumped at her sides, and her hair flew behind her. Determination lined her face.

Her eyes glowed bright enough to light the hall.

Even the Master stared at her in wide-eyed shock. She pushed past me to face him. Entranced by the power she emanated, I was too late to stop her.

"Let her go," Cadence demanded.

It was *her* voice, but not. Power amplified the words. The dungeon's halls rattled from the force of it.

The Master sneered, but his expression wasn't as venomous as before. Fear softened it.

"Be gone, witch," he ordered. "I'll even let you keep your

human."

Cadence smiled, and it wasn't recognizable in the slightest. Gone was the little girl in her eyes. Magic and vengeance swirled in their depths.

"Wrong answer."

She pointed a single finger at him and said a single word.

"Trap."

Huge roots grabbed the Master's feet. While he was distracted, Freya wrangled an arm free and elbowed him in the nose. His grip loosened just enough for her escape him. She ran to my side and watched my sister's—

My sister's spell.

"Help me!" the Master yelled at his followers. "You imbeciles! Help me *now!*"

They glanced at Cadence and didn't move an inch.

Huge, pink-speckled, green walls grew from the roots, until they towered over the Master. Screaming like a caged animal, he clawed and pushed at them. Their membranous walls stretched but held strong. He tried to climb them, but they were too tall and too slick. Long spikes grew on the tops of the walls.

"It's a flytrap," Freya whispered. "She summoned a whole godsdamned Venus flytrap."

Beyond the Master, a similar green wall covered the entrance, and the vampires who'd crept into the dungeon hall now clawed at it to get *inside* the castle halls. None of those on the other side fought to escape. The Master continued to thrash and scream, but his words were too muffled to understand.

Snap.

The trap snapped shut, and he went completely silent.

Just as quickly, Cadence collapsed. I caught her just before her head hit the stone.

I gasped. "Cadence!"

"She's fine," Freya promised. "Every witch is exhausted after her Awakening."

I nodded, though it felt like far too normal of a response to what had just happened. I'd always feared getting Cadence through human-puberty—I was *far* from prepared to get her through a witch's coming-of-age.

"We need to get out of here," Freya said.

The Master pounded against his trap.

"As badass as it is," Freya said, "it won't hold forever."

With Cadence in my arms, I hurried as fast as I could down the hall to where Arion still impatiently waited. The demon stamped his feet and growled relentlessly.

"How are we going to get across?" I asked. "Arion can't carry all of us."

"Not in this form," Freya answered and sighed. "It's time to give us all you've got, friend. You up for it?"

Arion shook his coat and roared. I didn't speak familiar, but it sounded like *hell yes*. That gave me even less confidence in this plan, but given I had nothing else to offer, I couldn't argue.

Arion roared again, but this time, the challenge transformed into a neighing sound. He stamped his paw, and it shifted into a dark, glossy hoof. His once thick legs slimmed into muscular, refined things. He shook his coat, and it became midnight black. His body conformed into a slightly smaller but no less impressive shape. His neck stretched into a long but proportionate head.

"His other form," I said, "his most *dangerous* form is a horse?"

Arion pawed at the ground and glared at me. His forelock moved and revealed a single white star that decorated his masculine face. His eyes remained amber, just like a cat's. It was freaky as hell, but other than that, he was one beautiful horse. Still, I'd never felt more at ease with him, even in his cat form.

"You'll see," Freya promised. A mischievous grin lightened her ash-covered face. "Arion's going to get us off this goddessforsaken mountain."

"He can carry all of us?" I questioned.

Did Freya hit her head? The tiger would've had a better chance.

Arion snapped at me with his large teeth.

"Okay, okay," I said. "I believe in you, big guy."

Arion bowed, and we climbed onboard. Freya sat in the front. We put Cadence—who was still out cold—in between us.

"Hold on tight," Freya instructed.

I reached around her and grabbed Arion's mane with both hands, then squeezed his barrel as tightly as I dared with my legs.

He stomped his hoof one more time, then blasted off.

We left my stomach behind us.

CHAPTER NINETEEN

Walker

The world raced by in a blur.

We soared down and up, then down again. Where we'd carefully placed each step on the brittle mountain path, Arion's hooves flew so quickly over the ground, it never even had time to break away. Maybe it did, but we were too fast to witness it.

I gripped his mane with white knuckles and held on for dear life. I kept my seat planted, which was a challenge. All things considered, Arion was a smooth ride but sitting on his hindquarters nearly threw me off him. His every stride was loftier than anything my quarter horse had ever achieved. Our speed threatened to push both Cadence and me off. I gripped him tighter, despite the cold air that threatened to strip me of warmth and numb me all the way down to my bones.

Cadence's head lulled to the side, and I worried it might snap, but I couldn't afford to loosen my grip. I'd broken bones falling off normal horses. I wasn't sure either of us would survive a tumble off Arion.

We reached the lake in mere seconds, and I prepared myself to go under water. I held in a huge breath and closed my eyes, but a gentle spray was the only water to touch me. I opened my eyes and nearly passed out.

Arion's hooves raced across the lake—so fast not a single hoof was submerged beneath the water.

What am I on? Horse-Jesus?

As we traveled through the forest, I realized why this was

Arion's most dangerous form. If you could ride him, he could take you anywhere in the world in only minutes. Maybe even seconds.

And I thought *my* horse was cool.

*

Freya

We reached the cottage in no time, though I had to pull Arion to a rather abrupt stop. As Walker and Cadence flew forward, I braced myself against their weight. I barely kept from toppling over Arion's shoulder.

When I was sure I wasn't going to fall, I caught my breath and studied the familiar cottage. Its thatched roof was still in perfect condition, and its brown walls were covered in green vines. Purple flowers bloomed on them. Flowers of all different colors lined the stone-paved path that led to the tiny building. The grass was as perfectly neat as it always was spelled to be.

Some of it was thanks to our family's magic, but most of it was because of Josephine. Her family was known for its earth magic.

Magic like Cadence's.

Arion snorted and stomped his feet. He already wanted to run again.

"Calm down," I whispered to him and patted his neck.

Arion was always hardest to communicate with in this form. He lost himself in his own speed. Left to his own devices, I wondered if he'd run his heart out.

"Is it safe to get off?" Walker asked.

I laughed, and it bordered on hysterical.

"Yes, cowboy," I answered. "Do you know how to get off a horse?"

I couldn't see him, yet I knew he rolled his eyes.

"Just hold onto Cadence, would you?" he grumbled.

I reached back and did as he asked. Cadence was light in my arms. It was incredible that such power had erupted from such a tiny body. It made me think of my own Awakening—I'd launched a tornado at an Elder in the middle of a ceremony. She had told me I was too young to participate.

She was wrong.

Mom and Josephine had never been prouder.

"Goddess," I whispered, "I wish you two were here."

Walker swung his leg over Arion and stuck the landing on shaky legs.

"Huh?" he asked.

"Nothing," I snapped. "Take her. I can give her some herbs inside. They'll help her regain her strength."

He grabbed his sister. It was normal to pass out for several hours after an Awakening, but it was hard to imagine sleeping through a ride on Arion, no matter the circumstances. I threw my own leg off my familiar and swung myself down. I wasn't much more coordinated than Walker, though I would never admit it to him.

"Okay, friend," I said. "Time to change back."

Arion snorted at me.

"Please," I added. "You won't be able to come inside in this form."

He snorted once more, then quickly shifted into his cat form. I was grateful he bothered to listen to me. I needed some cuddle-time with my feline friend.

The day isn't over yet, I reminded myself.

Walker waited for us with Cadence in his arms. Exhaustion made his shoulders sag, and worry furrowed his brow.

I sighed. "I'm sorry for snapping at you."

"You don't owe me an apology," he said. "You have every right to be angry with me."

I stopped in my tracks.

"Why would you say that?" I asked.

He switched Cadence to his other arm and refused to meet my stare.

"I almost got us killed, Freya," he explained. "Worse, I almost got you *captured* by those things."

He clutched Cadence closer and covered her head with his

hand, as if she needed his protection then or now.

"Freya," he continued. "You tried to stop me, and I didn't listen! You *shouldn't* forgive me. I could've wrecked all of us."

I shook my head. "You were trying to do the right thing, cowboy."

"You're not going to tell me I'm reckless?" he asked. "Or stupid?"

He actually *wanted* me to berate him.

"You *are* reckless," I said. "And maybe a little stupid sometimes, but you can't help it. You're a man—you're a good man, though. That's what matters."

He still didn't look convinced.

"Walker," I said and sighed. "You're going to make me admit this. I didn't want to leave that guy because I knew he was a vampire—I wanted to leave him to save our own asses. I didn't know he was a vampire."

Shame caused my cheeks to heat. Walker stared at me too intently, and I squirmed under his gaze.

"You were thinking of everyone," he said. "You do that a lot, even though you don't admit it."

I frowned. "Enough of that, Walker. Let's take care of your sister."

I swept past him to the front door.

"If only you could take a compliment," he complained.

"No one has it all," I retorted.

He laughed at my antics but followed me. Cadence groaned in his arms. I was grateful for a sign of life from the girl, but it meant I needed to get those herbs faster. Waking up from an Awakening was no walk in the sunshine.

I took a deep breath and opened the blue-painted door.

"You don't lock it?" Walker asked.

"Not with human locks," I answered. "The whole place is spelled to only open to Redfern family members or those invited in by Redferns."

"So," he said. "Are we invited?"

I pretended to contemplate and scratched my head.

"I suppose."

He rolled his eyes and chuckled. As we entered the cottage, his laughter stopped, and his jaw dropped a little. I couldn't blame him. If the vampires' castle was plucked from a nightmare, our cottage leaped from the pages of a fairytale.

Before us sat the most comfortable sofa in existence, and across from it were two high-backed chairs, whose light blue upholstery hadn't faded in the decades they'd been there. Behind the chairs were two bookcases filled with spell books. The entrance to the hallway split them up. Mom and I's bedrooms were down the hall.

"You can set her on the sofa," I told Walker.

I headed for the kitchen and smiled at the familiar scents that filled my nose. Shelves and shelves of herbs lined the walls. Potted plants sat in the windowsill above the farm sink. Jars of cookies, crackers, and other food sat on the counter. To my left, a backdoor led to the garden where even more plants could be found.

I ran my finger across the wooden countertops. There was no dust to be found. I snapped, and a light that hung on the wood-paneled ceiling flickered on. I scanned the shelves for the ingredients I needed and tried to ignore the ache in my chest.

Most of the jars were labeled with Mom's handwriting. I'd always failed to imitate her swirling letters.

"What are you making for her?" Walker asked.

I nearly jumped out of my skin. I hadn't heard him approach me.

"My mother always called it an R and R spell," I answered and smiled. "It increases healing in the body and cultivates a deeper, more powerful rest."

"Sounds like something we could all use after today," he said.

I plucked some chamomile, peppermint, and a few other things from the shelf, then searched the cabinets for a mortar and pestle. Mom always kept everything in the same place, but I'd never bothered to learn where it all went. She'd chastised me endlessly for my inability to keep the kitchen organized, but I had never imagined her not being here to tell me where to look or where to put things. I blinked away tears and tried to focus on the task at hand.

"I've never mixed it for a human before," I told Walker. "I could just as easily put you down forever."

I finally found the mortar and pestle and set the tools on the counter.

"But your usual mix will work for Cadence," he said and sighed. "Because she's a witch."

The sadness in his voice grated on my frayed nerves. I couldn't understand how someone who so honestly gave me compliments could be so opposed to his sister being one of my kind. I tossed some herbs into the mortar and ground them with more force than necessary.

"It's not the worst thing for her to be," I huffed, "and I can help her master her power."

"She shouldn't have to worry about mastering anything!" he argued. "She's just a kid."

I sighed and faced him.

"You denying what she is—what she's capable of—it isn't going to make this any easier for her."

Walker ran his hand down his tired face.

"You don't get it," he insisted. "How am I supposed to protect her from her own—her own *magic?*"

He said magic like it was a dirty word, and I threw my hands up in disbelief. I was too raw with grief to be having this conversation—to hear him insult the very thing that ran through my veins. Through my *mother's* veins.

"Maybe she doesn't need your protection!" I said. "Maybe she just needs you to stop acting like she's a monster!"

Slack-jawed, he stared at me. The kitchen suddenly felt too small for both of us.

"I'm only worried about what kind of life she'll have," he said, as if that would make it better.

As if there were something so clearly wrong with *my* life.

"Just go mope about your poor witch of a sister elsewhere," I told him.

His tense stance deflated. He clutched his hat in his hands. "Freya."

"Don't say my name like that," I whispered.

"Like what?"

I swallowed the lump in my throat.

"Like I'm someone you care about," I answered.

"I," he said and cleared his throat. "I do care about you."

I scoffed. "I'm a witch."

He sighed and paced the small distance between us.

"It makes sense for you to be a witch," he argued. "I mean, think about how we first met. Everything about you is..."

"Is what?" I asked.

"Power."

I was a stupid, horrible fool.

I'd never wanted to be seen as anything but what I was, and I would never feel shame for who I was, yet something in my chest cracked at his words.

All this time, I'd thought Walker saw me as a girl—not the heir to Hecate's coven or role model for the younger witches or even the great Sybil's daughter.

I thought he saw *me*.

I recalled my mother's warning to me after my Awakening. They were words that still rang in my ears years later.

"From now on, everyone is going to look at you and see power. Some will desire you for it, some will envy you for it, and many will fear you because of it. It's why you must hold onto you, my darling. No one else will remember for you."

Maybe there was something wrong with my life—a witch's life—but it felt like a betrayal to even think it.

"Not all of us can see in black and white," I said.

"And what's that supposed to mean?" he asked. "Just because my first instinct isn't to *kill* people?"

I didn't give him the satisfaction of even frowning. As I

stared him down, ice covered the raw ache of my hurt.

"It means that not all of us get to save vampires from cages without a second thought," I said, "that some of us have to think of the people we're responsible for—something I thought you got, but you can't even get over your own fear to help your sister."

My words hit their mark, and he winced, but I couldn't find it in myself to feel satisfied. I couldn't apologize either.

"I just found out," he argued. "Can I not have a moment to process? Can I not be scared *for* her?"

"Don't lie to yourself," I said. "You've known since she dream-shared in the cave, and you've probably suspected something was different about her long before then. You just can't run from it anymore."

"Excuse me then," he said and sneered. "We can't all be as perfect as the great Freya Redfern."

Anger and hurt marred his boyish features into something unrecognizable. I turned back to the counter and picked up the pestle.

"There you go again," he said. "Shutting yourself off as soon as anything gets real. Maybe you should ask yourself who's the real coward here."

I flinched at his words and ground the herbs together. At least I managed to hold back my tears until he finally sighed and walked out of the kitchen.

CHAPTER TWENTY

Walker

Freya poured the green potion or whatever it was into Cadence's mouth, then promptly disappeared into her bathroom down the hall. A shower turned on. When she emerged, her curls were still damp. She wore black tights, and a comfy-looking sweatshirt.

"You should shower," Freya told me. "You stink. There are clothes in there for you."

With that, she vanished into the garden. Though I hated doing what she'd practically ordered me to do, I was sick of sitting in my own filth. Ashes and blood clung to not only my clothes, but my hair and my skin.

I walked down the hall. Paintings and portraits lined its walls, which made it feel as homey as the rest of the cottage. I studied the portraits. Many of the women had Freya's bright eyes, and a few of them had her flaming hair.

Guilt gnawed at me for the harsh words we'd said, but not enough to make me apologize. She'd put up her defenses well before I had.

Keep telling yourself that.

At the end of the hall, the bathroom was small, but not cramped. Warm light cast over the sandstone floor and shower. A stack of clothes waited for me on the black quartz countertop. In the sink, I scrubbed many of the stains off my brown Carhartt coat. The amount of ash and blood that came out of it was impressive.

It really is an honest value for an honest dollar, I thought and smiled to myself. *I should try to get an advertising gig with them.*

I noticed the small red stain on the collar, and my smile died. I still didn't understand how Freya's mom's blood had gotten on my coat. My head pounded, and I abandoned the thought. I hung my jacket on the towel rack to dry and was relieved to learn that witches used normal shampoo, even if it had a sweeter scent than my usual brand.

When I emerged from the steaming water, I found that the clothes left for me must've once belonged to a pretty bulky dude. They hung on me awkwardly but looked familiar.

Anger reignited in my stomach.

Ryder.

I wore Ryder's clothes.

Though I loathed wearing anything of that prick's, I couldn't afford to be picky. I was lucky Freya had found me anything to wear. Still, I couldn't shake my pissy mood. I stormed out of the bathroom to resume my post at Cadence's side. Hours passed and, though I'd had one of the longest days of my life, I couldn't bring myself to sleep.

I bet she's cold.

Night had fallen a while ago and the temperatures had dropped, even inside the cottage. A fire had magically lit, nearly scaring me to death. I hadn't even noticed the fireplace nestled in the corner of the living room. Its heat quickly filled the cottage. The burning wood snapped and crackled.

If not for Cadence, I would've already doused the thing. The warmth was nice, but it reminded me too much of dying undead creatures.

Every time I closed my eyes, I saw the fear in their eyes as they burned. I remembered feeling relief at the sight of it.

I watched Cadence sleep and considered asking Freya for that potion. Even if it killed me, at least I'd get some peace. I wouldn't have to mull over the fact that my baby sister was a *part* of this world—a world with incredible magic, snarky werewolves, and undead monsters.

Hell, I thought, *a world with a shapeshifting cat.*

When I'd started this quest, the goal had been to *keep* Cadence from all of this, not introduce her to it. All I'd wanted was to solve some witch murders and go back to my regular job on the ranch.

As if you still have a job.

It was unlikely. Nathan wasn't the forgiving type, and I'd missed quite a few days without notice. Regardless, being unemployed was a problem I craved. There were plenty of other ranches to work at, but only so many beings who could train a witch. Freya had offered, but I had no clue what that entailed.

What if she joins a coven?

It wasn't like I could join with her.

A door clattered shut behind me, and I jumped to my feet.

It was only Freya. She stormed out of the kitchen and into the living room. She almost passed me by without a word but stopped when she reached the hall between the bookshelves.

"I'm not a coward," she said, "and neither are you."

Freya faced me. Her eyes were red-rimmed and puffy. Her curls were frizzier than normal, as if she'd run her fingers through them too many times. She almost looked human. I wanted to take back every mean thing I'd said to her, but my mouth operated faster than my brain.

"Is this your version of an apology?" I asked.

She rolled her eyes and put her hands on her hips.

"Is this your way of accepting it?" she shot back.

I glanced at Cadence, whose little chest rose and fell in a perfectly steady rhythm. Freya followed my gaze.

"She's stronger than you give her credit for," Freya said, "even if she is a *witch.*"

"There's nothing wrong with being a witch," I told her, and she raised her eyebrows. "Except that I have no idea how to help her be a witch! I-I'm barely surviving as a witch's sidekick."

Freya stared at me in shock. Then, she laughed in my face.

"You," she said and wheezed. "You just willingly called yourself my *sidekick?*"

Heat rushed to my face, and I scratched the back of my head.

"Your very much equal partner-in-crime," I corrected.

"You can't take it back now," she said and smiled. "Sidekick."

When she laughed, her whole face lit up. It almost made my embarrassment worth it.

"I can see your head swelling from the weight of your ego," I said.

"You know you've saved my ass as much as I've saved yours, right?" she asked.

I shifted my weight. "I don't know how to be there for her with this."

"Walker." Freya rolled her eyes. "Just do the same thing you've always done. You're a good brother."

"Yeah," I said and sat in one of the large, high-backed chairs. "But I can't be a witch. I don't even understand how it's possible that *she's* a witch. I'm sorry for taking that out on you."

Freya sighed and sat next to me. It was a tight squeeze with the both of us in one chair, but I didn't mind her nearness. Her lilac-scented shampoo tickled my nose. It smelled better on her. She laid her small hand over mine.

"I'm not really sure how she's a witch either," she admitted, "but I'll help you figure it out."

"Maybe it would be better for her to join your coven anyway," I said. The truth fell from my lips before my mind even caught up to it. "Being raised by a teenage brother and a drunk isn't much of a childhood."

I'd never acknowledged Dad's condition to someone other than Cadence, at least not in so many words. A weight lifted off my chest, though a part of me wanted to hide from Freya's stare. Her coppery eyes bore into mine with the heavy weight of sadness.

"You were a little bit right," she said. Her lip wobbled, and she cleared her throat. "Growing up a witch is not the easiest thing for a child, especially with power like Cadence's. When I was only fourteen, I sent a rather rude girl crashing down the stairs without even trying to. She broke her arm, and I got three weeks in the cuffs."

"Cuffs?" I asked.

She sighed. "They're what witches use to bind each other's magic when the situation calls for it. They're reserved only for severe punishments."

"That must've been frightening for you," I said.

"It was almost a relief," Freya whispered. "I didn't have to worry about losing my temper and hurting anybody. But when the other girls realized it was a perfect time to exact any revenge plots they had for me, the relief quickly ended."

"Freya," I said, "how many girls did you piss off?"

She laughed and shrugged.

"Probably too many," she admitted. "That's when my mother decided it was time for me to hone my physical combat skills."

She tucked a curl behind her ear, and it sprang free immediately. I couldn't stop myself. I coiled it around my finger.

"The point is, I get it. Though I love my mother and my coven, sometimes…"

She let the sentence trail away.

"You still wonder," I said, "what it would've been like to grow up in a different family. In a different life."

Freya nodded but didn't meet my gaze. I dropped her hair.

"I wonder too." I glanced at my sleeping little sister. "What having a normal family must be like."

She heard what I didn't say.

There was no judgement in Freya's voice. "One where you got to be a kid instead of a caretaker."

"We still turned out okay," I said and smiled. Reluctantly, she mirrored my expression.

"Yeah," she said and looked at Cadence. "And she'll be okay too."

We sat in comfortable silence, only filled by our steady breaths and the crackling fire. It didn't seem quite so jarring anymore. I couldn't believe only days ago, Freya and I were enemies.

I couldn't believe there was no one else I'd rather be next to right now.

Freya leaned her head against me, and I slung my arm over her shoulders without a thought. She stiffened, and I wondered if I should move. Just as quickly, she relaxed and casually rested her hand on my thigh. Suddenly, my comfort was replaced by heat. Flashes of our kiss rushed back. Thoughts of what could've happened, if not for Ryder's damn interruption, were even more potent.

Get a grip, I told myself. *She's not interested.*

Her fingers trailed shapes on my leg, and I tried to ignore the images of where else her hands could touch me. Freya was exhausted and lonely. Though she put on a brave face, grief was a heavy thing to burden. She would've sat with anyone to avoid being alone in her dead mother's home. Just thinking about it made me feel like an ass for wanting to kiss her.

And I'm back to thinking about kissing her.

"Witches don't believe in romantic love," she said softly, "did you know that?"

I cleared my throat. "No. That sounds lonely."

"I never thought so before," she replied.

Before?

"Not," she rushed to say. Her hand quit moving. I wasn't sure if I was relieved or disappointed by both her answer or her actions. "Not that I think differently now. I just...I was wondering what you thought about it. That's all."

"About love?" I asked.

Freya nodded. Seeing her soft and sleepy was doing something to me. I didn't want to make stupid jokes and or change the subject. I wanted her to know me, like she was letting me know her. With my thumb resting on her arm, I softly kneaded her skin. I couldn't allow myself to try to know her body. I'd indulge her thoughts instead.

"I don't know," I answered honestly. "I always figured

I'd find someone someday, but seeing how losing my mom destroyed my dad? It hasn't put me in any rush to give myself over to someone like that."

Another question came to mind. "Is that why you don't talk about your dad? Your mom was never really...*with* him, with him?"

"Yeah," she said. "The only role he's played in my life is sperm donor. I don't even know his name."

"Do you know *what* he is?" I asked.

"Human," she answered with confidence. "Hybrids are rare between werewolves and witches, plus I don't have the characteristics of them. Vampires can't father children."

"Could he be a witch?" I said.

She chuckled and patted my leg. "Of course not. There are *no* male witches."

"Silly me," I muttered.

Our conversation trailed away, but neither of us got up. I rested my chin on top of Freya's head. My breath brushed past her ear, and she shivered. That reaction lit my whole body with awareness. Freya turned her face to mine.

What the hell?

Did she actually want me to kiss her?

Giving her plenty of time to turn away, I slowly leaned closer. Freya's gaze flicked to my lips, then back to my eyes. She tilted her head toward mine. Her breath was warm against my skin. I savored the journey to her lips, determined not to screw it up this time.

Cadence jolted, and I snapped back into reality. Cold water wouldn't have been as effective. Freya's breath caught, and she pulled away. I released her from my hold. I hadn't even realized I'd gripped her waist. Cadence relaxed once more and continued to rest blissfully unaware, but the moment was gone.

"Better get some sleep!" Freya said in an uncharacteristically high pitch and hurried to her feet. "I'll go grab some blankets."

CHAPTER TWENTY-ONE

Freya

Without looking back, I hurried to the cabinet full of blankets down the hall.

Goddess save me.

I stood in front of the cabinet and tried to douse the heat of my skin. I'd sat next to Walker with all good intentions, but those had quickly fled to the wayside. It had just been so *nice* to talk to someone and to lean on him. I'd never had many friends and certainly not many male ones. I'd never gotten so close to someone toned from days of honest, hard work or whose smiles made *me* want to smile.

More than anything, Walker made me feel safe.

I'd only wanted to crawl into that feeling.

You can't, I reminded myself. *You're not safe, and you won't be until the witch killer is gone.*

Neither long talks nor long make-outs with Walker would solve that problem. I *had* to stay focused. That started with grabbing the cowboy some blankets, so we could all get some much-needed rest. I grabbed what I needed and faced Walker.

"You're welcome to use my bed," I offered then cringed. "I mean, you can sleep in there and I'll sleep on the floor."

I couldn't bring myself to suggest sleeping in Mom's room.

Walker insisted on sleeping in the living room with Cadence, despite my assurances that the cottage was so warded, the High Witch herself couldn't get in. Refusing to be awkward, I helped him set up a pallet of blankets in front of the fireplace, then headed to my own bedroom. It was a short trek down the dimly lit hall.

I turned the brass handle of my bedroom but couldn't bring myself to open the door. I would see the multi-colored quilt Mom and I had made together. I'd remember all the long chats we'd had on my brass-framed bed. I might be tempted to listen to the jazz records she bought me years ago.

I didn't want to be alone in a graveyard of our memories. Not when my nerves were still so frayed from my conversation with Walker.

I couldn't open the door.

I muttered some curses and walked to the end of the hall, where the cupboard of extra blankets was. After grabbing what I needed, I walked back into the living room.

Maybe he's already asleep.

The boy was seemingly able to sleep on command. He'd slept like a baby on the hard cave floor.

It's a cowboy thing, he'd told me.

I quietly laid out my blankets, then crawled under a couple of them. Arion came in through the cat door I'd installed a year ago and curled up at my side.

Hopefully, I would wake before Walker, and he would never know I slept out here after I ridiculed him for doing the same. With a smile, I closed my eyes and focused on the crackling of the fire.

"Night, Freya," Walker said. He didn't try to mask the smugness in his voice, but he didn't turn to gloat either.

I smirked. "Good night, Walker."

*

"Walker?" a young voice said. "Walker! Where are you?"

I rolled over, away from the sound, but sunshine streamed in through the window. With a groan, I sat up and rubbed my eyes.

"Freya?" a girl asked.

I opened my eyes and blinked away the dark spots that danced in my vision. Cadence stared at me from her seat on the sofa. Her skin was paler than usual, and her eyes were wide with fear. Ash and blood still stained her clothes and clotted in her hair.

"What happened to me?" she whispered.

Walker snored to my left.

Oh well, I thought, *she needs to hear the truth from someone.*

"Your powers awakened," I answered. "Cadence, you're a witch."

Her jaw dropped. "Like you?"

I nodded.

Please don't start crying. I casually stepped closer to Walker and nudged him with my foot. He choked on his snore and sat up.

"What?" he asked. "Who's here?"

He opened his eyes and noticed Cadence staring wide-eyed at both of us. Her lips were pursed in concentration, and her brow was furrowed. She fiddled absentmindedly with her sleeve.

"So," Cadence said. A smile slowly appeared on her face. "I have powers?"

Walker and I nodded. She pondered this for all of three seconds.

"That is *so* badass!" she exclaimed.

I couldn't hold back my laughter.

"Cady!" Walker chided. "Language."

She rolled her eyes. "I have sick powers, and you're worried about my potty mouth? Let's put things into perspective."

Walker was dumbfounded, which only made me laugh harder.

Poor guy, I thought. *He really isn't equipped to handle this.*

"I don't care who you are or what you are," he said. "You're still eleven, and I'm still in charge."

I turned so Cadence wouldn't be able to hear me.

"You sure about that, sidekick?" I asked. Walker cursed

under his breath.

With that, I slipped on some shoes and walked into the kitchen to make breakfast. I grabbed some yogurt out of the fridge then found some granola on the countertop. Behind it was a stray jar of herbs.

"That's odd," I said.

Mom was the most organized creature I'd ever met. She never would've left this here by mistake.

I opened the jar, and sweetness flooded the air. I picked up one of the browning flowers that filled the jar. From the looks of the thin, fluffy petals, they were dahlias. I recalled the hours of boring botanical theology I'd been subjected to.

Betrayal—dahlias represent betrayal.

I sifted through the jar and found a small, folded piece of paper nestled inside. My heart pounded in my ears, so loudly it nearly drowned out Walker and Cadence's conversation in the living room. It felt like they were a whole world away.

I held my breath and opened the folded paper.

To my darling Freya, it began.

It was written in an ancient language Mom had forced me to practice for years. Even Josephine didn't know it and had argued it was unnecessary, but Mom wanted us to be able to communicate with only each other. It was why I'd finally given into her wishes. I'd cherished our secret conversations, even if they'd never held any importance until now.

I took a deep breath and read on.

I'm sorry this letter has found you. I never wanted to leave you, but do not despair. There is no time, and there is no need. As I lived, I die without regrets.

As my last defiance of my mother's wishes, tears rolled down my cheeks. I read more, even though part of me wanted to stop. My world was about to change yet again—I could feel it.

I have to write this cleverly for I can't reveal powerful truths to clouded minds. Still, I offer this warning—you must trust your foes and not your friends. Trust the one you'd rather not, for in his history lies answers.

And Freya darling, do not forget to keep your chin up.
With all my love,
Sybil

"What in all the realms does this *mean*, Mother?" I snapped at the letter.

My mind raced. I hadn't trusted my friends—that was why I'd been on the run all week.

Because of Walker.

It was *his* history I needed to learn. He was from a family of witch hunters after all. I had wondered about his true heritage ever since discovering that Cadence was a witch. Not to mention, I still didn't understand his involvement in Mom's death. Her blood stained his jacket, but I knew in my bones he hadn't been the one to end her.

I needed to unravel Walker's history, but, even if I did, I was still left with a slew of questions.

Mom and I had both been wary of some coven members before her death. Namely, the Elders. I'd practically blamed their inaction for her murder.

Maybe they're not the problem.

Perhaps, they were foes who were actually friends.

"But who are the true betrayers?" I wondered out loud.

I didn't have many *real* friends to choose from. Arion was my familiar—he couldn't do such a thing. We were magic-bound. I wasn't particularly close to any of my peers. Thea was my friend, but I didn't trust her enough not to suspect her. The werewolves were innocent.

No.

No, no, no, no, no.

It couldn't be Josephine.

But the letter was placed in a jar of flowers—surrounded by earth magic.

"Freya," Walker said from behind me. I glanced at him. He'd put on his jacket, boots, and hat. "You need any help? Cadence is cleaning herself up, but she already informed me she's practically starving."

I quickly wiped the tears from my face. I couldn't find the energy to lie so I said nothing. Something was still amiss in the letter.

Keep your chin up. My mother never spoke in clichés.

"Keep your chin up," I whispered.

"What?" Walker asked.

I lifted my chin and stared at the wood-paneled ceiling.

Each panel was in perfect condition, thanks to the magic that coated every inch of the cottage. I searched and searched the panels for any sort of discrepancy.

A shiny cobweb grew in the corner of the room, where the ceiling met the wall.

Impossible.

All insects were magically repelled from dwelling inside the cottage, yet there it grew. Silky strands stretched across the corner of the space. A black widow trailed over the web. Her large, dark body moved with unnatural grace, and the red spot on her stomach gleamed like a ruby.

"Shit," Walker said.

He stared in horror at the spider and her web.

"Language," Cadence told him.

She walked to his side and searched for what held our attention. She was finally clean of ash and blood, and her damp hair hung limply around her pale face. She stared at the spider like she recognized it.

"That thing," Cadence said, "feels powerful."

"It does," I agreed then turned my gaze to the spindly creature. "Who are you?"

Its dance across the web halted, as if it were pausing to consider my question. A talking spider wouldn't have been the craziest thing I'd seen, but disappointingly, it carried on about its way without a single word.

"Wait," I said. "I *do* know you."

"You *know* a spider?" Walker asked and shook his head. "I'm not even really surprised."

I hurried past him to the left bookshelf. The top shelves

were lined with books about combat magic, but the lower ones were all about the gods. Some of them were original accounts from centuries ago, though Mom had rarely let me touch those. Magically held together or not, they were too valuable to be messed with.

There, I thought.

Arachne by Ovid. Luckily, it was a new copy and written in English—I would've hated to be slowed down by my lackluster Latin.

Cadence peeked over my shoulder and gasped at the title of the book.

"No way," she said. "You don't think that's her, do you?"

"And of course you know the spider too," Walker said and sighed.

They gathered closer to see over my shoulder. I flipped rampantly through the pages.

"Arachne is the goddess of spiders," I explained. "She was a talented weaver cursed by Athena for daring to consider herself better than the gods."

"Walker," Cadence chided. "How can you *not* know this? You really should brush up on your mythology."

"She's not a myth," I corrected and finally found the page I was searching for.

We stared at the beautiful ink portrait of a black widow with an unusual red spot.

"I think she's in my kitchen."

CHAPTER TWENTY-TWO

Walker

I stared at Freya in shock. My mind couldn't catch up with reality. Freya was barely better off. Her eyes were wilder than I'd ever seen, and she moved frantically, instead of with her usual grace. Cadence was merely intrigued. Her reaction only further proved what Freya told me was true—she would be just *fine.*

"Okay," I said slowly. "Sure, I can get that Arachne is real, but why would she be here?"

"My mother must've summoned her," Freya explained. Her hands shook so badly, she nearly dropped the book. "She's trying to tell me something or-or give me something—I'm not sure, but I *know* that's her."

Freya and Cadence flipped through the book for answers. When I walked back into the kitchen, they were too engrossed in their research to notice. I didn't exactly want to be alone with a goddess, but it seemed unwise to leave her unattended.

"Whoa," I said.

That spider really was talented.

With her silky, silver web, she'd weaved a brilliant depiction of a battle between two women. One of them was curly-haired and threw her arms up to shield herself. The other woman—taller and grimacing—hid a knife behind her back. Between them was a wispy shield.

"What is that?" I asked the spider.

Arachne tapped each of her dark legs in exasperation, as if she couldn't believe I *still* didn't understand. The spider crawled over to the wispy thing between them, then walked back to the curly-haired girl who looked uncannily like Freya, right down to her fierce expression. Arachne paused, and I once again got the sense that she was questioning my intelligence.

I see your lesson on arrogance didn't take.

She hurried back to the knife in the other woman's hand.

"Oh," I said, "that thing you spun is supposed to be a shield."

Arachne twirled.

I studied the carefully woven lines of the shield and realized I really was an idiot.

"Your web," I said, "it's a shield?"

I studied the image even further and gasped.

"Even against the Bloodblade," I said.

If spiders could sigh, I was confident Arachne would've.

When I took a breath to call for Freya and Cadence, the jars on the countertops rattled. I frowned.

Odd time of year for an earthquake.

An image flashed in my mind—I stared at the forest floor, lit only by the moon. My hands braced myself against the shaking ground, and dew clung to my cold skin.

A headache nearly split my skull.

"Walker!" Cadence cried.

She and Freya raced into the room and brought me back to the present. My strange daydream dissipated.

"Did you feel that?" Freya asked.

I nodded and rubbed my pounding forehead. Unfortunately, I didn't think now was the best time to ask for an Advil.

"Someone's tearing down the wards," Freya said in disbelief and muttered to herself. "How are they doing this?"

The walls shook even harder, and some of the spices fell off their shelves. Arachne watched us with keen eyes. She was completely unbothered by the looming threat.

"Can you tell who it is?" I asked Freya.

"I already figured out who's behind it." Fury burned in Freya's eyes. "Josephine."

"Your witch-friend?" I asked. "You didn't think to mention this?"

She glared at me. "I got a bit sidetracked by the *goddess!*"

Fair enough, I thought.

Something pounded on the front door of the cottage.

Boom...boom...boom.

"Are they hitting it with a *log?*" I asked out loud, then shook my head at myself. "It doesn't matter. What matters is we need to go."

Cadence nodded enthusiastically, but Freya hesitated. I couldn't blame her. This cottage was her family's prized possession and had been the home she shared with her mother. Whoever was on the other side of that door wouldn't give a second thought about destroying it. She fiddled with the book in her hands.

"You're right," Freya reluctantly admitted. "We can ride Arion again."

She spun in a circle, and it occurred to me that I hadn't seen the pesky cat in a while. Freya set the book on the counter and raced through the cottage. Cadence and I followed her into the living room and searched for the cat, but he was nowhere to be found.

"Arion!" Freya called.

I looked frantically for him but came up with nothing. Scowling, Freya emerged from her bedroom. Colorful and admittedly creative language rolled off her tongue. I was tempted to cover Cadence's ears.

"This is why he doesn't get to shift forms whenever he wants!" Freya exclaimed. "And this is why he *never* gets to be in his favorite one. Damn cat loses all sense of reason. He's probably off on a joy ride right now!"

Freya continued to curse him, and it didn't seem like she had any intentions of stopping. I racked my brain for an escape plan. The pounding on the door grew louder, and the floor shook beneath my feet.

Crack!

The front door flew off its hinges so violently, splinters of wood hit me in the face. I blinked the debris out of my eyes and squinted to see whose footsteps thundered into the living room.

"Golems," Freya whispered.

Four hulking figures stomped into the room. Sand seeped from their skin and left a trail where they walked. They grew closer, and I got a better look at them.

No way.

Their skin *was* sand.

The golems' faces were bulky and square, like the rest of their bodies. They wore rough-hewn clothes that barely stretched over their massive forms. They stood at least a foot taller than me and could probably grab my head in one hand. As they scanned the room, their dark brown eyes lacked pupils and any signs of life. They moved as one. When they saw us, they grunted in sync and charged farther into the cottage.

"We have to get to the portal," Freya ordered.

We backed into the kitchen and slammed the door shut. The golems' slow, steady march shook the ground.

"Where's that?" Cadence asked.

Freya grabbed a long kitchen knife off the counter and handed it to me. "Aim for their heart."

She looked at Cadence. "My mother's room."

Without further preamble, Freya raced into the living room.

"Wait!" I called after her, but she was already gone.

"What?" Cadence asked. "Walker, we need to get out of here."

I handed Cadence the knife and tried to remember she'd trapped a powerful vampire with her magic.

"Go," I told her. "There's something I need to grab. I'll meet you at the portal."

Cadence hesitated. Something crashed in the living room,

and she rushed to help Freya. Praying to God she'd be alright for just ten seconds, I faced the spider goddess.

"Please don't bite me," I whispered and reached for her web.

CHAPTER TWENTY-THREE

Freya

With a gust of wind, I knocked the first golem in my path on his back. Golems were slow but strong creatures. They were created and operated by only the most powerful of witches. I'd been training to fight them since I was fifteen.

It made it easy to recognize Josephine's work.

I was, however, offended that she'd only sent four.

I tried to knock the second golem back, but he'd learned from his friend's mistakes and braced himself. Cadence rushed to my side, clutching the knife I'd given to Walker. With her free hand, she grabbed pillows from the sofa and lobbed them at the golems. It was enough to distract them, so I could knock them down with wind. As they fell, they destroyed precious furniture and cracked long-standing walls. I didn't have time to mourn any of it. We needed to get out of here.

"Where is your brother?" I hissed.

Cadence didn't answer. She'd run out of pillows.

"Don't let them catch you," I told her. "Use the knife if they get too close."

Without further hesitation, I lunged for the fire poker. As Cadence darted around the small room, the golems thumped into each other. I muttered a quick spell to strengthen the poker and slashed it through the two closest to me.

With perfect timing, Walker emerged from the kitchen

and snagged Cadence by the waist, right before a golem struck her. I severed the golem's legs, and it crumpled to the floor.

"Took you long enough," I said.

Walker and Cadence sidestepped the golem. The golems shifted on the floor and tried to piece themselves together. It wouldn't be much longer until they were back in action.

Walker held out a glimmering web. "I thought we might need this."

I balked. "You took Arachne's web?"

"It's a shield," Walker explained, "against the Bloodblade."

"That's why mom summoned her," I said. "Let's get to the portal."

As I skirted between the fallen golems, Walker took the knife from Cadence, and the siblings raced after me. Unfortunately, the first golem had finally recovered. It charged from the left and blocked the path down the hall. Its huge hands swiped at me and knocked me to the ground. Walker struck the blade into its chest and twisted it. The blade clanged as it collided with golem's stone heart, and the creature crumpled into a pile of sand at our feet.

Walker stared at its remains in shock.

"Nice," I admitted and rose.

The other golems roared behind us. We quickened our pace. We reached my mother's doorway, and nausea turned my stomach. My hand wrapped around the brandished handle but failed to turn it. The golems footsteps grew louder.

I cursed myself for my foolish emotions and turned the damned handle. I didn't let myself look at her silky maroon bedspread or the jewelry still on her vanity. I didn't inhale her familiar vanilla perfume or glance at the closet full of her clothes. If I did, I wouldn't have the heart to leave this place in the hands of these monsters.

Instead, I grabbed Mom's emergency bag from her armoire and ran to the mirror that stood proudly on the right side of the room. No one would know it was over a century old. Its bronze frame gleamed, and Mom's magic still emanated from it like a familiar lullaby.

I whispered the first spell my mother ever taught me—the one that unlocked our emergency portal.

A kaleidoscope of light and color swirled in its depths. Tears burned the backs of my eyes. The portal had my mother written all over it. It was beautiful, but well-concealed, and I knew it wouldn't fail me.

Walker hissed in pain. I searched his body for an injury I might've missed.

He shook his head. "I'm fine."

The golems burst into the room. They splintered Mom's doorway and barreled into her antique dresser.

I tried to cast a sleep spell to keep them from breaking anything else, but it didn't work. They weren't mine to control, and they'd clearly been commanded to follow us. They would do as their master instructed.

I glanced back at the portal. Its thrumming magic was a song to my ears.

The last existing spell of my mother.

A tear slipped down my cheek.

I knocked the charging golems back with a powerful blast of wind and winced when they collided with Mom's furniture.

"Close your eyes."

I grabbed the siblings' hands and leaped through the portal.

Just before jumping into its familiar warmth, I closed my eyes and envisioned Walker's front yard exactly as I'd last seen it. I recalled the gravel driveway, the mountains that nestled the property, and the fresh air that wafted through it.

The portal's magic moved through my body like air moved through my lungs. It became an extension of myself, and I welcomed its heady power. As we spun through time and space, I gripped the Reids' hands like they were a lifeline and willed them to stay with me.

Wind whipped my body and threatened to loosen my grip on them, but I held tightly and focused on my destination.

Walker's house, Walker's house, Walker's house...

I ignored the urge to turn back to my home. My mother wanted me to forge ahead. I would not disappoint her.

Even if it broke my heart.

Finally, my feet crunched against gravel, and sunlight burned my eyes. As soon as we landed, I whispered the second spell mom ever taught me.

"An escape route is only useful if you can't be followed."

With one whispered spell, the portal and the last remnant of her magic was destroyed forever. Even if the golems had already crossed into it, they'd be lost in the gaps between time and space forever. If they had brains of their own or any real emotions, I would've almost felt bad for them.

Almost.

Cadence and Walker gasped beside me, but neither of them threw up. I considered it a victory.

"That." Walker rested his hands on his knees and fought to catch his breath. "Was. Insane."

His skin was sickly green, and I wondered if I'd celebrated too soon.

Cadence took in her familiar surroundings and frowned.

"Why here?" she asked.

As he too realized where we stood, Walker's shoulders stiffened.

I swallowed. "Answers."

*

Walker

My driveway stretched longer than I'd ever noticed. Freya quickly explained the contents of her mother's letter, and one truth stuck out to me. We would have to consult my father for answers about my history.

I hadn't relied on him in years. It felt wrong to turn to him in such a dire situation, but I had no choice. Clearly, Josephine would not stop her hunt for us.

"Can I put this in your bag?" I asked Freya and held up the web.

Its power thrummed in my hand and sent reverberations down my arm. It was softer than I'd expected, but slightly sticky. Its clinginess made me claustrophobic. Freya held open her duffel, and I dropped it inside.

My house loomed in front of us. It seemed especially mundane and dingy after seeing Freya's cottage. At least the chipped white paint and expansive porch was a familiar sight after so many days away from anything I'd ever known.

I glanced at Freya and noticed how shiny her eyes were under the bright sun. I wanted to curse myself for being so selfish. Just last week, Freya lost her mother and now the closest thing she had to family had betrayed her.

I knew that reality all too well.

I could still remember the days and weeks following Mom's death. I'd been so sure that Dad would get out of his depression eventually. I just *knew* he'd wake up one day and make us breakfast like he used to, and I wouldn't be alone to care for my sister. He'd choose us—his family—over a drink.

That day had never come.

As we marched toward my house, I brushed my hand against Freya's. It was the only small show of comfort she'd allow, and the only one I was brave enough to offer. Her gaze met mine, and she offered me the tiniest of smiles. My chest ached at the sight.

I wanted to ask Freya if she was okay, but I already knew the answer. I wanted to do something to help her, but nothing would—nothing except for the truth. If the only thing I could do to help her was pry answers out of my sorry excuse for a father, I would do it.

We finally reached the front steps.

"I'll go see how he is," I said and gestured for the girls to wait.

Freya nodded in understanding, and Cadence shifted uncomfortably. We hadn't invited anyone over to the house in years. The last time we'd tried was Cadence's only sleepover she'd hosted, back in the fifth grade.

When one of her friends spilled orange soda on the carpet, Dad had lost mind. He'd been too drunk to speak coherently and too belligerent to shut up. All the girls went home before the night was over. I could still see their parents' pitiful glances as they'd picked up their kids.

The steps creaked under my feet, and the door swung open easily. We'd left it unlocked. I had figured that was how we'd find it.

Dad's snores rattled the entire house. He was passed out in his recliner. It was so worn-out that the once dark leather was now an ugly purplish color. Mom had bought it new for him, and none of us had ever discussed getting rid of it. Next to it was her rocking chair that only Cadence was allowed to sit in for fear that it would break. It was a miracle Dad hadn't torn it up yet in one of his many tumbles out of his chair.

An equally old couch was pushed against the right wall. Sunlight streamed into the room from a window behind the couch. It cast the grayish-blue painted walls in dim light. Though it wasn't at all hot, a ceiling fan rotated overhead.

I shook his shoulder. "Dad."

He choked on his snores but didn't awaken. I shook him harder, but still no luck. I sighed then headed into the kitchen to get a glass of water. Flies buzzed around the trash can, which clearly hadn't been emptied in the days we'd been gone. Trash and crumbs littered the counter. The bread had been left unwrapped, and a knife covered in old peanut butter sat beside it.

At least he shut the fridge door.

I grabbed the trash and took it out the backdoor to the dumpster, then scooped what was left on the counter into a new bag. I grabbed the empty beer cans and vodka bottles next to his chair and threw them away too. The carpet was still a mess, but I feared Freya would soon lose her patience and barge in anyway. I sighed and filled a glass with cold water.

I carried it to Dad, who still slept like the dead. He smelled like sweat and liquor. His graying beard needed a trim, and crumbs covered his bloated stomach. His kids had been missing for days, and he hadn't even bothered to shower. I wasn't sure he'd changed clothes.

I wasn't sure he'd noticed we were gone.

I wasn't surprised, but some disappointments never got old.

I shook his shoulder one last time. His snores continued. Without an ounce of guilt, I splashed cold water all over his face. He jerked awake, and his dull green eyes met mine. He blinked several times, as if he couldn't believe I stood before him. For a second, I thought I saw relief relax his face into the dad I once knew.

His face morphed back into its typical scowl.

He looked me up and down. "So, you decided to come home?"

I rolled my eyes. "Good to see you too, Dad."

I took the empty glass back into the kitchen and filled it again. When I brought it back, Dad sat straighter in his chair.

"Splash me with that shit again," he threatened, "and I'll make you wish you hadn't wandered back home."

"Sure you can aim well enough to hit me?" I shot back. I shoved the glass of water in his face and turned to the kitchen. "Sober up. We have company."

He mumbled something undoubtedly rude under his breath, but I ignored him. I put on a pot of coffee and went to check on Freya and Cadence. They stood in silence on the front porch. Neither asked me what took so long, but Cadence had a knowing look on her face. As I led them inside, I noticed Freya appeared to be making a conscious effort to keep her expression neutral. She bit the very corner of her bottom lip in concentration.

"Cady?" Dad called.

It was one of those rare times he said her name with affection. Her lip quivered. She'd wondered the same thing I had.

Did he notice I was gone?

He had. He just hadn't really cared.

My sister rushed into the room to greet him, but I hung back and poured a few cups of coffee. Cadence's excited chatter echoed into the kitchen. She'd always been better at forgiving him than I was. Freya hung back with me. She leaned against the counter with her arms crossed and her gaze vacant. She still gripped the small, leather duffel she'd grabbed from the cottage. The golems' sand clung to her hair and clothes. For once, she wasn't a perfectly put-together warrior.

"Coffee?" I asked.

The question pulled her from her reverie, and she straightened. She didn't answer but set down her bag and reached for the mug from my hands. I pulled it out of reach, and she raised an eyebrow at me then sighed.

"Walker," she crooned. "I would be *most* grateful for a cup of delicious, freshly-brewed coffee."

I laughed and coaxed a ghost of a smile out of her.

"I'm sorry we had to leave it behind," I said in all seriousness.

Her smile deadened, but at least she was no longer a million miles away.

"Me too."

Her quiet words were oddly loud. The conversation in the living room had stopped. My father's heavy footsteps pounded across the floor, and the house creaked in response.

All kindness left Dad's voice. "Who's there?"

As Dad barreled into the kitchen, Freya stiffened beside me. My dad had been an ass for a long time, but I'd never seen him stare at anyone with such *hatred*. His scowl carved lines into his face, and his hands clenched into fists.

"What is this *thing* doing in my house?" he practically growled.

I stood between him and Freya and held up my hands.

"Dad," I warned, "calm down."

He reached under the cabinet to his left and pulled out a gun I hadn't even known had been taped there.

"Dad?" Cadence called from the living room.

My father raised the gun at me.

He clicked the safety off. "Get out of the way, Walker."

I stared at him in utter shock.

Freya stepped to my side. "You know witches can't be killed by little guns, hunter."

He scoffed. "If you know what I am, then you must know I wouldn't bother wielding a regular gun."

I moved in front of Freya again. Regardless of our less-than-stellar relationship and the secrets he'd clearly been keeping, Dad wouldn't shoot me.

I hope.

"She's here to help," I promised. I gestured to the gun. "Please."

Cadence burst into the room behind him. Her head swiveled back and forth between the gun in my dad's steady hands and its target.

"She's my friend, Daddy," she whined.

Cadence hadn't called him that since she was six, but the endearment didn't hurt. The gun wavered in his hands. Dad refused to tear his gaze from Freya, who stood as still as a statue behind me.

"She's a monster," he said and clenched his teeth.

Cadence's little jaw dropped. "Because she's a witch?"

Dad finally glanced at Cadence. "You don't understand."

"No," Cadence argued. She moved in front of me and put her hands on her hips. "*You* don't understand. Because if Freya is a monster, then so am I!"

Dad's eyes widened in fear, and the rough lines of his frown smoothed. He hadn't looked so young in years.

"You know?" he asked. He ran a hand through his unkempt hair and lowered the gun. "It's too late."

"Too late for what?" I asked.

Freya whispered something behind me, and the gun flew from my father's hands and into hers. She sighed in relief, but Dad looked ready to take her on with his bare hands.

"Easy," Freya told him. She tucked the gun into her

waistband and held her hands up. "I just wasn't feeling very welcome with this thing pointed at my face."

"Have your jokes, witch," he snapped. "None of us will be laughing for long."

"Why?" I pressed.

Dad looked at Cadence. "She'll come for her. It's time."

CHAPTER TWENTY-FOUR

Walker

"Cut the theatrics," Freya snapped. "What do you know about Josephine?"

She appeared to be at the end of her patience with my father, who continued to stare at her like she was an invasive cockroach he'd like to step on. I thought he might refuse to speak to her altogether, but he finally replied.

"Not much," he answered. "I didn't even know that was her name. I only know of the curse."

"What curse?" Cadence asked.

Dad wiped sweat from his brow and sighed.

"Why don't we take this into the living room?" he asked. "I'd hate for our guest to feel unwelcome."

Without another word, he grabbed his cup of coffee off the counter and headed into the living room. Like always, his gait was sluggish and messy. Watching him shift from hopeless drunk to ruthless hunter and back was disorienting.

After Cadence and I shared a confused look, we followed him. While Cadence eased into the rocking chair beside my father, Freya and I sat on the couch. We waited in strained silence, and my dad refused to meet my gaze.

"Start talking," I ordered.

He sighed and looked at his coffee in distaste. I wanted to slap him. Now was not the time to be drinking anything stronger.

"You two know our family's history?" Dad asked Cadence and me.

"Bits and pieces," I answered.

He nodded. "The Reids have been witch hunters since long before Hol Creek was founded. And witches have lived in these mountains for even longer than that. It's what drew us here— the magic in these mountains. We ensured that no humans were hurt to amass more power for them."

He practically spat the last part at Freya, but she didn't flinch.

"You didn't always kill killers," she argued. "No one's innocent in a witch hunt."

He kneaded his hands in his lap. "Things got out of control a few times."

Freya scoffed but didn't interrupt him again.

"So," Cadence said. "Where do I fit into this?"

Dad stared holes into the floor.

"We were some of the most talented hunters for centuries," he continued. "It's no surprise that we acquired quite a few enemies in that time. Enemies that hadn't found forgiveness by the time your ancestors decided to give it up."

We all leaned forward in anticipation. I couldn't remember a time I'd been so wrapped up in a conversation with my dad.

He took a swig of coffee. "Your great, great grandpa was the one who ended our dynasty."

"How?" Cadence urged. The same question nearly tumbled from my lips.

"He fell in love with a witch."

All of us gasped.

"For her," Dad continued, "he gave up hunting. And she gave up her craft."

Freya's jaw dropped, and she leaned forward.

"She left the coven?" Freya asked. "For a human? I wasn't even aware such a thing is possible."

Why should she be?

Freya would sooner give up her right leg than her magic.

"It wasn't," Dad said. "Isn't, and especially not for a hunter, whose family had killed its fair share of their coven over the centuries. But they loved each other. They were ready to damn any and all consequences to be together."

"What happened to them?" I asked.

Dad laughed, but there was no humor in it. "To them? Nothing. They got married, had a child, and died like any other humans. But the witches knew they'd be around to see their curse come to fruition, whether it strike in that century or the next, or the next after that."

He leaned forward and put his head in his hands. Dread pooled in my stomach at what he would say next.

"Those witches also knew that even though their sister gave up her extended life and her practice, magic did not disappear. It would be passed down through our family, until it appeared in the next girl born. She would be a witch."

Cadence grew very still. For once, she understood the weight of the situation. To my shock, Freya's hand grabbed mine. I gripped it tightly.

"And she would be killed by her own blood," Dad finished.

My stomach dropped. I'd known Cadence was at risk of getting killed by the witch killer, but I hadn't known she'd been the *target.*

By her own blood, I thought.

Green eyes flashed through my mind, and pain laced my head.

"Josephine," I said. "She's related to Cadence?"

"What was the witch's surname?" Freya asked. "The one in your bloodline?"

"Moonflower."

Cadence perched on her chair with unnatural stillness. I reluctantly let go of Freya's hand and knelt by my sister's side. She refused to meet my gaze, so I tucked my finger under her chin.

"No one is going to hurt you," I told her. Her too-green eyes met mine. "No one, okay?"

She nodded, but her face remained in an unsure frown.

"We will protect you, little witch," Freya promised and forced a smile.

Cadence nodded again. "I can help fight her too. You did say I was powerful."

This time, Freya's smile was genuine. "I like the confidence."

I rolled my eyes.

The duo the world is not prepared for.

Freya's smiled faded. She paced the room and chewed on her lower lip in concentration.

"Something still doesn't make sense though," Freya said. "There's no way Josephine is doing this just to right a vendetta against your family. She has an end-goal. She always does."

Sometimes, I wondered how Freya had ever loved someone so selfish and cold, but then again, no one's family was perfect. I glanced at my dad and mulled over his words some more. A realization hit that made my blood boil.

"How long have you known about this?" I asked.

He tensed but didn't answer me.

"How long?" I repeated.

Dad exploded out of his chair, and things almost felt normal.

"Don't take that tone with me!" he yelled. "You don't know how hard it's been to carry this around, not knowing what to do to fix it!"

"Yeah?" I said. "And how long have you carried it?"

The fight drained out of his body, and Dad hung his head in shame.

"My whole life."

I jumped to my feet.

"You've known all this time," I said. "And your solution was to get *drunk?*"

Dad blanched. "It's not all my fault, you know. I tried and

tried to warn your mother, but she refused to listen. I said that if it was a girl, we had to get rid of it before she was born. She called me a superstitious monster. It nearly tore us apart!"

"Get rid of it?" Cadence said quietly.

Tears slipped down her cheeks, and she ran into the kitchen. The front door quickly swung open and slammed shut. I moved to follow her, but Freya shook her head.

"I've got it," she said and hurried out of the room.

Dad and I faced each other.

"I've forgiven you for a lot of shit," I said. "I've stepped up where you failed for Cadence. Hell, for myself. I've made sure you didn't choke on your own puke, and I've picked you up from jail. Throughout it all, I knew you were a coward. I just didn't know you were this big of one."

I expected him to lash out at me, with either his words or his fists. I didn't care which. I itched for a fight.

"You're right," he admitted in a voice so small and quiet, I barely recognized it. "For years, I tried to find out how to break the curse, but no witches were willing to help a retired hunter with no favors to offer and not a lot of cash. This Moonflower witch is in one of the most powerful covens in North America and maybe even the world! I was too scared to take her on alone. And then your mother died…I wasn't sure how to care for either of you, much less keep you from dying. It was too much for one man—for me."

I stared at him in shock. Slowly, some things became clear.

"That's why you've been worse," I said. "These past few months, your head's been so far in the bottle, I don't know how you haven't drowned in the stuff. You knew she'd Awaken soon."

Dad nodded. "Her power is like a beacon to witches. Now, that witch can track her anywhere. We might as well paint a target on her back."

I wanted to snap at my father or yell some more. I wanted to sit down and drink until I couldn't remember my sister's life was in danger. I couldn't bring myself to do any of it. If I resorted to his bad habits, I would be no better than him. I wouldn't let this break me as clearly as it had broken him, but, for the first time, I understood my father.

"You were so angry after Mom died," I said. "I always thought it was just grief running its course, but that's not true. You were mad she left you to deal with this by yourself."

He sat back down in his chair with a huff.

"I didn't mean to hurt your sister's feelings," he said, "but I never wanted this. Not just for me, but for her. No child should fear her life like this. This isn't the life I wanted for her."

I sat too, though more gracefully than he had done.

"And it's not just because she's a witch?" I asked.

I wasn't sure what prejudices my dad held onto from our ancestors. After today, I was confident there was a fair number of things I didn't know about the man. It was a scary new reality, but one that offered a flicker of hope. For years, I hadn't allowed myself to dream that he could be anything but what he was—a drunk.

"I only care that she's a witch because it puts her in danger," he said.

I believed him.

Looking back, I saw how desperately he'd tried not to love my sister, especially after Mom died, but Cadence was too charming for her own good.

Too bad I'm not the one that's cursed, I thought. *He certainly never had a problem pushing me away.*

My heartbeat pounded in my ears. I couldn't shake the headache that had plagued me since we left Freya's cottage. It was like my brain struggled so badly to understand everything I'd learned in just one day, it might explode.

I tried to blink away the pain, but brilliant green eyes flashed through my mind.

"Walker," Dad said. "You all right?"

I nodded. "It's been a long day. A long *week.*"

A long freaking life. Dad heard what I didn't say.

"I'm sorry, son."

I jolted in shock and stared at him. His glassy eyes stared

unflinchingly into mine. I didn't know what to say or what to do or even how to breathe.

For years, I'd longed for those three short, simple words.

I'm sorry, son.

The pain in my head grew worse, but it didn't dull this moment. Nothing could. I waited for the punchline to come or his scowl to return, but he just stared and stared at me.

Dad swallowed. "I should've found a way to save Cadence. Hell, I should've *raised* her. I should've raised you. I–"

"Okay," I said. If he said it again, I might have to pinch myself to check if I was dreaming. "Just help us now. Okay? Help us fight Josephine."

Dad nodded enthusiastically, and a small smile took shape on his face. It was awkward, as if he couldn't quite remember how to do such a thing, but it was there.

"I have something to show you."

I sighed. "Dad, I'm excited to see all the secret badassery you've been hiding over the years, but I really should go check on her."

Dad scowled and crossed his arms. "Which girl?"

I rolled my eyes and turned my back on him. I wouldn't give him the satisfaction of a reply, though the answer was obvious.

Both.

CHAPTER TWENTY-FIVE

Freya

I raced after Cadence. The girl shouldn't be off on her own, and I needed an excuse to get out of that house. I wasn't having a fantastic day before meeting Walker's father, and it surely hadn't improved since then. Clyde Reid had worn my patience thin. I couldn't fathom how a man could so terribly fail his children but have the nerve to call *me* a monster.

I couldn't imagine mentioning aborting my daughter right in front of her either.

I swung the front door open and spotted Cadence running for the woods to the left side of the front yard.

"Wait!" I called after her, but she didn't listen.

I ran down the grassy hill in pursuit of her. The pine-scented air burned in my lungs, and the sun warmed my skin. It countered the effects of the bitter wind that cut through the mountains.

As we grew closer to the woods, my stomach turned. Somewhere out there, Josephine had killed my mother. Or maybe that had been a lie too.

My goddessmother *had* been the one to tell me that's where she'd found the bone. I shook my head at myself. That part had been true. I'd felt the echo of magic that stained the land weeks ago, and I felt it again now. The wind carried an extra chill. The plant life was a little duller. Few animals scurried nearby.

Cadence came to an abrupt stop at the edge of the forest, and I halted a few feet behind her. My heart pounded in my ears. The little witch was fast. I'd actually had to exert some effort to keep up with her. After her sprint, Cadence's chest heaved, so I took the opportunity to speak.

"He only meant he didn't want to see you in fear," I told her. "He loves you. It's clear as day."

It was. His bloodshot eyes brightened when they looked at his daughter. It was also painfully clear that when he looked at Walker, he didn't allow himself to feel anything but shame. I would be embarrassed too if someone with no guidance at all managed to become a better person than I could ever dream of being.

When I looked at Walker, maybe I felt shame too.

He was so godsdamned *good.*

I shoved that thought aside and focused on Cadence. She still faced the forest, though she finally caught her breath.

"I know," she answered. "It's not that."

I waited for her to continue and sat on the grassy hill. Perhaps I was a coward, but I refused to get any closer to the woods. Cadence heard me sit and joined me. As she spoke, she wrung her hands in her lap, just like her father had done.

She's not all witch after all.

"Everyone wants to protect me," she said, "but what if it only gets you killed? All Walker ever does is take care of me. I don't want him to die because of it."

Her voice cracked, and I pulled her into a hug. I wasn't sure what the Reids had done to make me so ridiculously affectionate, but I couldn't watch Cadence cry without doing something about it. She sobbed into my chest, and I ran my hands through her tangled hair, just how my mother had consoled me.

"He won't die," I promised her. "I won't let him."

I meant it with every fiber in my being. Though he lacked a lot of survival instincts, I wouldn't let Walker get himself killed.

This was my coven's mess to deal with, not his. At least not his alone.

Cadence pulled back to look in my eyes. "You can't die either, Freya. Who will teach me how to be the most badass witch ever?"

I laughed. "You should watch your potty mouth, badass."

She giggled and finally released me.

"Thanks, Freya."

"Anytime, kid."

"I hardly believe my eyes," a deep voice drawled behind us. "The wicked witch has a heart after all."

I shot a glare at Walker over my shoulder and fought the urge to cringe away from Cadence. Mom had taught me to be strong in the face of danger, but she'd also wanted me to be warm and gentle with those I loved. She'd found a balance between the two things. It was time I did as well.

Walker stood with his hands in his pockets and wore a knowing smirk. Clearly, my discomfort was not as camouflaged as I'd hoped.

"It's alright, sweetheart," he said. "I won't tell the rest of the world."

Sweetheart?

The endearment chafed me and enthralled me all at once. I wanted to know if he said it with any degree of sincerity, but his focus had already shifted to his sister. I was quite positive, however, the flush that crawled up his neck wasn't from Cadence.

Sweetheart. Ridiculous.

He walked farther down the hill. "Dad's real sorry, Cady-Cat."

Cadence wiped the last remnants of tears off her face and nodded.

"He always is," she said, though her voice lacked any vehemence.

Walker sighed and stared into the woods, then winced. He clutched his head in his hands.

I rose to my feet. "Walker?"

While Cadence rushed to his side, I searched our surroundings for any signs of an attack. Nothing hummed in the air, and nothing scurried through the forest other than a rabbit or two. I cast my magic like a net over the forest and searched for tiny hints of magic. Even the dark witches left a small trace, if you knew how to look. My magic touched every tree and weathered rock. Everything seemed in perfect order—there was no excess of wind or earth or energy. I found nothing but the faint echo of the Bloodblade's power.

Walker suddenly straightened. His expression was crafted into grim determination. He gently pushed his fretting sister aside and walked toward the woods.

I stood in his path. "Walker."

He stared at me in confusion. As if I were a rock in his path, he grabbed my shoulders, picked me up, and moved me out of his way. He continued down the slope of the mountain and into the thicket of trees.

Something was very wrong.

"Cadence," I ordered. "Go get your father. Tell him to prepare whatever weapons he has."

She hesitated. Her gaze darted to her brother, but she sighed and raced back to the house. Left with no other options, I followed Walker into the goddessforsaken forest.

Walker charged through the brush and foliage. Branches scraped his skin, but he paid them no notice. His focus remained fixed on something in the distance. As I weaved around rocks, trees, and bushes, I kept my gaze firmly on him and my senses on high alert.

Pine and dirt and the musk of animals was all I could smell, but something darker lurked ahead of us. It was the stain of dark magic, intermingled with the Bloodblade's power. It made the hairs on the back of my neck stand and left a sour taste in my mouth. A vague ringing pierced my ears, and my heart raced rampantly.

We walked and walked, until I wondered if I'd need to use

force to stop the cowboy.

Walker halted.

It was so abrupt, I nearly stumbled into his back, but I caught myself.

Trees ensconced us, but their branches drooped to the ground. The grass beneath my feet was brittle and brown. The frosty air was completely still. That lingering magic called out to me from afar. Like a dissonant chord, it rang louder in my ears. My gut churned, and everything screamed at me to run, but I could *feel* I was on the cusp of discovering what really happened the night my mother perished.

Walker crouched to the ground and picked up a stray log. He cradled it to his chest and stared at it as if it held the world's secrets. The log fell from his hands, and he hissed in pain.

Panic and hope warred inside me. I couldn't let Walker get hurt, but I couldn't tear my gaze from the small smear of blood on his coat. My mother's blood.

What if he remembers something?

He crumpled to the ground and groaned. All my foolish hope subsided, and I crouched to his side. It didn't matter what he might or might not know. Walker was in pain.

I rolled him onto his back. "Okay, cowboy."

He groaned.

"Time to come back to the present," I ordered.

I grabbed his face to get him to focus on me and gasped. Magic coated Walker like a second skin. I'd never sensed a spell so concentrated to one individual. It couldn't have been cast recently.

Golems were incapable of casting their own spells, and I would've sensed if Walker had wandered into someone's curse while I was with him. It wasn't the dark magic I'd sensed either. This was so personally crafted, it almost felt like Walker himself —powerful, but understated. Clearly of this earth. It was why I'd failed to notice it for so long. Now that he was on the cusp of breaking it, I could finally feel it.

As Walker's eyes snapped open, he sat up and gasped.

"Freya," he whispered. "I remember."

My heart stuttered.

Tears brimmed in his eyes, and a furrow formed on his brow. He broke his gaze from mine and stared at his hands.

"What do you remember?" I asked just as quietly.

I already knew the answer, but I asked anyway. The truth I'd longed for had become all too attainable. I didn't want to know if Mom had screamed or if she hadn't even seen Josephine's attack coming. I didn't want to know if my brave, fierce mother had been afraid. I didn't want to know if my own goddessmother had truly been the one to end her.

But I needed to know.

Walker wouldn't have been drawn back to this place if we weren't meant to uncover the full truth of that night.

"She told me to run," Walker said. His eyes searched mine. "I didn't listen."

A laugh crept out of my throat. "Of course you didn't."

My smile was short-lived. My lips wavered.

"What exactly did you see?" I asked.

Walker swallowed. "I didn't see the killer, but it sounded like a woman. Your mom, she was trapped. She…she called her attacker her friend."

He squinted and rubbed his fingers on his temples. I waited for him to continue and fought the urge to puke. My stomach became a sinking ship.

"Your mom said the only way she could've bested her was to be high on death," he said. "The death of her kind."

I gasped.

"Your family's curse, the dead witches, why my mother was even here," I said. "How that bitch actually managed to kill Sybil! It all makes sense."

Horrific, terrible sense.

Walker squinted at me in confusion.

"She Embraced them," I explained. "Josephine—she was killing the witches and stealing their magic. That had to be why she came here. For Cadence."

Walker's confused expression softened. "Your mom stopped her."

I nodded, and some of the anguish that gripped my heart eased. My mother had died doing what she'd always done—protecting witch-kind.

"Josephine's power must've been knocked down after facing my mom and wiping away your memories. She couldn't have performed the spell to steal your sister's magic, even after Embracing so many witches."

I wiped away a tear that slid down my cheek.

"But why?" I asked. "Why did she need this power? Why send me to kill you?"

"I don't know why she needs all this damn power," Walker said, "but I was a loose end she needed tied She thought you'd be too lost in grief to think straight. She thought you'd kill me before realizing what an inept hunter I really am."

He chuckled softly, then his expression sobered. "Your mom already got in her way once. She didn't want you doing the same."

"So she sent me on a wild goose chase for the killer to clear a path to Cadence." My hands curled into fists. "She tricked me."

"Cadence said she felt watched," Walker said. "When she found us in the woods, she said she ran because she was scared. If she hadn't…"

"It doesn't matter," I said. "Josephine didn't get to her then, and she won't get to her now."

Despite my advice to let go of the past, guilt still gnawed at me. I'd been *so* close to killing an innocent man.

"Hey," Walker said and smiled. "At least you didn't actually kill me."

I sighed. "I suppose there's a bright side."

He playfully punched my arm and got to his feet. I sighed, then accepted his outstretched hand and rose. I was relieved that magic no longer coated his skin. I glanced around the wilted forest, and my relief scattered.

"Was she afraid?" I asked.

Walker shook his head. "She was trapped, but she was confident. Like she knew that even if she didn't make it out of the forest, everything would be all right."

He squeezed my hand.

"She knew you'd fix everything," he said.

I snorted and blinked away tears. "I've really let her down then."

He gently pulled me closer and tilted my chin up with his free hand. I hadn't realized it had fallen.

"You're still here," he argued.

"With no familiar, no coven, no wolves, and nothing but my own magic."

My heart ached from the weight of it all, but especially for Arion. The little demon had run away before, but he'd never stayed gone for long. He'd never abandoned me in a time of need.

I prayed to the goddess that he was okay, then I vowed to ring his neck for leaving me to face this alone.

"Josephine will be here soon," I said. "Your father was right. Cadence's magic is a beacon. Any witch can track her bloodline with ease."

It was how I'd known my mother was dead. My tracking spell hadn't worked. Walker stood in silence beside me and mulled over my words. Like a flame sparking to life, his eyes brightened with a dangerous thing.

Hope.

"Then use your magic," he said. "Call for help. Surely, there's a way to do that, right? Astral whatever?"

I considered his words. Astral projecting required focus, lots of power, and time. Plus, I didn't have anything in my possession that could link me to my allies, other than some passed-down wolf's clothes. I doubted that would be strong enough to establish a link. I didn't pack any personal objects of my coven either. If she were still alive, my mother would've chastised me for not thinking ahead.

She's not alive though, I thought, *this is on you.*

"Astral projection won't work," I said. "Even if I had the

right objects for a spell, the receiving end must answer. It's like a phone call—someone has to pick up. I doubt my coven is dying to hear from me."

"We need a PSA," Walker amended.

That's it.

I grinned. "Walker, you're a genius."

A flush crept up his neck. "Those are words I never thought I'd hear you say."

"Don't get used to it." I tugged on his hand. "Let's get moving, cowboy. We've got work to do."

I hid my discomfort with spirit and forced my mouth to shift into an encouraging smile. One that Walker so clearly saw through. He quirked an eyebrow at me. Clouds moved over the sun and dimmed the light that filtered through the trees. I shook off the bad omen and headed for the dark magic that loomed ahead.

"Freya." Walker rubbed his thumb over my hand. "You sure about this?"

"You sense it too?" I asked.

The farther into the forest we ventured, the stiller nature grew around us. The air grew colder, and our breaths clouded before us. The chords in my ears reached a crescendo.

"This is where it happened," he whispered.

We stood before a small clearing of blackened earth. Trees had fallen to piles of ash. Tufts of grass fought to grow again and recover what my mother's magic had destroyed, but the very soil was poisoned by the magic that had killed her. Nothing would grow here for a long time.

Not unless it was removed.

A tear trickled down my face, but I didn't wipe it away. For once, I let my emotions pour out of me freely. Walker stood silently at my side. Instead of frivolous words, he comforted me with his presence. His steadiness.

I crouched to the earth and touched the charred grass. It was so cold it burned. These past days, this place had been trapped in this terrible magic, waiting for me to find it. To heal it.

I whispered a simple drawing spell, intended to pull poison out of wounds. Yet again, it was proven why the most basic spells were the most powerful. They were flexible.

As it poured into my veins, the dark magic screeched. It was thick like oil but colder than frostbite. The magic chilled me so greatly, it burned, but I didn't relent, not until the last drop of it flowed through my body.

Barely able to control my chattering teeth, I whispered the words of the amplification spell. My voice shook, but I managed to enunciate the throaty vowels. Instead of relying on my coven for more power, I used the dark magic I'd just contained. As it left my body, it transformed.

As if I were my own Sun, light shone from my limbs. The coldness was replaced by gentle balminess. It was like stepping into a warm bath or hugging my mother. Walker squinted at me in wonder.

I smiled. My jaw no longer shook. When I spoke, I prayed my voice reached every supernatural ear in the next hundred miles.

"Hear me," I demanded. "I am Freya Redfern, Heir to the Coven of Hecate, and I am asking for your help. We have been betrayed by one of our own, sisters, and we must put an end to her. We must protect our newest coven member, and we must avenge our fallen sisters. We must avenge our dearest Coven Mother, Sybil Redfern. Please, hear my cry and offer me forgiveness. Know that everything I have done, I have done for us. For the Goddess. Even for you, Arion. And wolves, please do not forget your allies of the last three centuries. Please hear me. To face her together is our only hope."

Once I finished the amplification spell, stark silence fell over the forest. Blood pounded in my ears, but no dark magic screeched. The sky lightened, and the Sun shone down on us. I touched a hand to the forest floor. At last, the charred earth warmed.

"Josephine will definitely know where we are now," I said.

"She would've found us anyway," Walker replied. "And

now that she knows you've called for help, she'll need time to gather her own forces."

I stood. Leaves crunched under animals' feet, and branches rustled. I might have healed the forest, but I wasn't convinced I'd saved us.

"They might not come."

"They will." Walker grinned. "That was quite the speech. Ever think about going into politics?"

I shoved his arm and fought back laughter. He didn't make the same effort to hold in his own amusement. With a smile tugging at my lips, I stormed off in the direction of his house.

"C'mon, cowboy. We have a battle to prepare for."

CHAPTER TWENTY-SIX

Walker

When we walked back to the house, Dad waited for us on the front porch. I was relieved that his gaze was still clear, and his stance was still steady. I'd half-expected to find him drunk. Cadence rose from her seat on the steps.

"That was incredible," Cadence said and grinned at Freya. "I'd just gotten home when I heard your spell. I figured I better wait here for further orders, Coven Leader Redfern."

"It's Coven Mother," Freya said and ruffled Cadence's hair. "And I'm not technically allowed to claim that title. Yet."

"Well," Cadence said, "you've got my vote."

Dad huffed. "Yes, it was quite the speech, witch. Now, it's time to introduce you kids to your heritage." He walked into the house.

Here goes nothing.

With Freya trailing reluctantly behind us, Cadence and I followed him inside. He surprised me by walking to end of the hall, to the linen closet. The only thing I'd ever seen inside of it were old blankets and a couple cobwebs.

Dad pulled a key I'd never seen before out of his pocket. It was old and delicately shaped, with an insignia imprinted onto its handle. He held it out to me, and I studied the rearing, fire-blazing dragon.

"Dragons have been symbols of protection for centuries,"

he explained. "That's what our family business is really about—protecting innocents from dark magic."

Freya scoffed but tried to disguise it as a cough. My father glared at her.

"You were showing us something, Daddy?" Cadence said.

Dad grumbled to himself but put the key in the closet door's lock. I'd always wondered why we would ever need to lock it. When he turned the key, instead of locking the door, the entire wall creaked. The doorway, crown molding and all, hinged forward but caught on the hardwood floor.

"It hasn't been opened in a while," Dad explained. "The house has shifted a bit in that time. Walker, help me pry it open."

We grabbed the corners of the door frame and pulled. It was heavier than I expected. It opened wide enough for me to jam my shoulder into it. With a final heave, the hidden door and the attached narrow closet swung open. A dark staircase greeted us.

Someday, I would get used to hidden passageways and creepy basements.

Dad ran his hand on the right wall and flipped a switch. Lights flickered on. He led the way down the concrete, dust-covered stairs. I reached out, squeezed Cadence's hand, then followed him. Cadence was right behind me.

When we reached the bottom of the stairs, Dad flipped another switch, but nothing happened.

"Come on," he grumbled and flipped the switch a few more times.

A huge, iron chandelier shined down on what could only be described as an armory. Throwing stars, swords, daggers, and weapons I didn't even have a name for lined most of the concrete walls. In the center of the room was a sparring ring. Thin, black padding laid on the floor, and low-hanging rope bordered its perimeter.

A wooden target hung on the far wall. It'd been there for a while from the looks of it. Several nicks chipped the paint, especially in its center. There was a closet built into the far corner of the room. It was padlocked shut.

"What sorts of stolen magical goods are you hiding in there?" Freya asked.

She stood in the doorway of the armory with her arms across her chest and an unfiltered sneer on her face. Somehow, she managed to appear unimpressed by my father's secret cache of weapons, not that I could blame her. Everything in here was designed to kill her kind.

Dad glared at the witch. "Cursed objects, weapons of mass destruction—the usual magical contraband."

Freya snorted. "Hunters, more like hypocrites. You kill witches, but you clearly needed one to keep all this hidden and your spoils locked away."

He rolled his eyes. "Witches, you think you know everything. Need I remind you that a witch married into my family? Or that other witches were the ones to curse her for it?"

"About that," I interjected. "If our family gave up hunting, why do you know about all this?"

Dad snagged a dagger from Cadence's hands and scolded her before answering me.

"We haven't killed anything supernatural in over a century," he explained.

Cadence grabbed an axe half as tall as herself. She nearly crumpled under its weight. I reached for it, but Dad was already there, prying it out of her hands. She laughed mischievously.

"But it didn't mean we became weak," Dad said. "The eldest son has always been trained in combat. It's our family way. We didn't want to be caught unawares."

Until now.

I winced, and Dad broke his gaze from mine. All those generations of trained warriors ended with me—the first person in centuries to actually need the training. I studied the thick layer of dust covering everything in the armory and tried to fight off the sinking feeling of gloom.

Freya stared down my father and snorted. "You're more of a screw-up than I realized."

"Freya," I warned, but she held up her hands.

"I know anger won't do us any good now," she said, "but he better start righting his wrongs."

"How much time do I have?" Dad asked her.

"Until sunset," she answered. "Tonight's a blood moon. Josephine won't waste an opportunity to draw on its power. Plus, vampires are their strongest after dark. That's when they'll attack."

Dad nodded and plucked yet another pointy object out of my sister's hands. Cadence giggled like a little sociopath.

Freya laughed. "C'mon, Cadence. I'll teach you how to really do some damage."

She stormed out of the room without another word. Cadence grinned and raced after her. I silently prayed the house would still be standing when we emerged from the armory.

"Let's get started," Dad said.

"No time like the present," I agreed.

We stood in awkward silence. I couldn't remember the last time we'd been in a room together, alone and completely sober. I scratched the back of my head.

"Combat," Dad barked.

He kicked off his boots and ducked under the rope that bordered the fighting ring. I did the same.

"We'll go over the basics in here," he explained, "then practice outside with shoes. It'll feel different, but the maneuvers will be the same."

He launched into an explanation of how to stand—with your left food just a bit farther forward than your right. He showed me some basic footwork to help me more efficiently dodge and parry an attack. It came naturally enough. Years of horse-riding had granted me good balance. We moved on to punches. Dad insisted I throw a real punch, instead of a *cowboy* punch.

"No," he said again. "Quit swinging from behind you. All that wind-up will slow you down, and the vamps will have a field day."

I sighed and dropped my hands. "What if I'm not facing a vampire? What good does any of this do against magic?"

"The witch." He sighed. "She wasn't entirely wrong when she called us hypocrites. There's always been magic in our blood to protect us from their kind—ancient charms of protection. You didn't think you've survived the past few days on good luck alone, did you?"

Maybe.

"Then we are hypocrites," I said, "because the only way we got those charms is from witches."

He nodded. "Son, you have to accept your ancestry. Our family hunted because as many witches who don't kill, there are just as many who do. Clearly, not even your new friend's coven isn't clean of blood. It was our sovereign duty to end those witches. That meant we had to become more than human to protect humankind. We can rely on those charms—on that magic in our blood, even stronger now with the Moonflower heritage—to hunt. To kill. You just have to give yourself over to it."

"What do you mean?" I asked. "Give yourself over to it?"

"Accept it," Dad explained. "Give yourself over to the dormant instincts in your blood. You've always been a protector. Hell, you've protected your sister from me for years. Now, allow those instincts to overwhelm you. Allow them to guide the swings of your fists and the arc of your sword."

"What sword?" I asked.

He grinned. "Let's practice your punches and footwork a bit more, then I'll show you."

*

Freya

Cadence sat across from me on the porch with her eyes squeezed shut. As she nervously shifted her weight, the old boards beneath us creaked and groaned. A wilted flower sat between us.

"Remember," I told her. "It's all about intent."

The Sun hung low in the sky and would sink past the

horizon in mere hours. I shifted, and the rough wood chafed my hands. Cadence opened her mouth to recite the spell I'd taught her and just as quickly snapped it shut.

For the fifth time, she repeated the same question.

"How does it go?"

I sighed. "You know how it goes. Just try it."

Finally, Cadence whispered the spell.

Nothing happened.

She peeked one eye open and groaned.

"Try again," I instructed.

Again, she whispered the spell. Then, again. And again. And again.

"Why isn't it working?" she grumbled. "I trapped a freaking vampire, but I can't make one measly flower come back to life!"

"Trapping a vampire demonstrated great power," I said, "but no control. You were acting on instinct alone. Think of what you did in the castle as a really fast, short sprint. Now, I'm asking you to do a marathon."

Cadence ran a hand through her hair, and I nearly smiled. It was a nervous habit that reminded me of her brother.

"Can't I just be a sprinter?" she asked.

"Sprinters don't last long in battle," I answered honestly.

Cadence considered my words and nodded. Again, she closed her eyes and whispered the incantation. She peeked then sighed in defeat.

"Hey," I said. "Look again."

The bottom of the flower's stem was green. A smile stretched across her face.

"Amazing," Walker said.

He stood in the doorway with an easy smile. Only Walker could manage such a gentle expression with a battle looming over our heads.

A sword was sheathed at his side. Its silver handle shined, despite the quickly fading sunlight. I rose to my feet and stretched my arms over my head to alleviate the tension gathered there.

"Keep practicing," I told Cadence. "Time to gather my own weapons."

I ruffled her hair then breezed past Walker into the kitchen. My duffel bag was gone. I nearly growled in frustration.

Thunk.

I turned around. Clyde stood in the doorway to the kitchen. My bag—my *mother's* bag—was beside him. He'd shaved and changed into fighting leathers. His hunter's clothes stretched over his beer belly, but his gaze was clear.

"Looking for this?" he asked.

I summoned a gust of wind, and the bag slid across the floor to me. I picked it up and checked its contents. The Kevlar suits, daggers, and protection charms were all inside, as was Arachne's web and my only other defense against Josephine.

Thank the Goddess Mom left that in there.

"Why'd you take it?" I said. "Did you think I spent my last week saving your kids just to bring a hex into your home?"

He crossed his arms. "I don't trust you."

"Yeah?" I said. "The feeling's mutual."

I studied his shaking hands. "You've abandoned your kids to get drunk before. Who's to say it won't happen again?"

He ignored me. "You're planning on striking against your own coven."

"I already have," I interjected, "to save your son's life."

"I know," Clyde said and sighed. He stumbled over his next words. "Thank you…for sparing him. If I'd done my job right, he would've been prepared to face you. I own that."

I struggled for a response. I hadn't expected Clyde to *own* anything.

"But this battle," he said, "it'll be different. You could be fighting your own sisters. I know you've helped my kids, but where will your loyalties fall when its your coven's lives pitted against theirs?"

"I won't have to make that decision," I said in a rush. Fear coiled in my stomach. "My coven will come to their senses.

They'll see Josephine for what she has become—a monster."

"And if they don't?" Clyde pressed. "Hell, even if they do, will you really be able to kill the closest thing you have left to family? Will you be able to kill Josephine?"

I shook my head. "I won't side with my mother's killer or anyone who supports her."

Clyde sighed. "I hope you're right."

I hope so too.

CHAPTER TWENTY-SEVEN

Freya

The blood moon hung low in the purple sky, and the trees seemed to cower from it. The air was unnaturally still, and the grass did not sway, as if nothing wanted to attract attention.

I stared at the sky and took calming breaths. Already, the blood moon's power heightened the air with untapped energy. Always, my coven had used the blood moon as a time for cleansing spells and peace. It was a way to rebalance ourselves. It had never felt so sinister as it did tonight.

Even the sky knew death was coming.

Walker, Clyde, and Cadence stood beside me in the Reids' front yard, several feet from the house. Walker looked like a true hunter, except for that damn hat he still wore. He was dressed in a leather jacket that molded to his skin and fitted, thick black pants. With discomfort clearly painted in his frown, he tugged at them. A sword was strapped to his side. Other than one brief lesson by his father, Walker was untrained to use it. I prayed his hunter's blood would be enough to save him.

With protection charms and crystals hanging around my neck, I stood proudly in my mother's Kevlar suit. Cadence wore my old one, complete with the Goddess's emblem stitched on the chest. Hecate's three faces blazed in swirling, golden embroidery. The suit was a hair too big on Cadence, but its durable material and intense defensive spells would protect her.

I hoped.

None of my coven had yet to arrive.

Arion hadn't shown either. I missed the little demon as much as I craved his support.

I double-checked that Arachne's web was hidden in the pocket on my thigh. My other last resort was nestled beside it, and daggers were strapped to both of my legs. Cadence squeezed my hand in a death-grip, but I didn't complain. She stared straight ahead and squinted in determination. I followed her gaze.

Vampires, golems, and dark witches walked leisurely through the front gates of the Reids' property. The golems' broad, sandy bodies cast huge shadows, and they wore their usual emotionless expressions. The vampires occasionally glanced at the monsters in disgust and picked at invisible flecks of dust on their clothes. Clearly, they would have no idea how to fight alongside each other.

It was one small advantage, but it was better than nothing.

Leading them was Josephine.

She was more stunning than usual. Her long, ebony hair shone in the dim light, and her red lips curved into a feral smile. She wore a green velvet dress with a slit that ran to her hip, and a neckline that dipped nearly to her belly button. A glimmering ruby hung around her neck, and power radiated from her.

Her once kind eyes promised violence.

I waited for her to arrive, though it made my skin itch to give her the grand entrance she desired. I needed to placate her for a while. If I could convince her to keep this fight between us, no one else would have to get hurt.

She grew nearer. Her cheeks were round, and her forehead was perfectly unlined. The few markers of age she'd developed throughout the centuries were gone, undoubtedly because of all the witches she'd so ruthlessly killed. Surely, she hadn't broken our most sacred law just for a face-lift.

She really had Embraced them.

Josephine must've kept the fallen witches' power somewhere safe, like a cauldron, and siphoned it over time. If she'd absorbed it too quickly, she wouldn't have been able to hide its effects for as long as she did. Now, the evidence shone through her like a beacon, and power shined from her very pores.

When Josephine was only ten feet away, she stopped. Her cronies halted in perfect unison. Amid the golems and vampires, witches shed their magical camouflage and flickered into existence. I studied their faces and was horrified by what I saw. The dark witches sneered at Josephine's side, but worse, a few of our coven members—*my* coven members—stood among them.

"Lydia?" I asked.

My peer—a girl I'd known since I was out of the womb—lowered her blonde head and refused to meet my stare again. As the other betrayers did the same, I ground my teeth.

"Good riddance," I snapped. "Our coven has no use for the disloyal, but especially not for cowards."

Great job placating her, I thought and cursed myself.

Walker brushed his hand against mine. It was a reminder of what was at stake if I failed.

Walker, Cadence, their father, my coven, the whole town...

When Josephine laughed at my display, I didn't flinch. I just met her wild, green-eyed gaze unflinchingly.

"You've always been such a hot-tempered girl," Josephine chided. The familiarity of her voice crushed my withered heart. "I've always known it would be your downfall."

"Really?" I said and casually strolled closer. Cadence reluctantly dropped my hand. "Because I thought my downfall was going to be trusting such an insufferable bitch."

The witches behind Josephine gasped. Though humans tossed the insult around like it was a common name, witches did not use *male* insults on each other, and *especially* not to their superiors.

"Call me all the childish names you can think of,"

Josephine snapped. "It won't bring your mother back."

I bit my tongue so hard it bled. Before speaking, I waited for the coppery taste to subside and counted to ten. Walker fidgeted in my periphery, and grass crunched under his feet.

"Why?" I asked. "Why did you do it? Why have you done any of this?"

Josephine's sneer melted. For a moment, the ghost of my goddessmother stood before me.

"I had no choice," she said and stepped closer. Only six feet separated us. "You must see that—you *must* listen to me."

"Don't," an old familiar voice said from behind me.

I half-turned and saw my coven. They'd portaled in soundlessly—and they stood on *my* side. Even Gloria, our oldest elder who I never thought cared much for me, had shown up. It was her gravelly voice I'd recognized. I'd never been so relieved to see the Elders and their persnickety velvet robes.

They came.

We were still egregiously outnumbered, but their mere support strengthened me. Despite my slip-up with Walker, they'd still shown. If not for me, they did it for my mother, and that was enough.

I mouthed the words 'thank you' and faced Josephine again. I twisted my expression into the foolish girl she thought me to be. As if there were any story she could tell that could make her betrayal bearable, I stared at her in earnest.

It wasn't too difficult to fake. I wanted more than anything to hear an excuse that could wipe my pain away. I just knew it didn't exist.

"It began years ago." Her eyes grew distant. "When I met Lilly."

I racked my brain for the name and furrowed my eyebrows at the memory.

"Lilly," I said, "she was that human girl you'd been seeing."

Josephine shook her head. "I wasn't just *seeing* her. I was in love."

I fought a gasp. Witches rarely fell in love, but witches like

Josephine *never* did. I'd never even heard her speak about her lovers beyond the physical level. Tears pooled in Josephine's eyes.

"I wanted more than anything to be with her forever," she said, "but I was willing to settle for a few more decades. I was *happy*. Then she got sick."

I recalled a lesson about combat magic I'd had with Josephine a little over a year ago. It was the only time I'd seen her make a mistake.

"I'm in too good of a mood," Josephine had said. "It makes draining things hard."

It was true that magic had the tendency to follow our moods, so I had dropped the incident. I certainly wasn't bringing it up after I'd chuckled, and Josephine had whacked me with one of her many plants. Now, I wasn't so quick to dismiss her slip-up or just how happy and distracted Josephine had been those couple years. She'd never attended every coven meeting, but she *had* skipped more than usual. Damning sympathy squeezed my heart.

Had Josephine really been in love?

"Did you try to heal her?" I asked.

It was against the rules to do such a thing for a human, but it happened here and there. If Josephine were truly in love, Mom would've turned a blind eye for her friend.

"Her body rejected all of it." A tear slipped down Josephine's cheek. "Your mother and I found the best healers in the world, and they couldn't do a damn thing about it!"

The Elders behind me scoffed at their insolence, but I couldn't tear my gaze from my goddessmother. Her green eyes blazed with anger, and her face twisted into something unrecognizable. She paced in front of me like a rabid dog, lost in her own rage. Now that I'd unmasked all the torment she'd hidden, it was all I could see.

She seethed. "They *failed* me."

Josephine stopped to stare at me. Like a simple shift of wind, her sneer turned into a pleading frown.

"There was no other option," she whispered. "I couldn't

lose her."

Slowly, the wheels in my head turned. Reality had become too fantastical for my mind to keep up with.

"You," I said. "You—"

It all made *too* much sense. There were only two atrocities my mother couldn't have forgiven Josephine for, and she'd done both of them.

"You turned her," I finally said. "You made her a witch."

I scanned the crowd for the madwoman Josephine had *saved*. Witches were not vampires. They were not meant to be created—they were *born.* My coven stirred behind me. They probably searched the crowd too, though I wouldn't turn my back on Josephine to check on them.

She *was* a rabid animal—so desperate and afraid she'd lost all reason.

"Josephine," I pleaded, as if I could undo the past. "You had to know it wouldn't work. *You* have warned me about Marie Laveau."

The crazy, demented witch had tried to turn her poor slaves into her followers, but it had gone terribly wrong just like it had for any other foolish witch who attempted the spell.

"That witch on *American Horror Story*?" Cadence asked. "She's *real?*"

I winced. Walker quickly tried to quiet her down, but it was too late. Cadence had already gotten Josephine's attention. My mentor peered around me at the young girl with matching green eyes. Her gaze turned hungry.

"She was real," Josephine purred. "And she was a failure, but you and I will be different. *We* will usher in a new wave of witchcraft."

"You'll do nothing with her!" Walker bellowed.

Cadence stared at Josephine with eyes as wide as saucers. Walker tucked her behind him, and she didn't protest.

"I didn't fault Sybil for much," Gloria chimed in, "but I always did doubt her for trusting you. She loved you too much to see how spoiled you'd become and how slimy you've always been."

What Gloria said was true, but I knew she spoke to try to protect the younger witch and her brother. We needed to keep Josephine distracted. If she really decided to take what she wanted—Cadence's powerful, young blood—she could overpower us in a flash. She was high on the magic of six fallen witches, but more dangerously, somewhere on her body, the Bloodblade was sheathed. She wouldn't have come without it.

Josephine looked Gloria up and down. The Elder stood proudly in her velvet robes and lifted her chin an inch. Finally, Josephine chuckled.

"I look forward to killing you," she said. She turned her focus to me.

"You can stop searching the crowd," Josephine said flatly. "It didn't work. Without your mother's help, it killed her. Your mother *betrayed* me!"

"Because she wouldn't let you hurt the one you supposedly loved?" I said. "You knew the risks. Most people don't survive, and those who do aren't witches or humans or anything that's really *alive.*"

My hands shook with rage, but I walked closer to her on steady legs.

"I'd figured it out!" She threw her hands in the air. "I just needed *help!*"

"My mother was kind enough to not report you," I argued. "She showed you mercy, and you *killed* her."

"No!" Josephine shook her head. "I showed *her* mercy, until she got in the way again! Don't you see, Freya? We shouldn't have to be bound by the rules of some far-off High Witch! We should be *free.* I thought your mother would see that, but I was wrong."

I waited for the High Witch herself to descend upon us from the sky, but everything remained still except for Josephine. She paced again, clearly lost in her own tragedy.

"I didn't want them to die." She wrung her hands. "But with change comes sacrifice. I had to amass enough power to face the most powerful of all witches, so I took it the only way I knew how."

"The missing witches," Walker said to himself.

"You Embraced them," I added, "you stole their very life source."

"Once I killed one," she continued, "I knew I had to kill another. I had to make sure they wouldn't die in vain. A couple of them understood. They gave themselves willingly to my cause. The others..."

Josephine licked her lips, and I nearly vomited. This was too much. Knowing she'd done something horrible and hearing her talking about it were too different things. I couldn't play this game of cat and mouse anymore. If things didn't end now, my wounded heart might actually kill me.

"I had almost gotten everything I needed," she implored. "I only needed to Embrace my family's greatest shame, and it would've been a done deal! The vampires had sworn their loyalty to me and loaned me the Bloodblade. With it and a fellow Moonflower's power, I would've been ready to face the High Witch."

"Mom stopped you from killing Cadence," I said. Tears poured down my cheeks. "She died protecting someone."

It was a noble death—the kind my mother deserved.

It didn't make losing her any easier.

"I didn't want to use the Bloodblade against Sybil," Josephine admitted quietly, "but your mother was relentless."

"You mean she was too powerful for you to Embrace," I snapped, "so you had to use a coward's weapon to kill her."

"I did what I had to do," Josephine argued. "Then the human showed up. You were supposed to handle him, but you failed me too."

My hands shook from the force of my rage. "Sorry I didn't kill an innocent man to cover your crimes."

"Calm yourself, child," Josephine crooned. "I'm not angry with you. I just need to know that you understand."

She took a step closer and another, until only a few feet separated us.

"Freya," Josephine said. My name on her lips startled me. "You understand why I did it. Don't you?"

It wasn't a question, but a demand.

I stared at my goddessmother. She was the only mother I had left. The memory of twinkling laughter rang in my ears, and images of us brewing new potions flashed through my mind. She'd given me healing herbs after my Awakening and trained me to use wind as an extension of myself. She'd watched silly human movies with me that Mom had refused to endure. She'd shown me spells to make mean girls trip and taught me how to convince the world I was strong, even when I was not.

She killed my mother.

"No."

Her face twisted into disbelief. Silence stretched between us.

Josephine sneered.

"Then tell your mother I said hello."

CHAPTER TWENTY-EIGHT

Walker

With a scream that pierced my ears, Josephine launched herself at Freya. I raced forward to help her, but Josephine's army moved with her. Witches crashed upon witches, fighting with steel and spells and sheer violence. Vampires and golems surrounded my family. The vampires flashed fanged-grins, and the golems stared at us with their lifeless eyes.

I pulled the Sol sword from its sheath. It instantly came to life—blue flames danced on the silver blade. Its flames would kill any vampire, at any time of day or night.

Gifts would never make up for Dad's behavior, but this one came pretty close.

Dad raised his own weapons—two daggers crafted of obsidian that could cut through almost anything—and attacked vampires with lightning-quick speed. He moved almost as gracefully as Freya and with swiftness that rivaled the vampires'. Cadence tucked close to my side and chanted the protection spell Freya had taught her. Careful not to hit Cadence, I swung the Sol sword at any golems or vampires within range.

It was working—Cadence's spell slowed any golem that got close to us. Overwhelmed by the Sol sword, vampires stumbled right into Dad's swinging blade. I was quick to finish them with the Sol sword's flames. I kept alert for any attackers that fought past the spell, but then Freya screamed.

I spun to find her. She had crumpled to the ground like a ragdoll and clutched a bloody wound on her shoulder. Witches launched flames, wind, and even electric currents at each other. Blood spattered across their bodysuits and robes. Across the chaos, Freya's burning gaze met mine.

"Look out!" she shouted.

Coldness seeped into my back. I spun around and found myself up close and personal with a vampire. Seconds before the vampire's rotting teeth sank into my throat, I swung the Sol sword into his midsection. His dying hiss echoed in my ears. Beyond us, I caught a glimpse of Dad. He killed so quickly, I could barely see him in the plumes of sand.

Ash rained down on us, and Cadence coughed. Two golems used her momentary distraction to come down on us. I recalled what my father taught me.

Two attackers—get them in a line. Make them face you one-by-one.

I shuffled around, and Cadence followed me perfectly. The golems were large and strong, but they didn't actually have minds of their own. They weren't great at anticipating movements.

The first one got frustrated with my antics and charged. I thrust my sword into his stone heart. The collision reverberated up my arm, but it did the trick. The golem disintegrated into a pile of sand. Cadence held her breath, then resumed her chant.

The next golem moved sluggishly, but he was significantly larger than his friend. He stood at least eight feet tall, and his earthy body was much thicker.

I struck his chest, but my sword sank into nothing but sand. When I tried to remove it, it wouldn't budge.

"Uh-oh," I muttered.

The golem roared and shook. I lost my grip on my sword and fell to the ground. Cadence dodged me and screamed her spell at the beast. The golem raised its hand to swat at her, and I lunged at the thing.

I tackled it—or, tried to. It only budged a few inches, but

it gave Cadence time to escape. I tried to retreat from the golem, but my left arm was gripped by its quicksand-body. In what I suspected was its version of laughter, the golem huffed. Curses tumbled from my lips.

Cadence's eyes brightened, until they were an unnatural green.

"Language," she chided me with a smile.

How is she smiling right now?

Cadence raised her finger and pointed at the golem. Its laughter stopped, and it froze under the weight of her stare. A single vine shot from her fingertip and wrapped around the golem's throat. More vines sprang from the one Cadence had created. They wrapped the golem's legs, then its feet. The golem struggled to break from their grip, and I was forced to move with it.

Cadence's smile widened.

The golem grew more frantic, and its hold on my arm lessened. I didn't hesitate to move my arm, but I didn't pull it out of its body. I plunged it deeper, until my hand wrapped around its stone heart, then I ripped it away. With one last bellow, the golem died.

Cadence's vines shriveled up, and her face paled. We stared at the pile of sand and struggled to catch our breath. The stone heart was heavy in my grasp.

"That," she said, "was awesome."

"You're insane," I told her, "but, yeah, it kinda was."

Cadence grinned at me, but it quickly faded.

"Dad!" she screamed.

He was only ten feet from us, laying all too still on blood-soaked grass. We rushed to his side, and I pressed my fingers to his throat.

Thrum...thrum...thrum...

A small, slow pulse throbbed against my fingertips.

"He's alive," I told Cadence.

She pressed her tiny hands into the gaping wound on his abdomen. Though we'd been given a momentary reprieve

—probably just to let us soak in this pain—fighting still raged around us.

"We need to get him out of here," Cadence said. Though her voice was steady, tears streamed down her cheeks. "He needs a healer."

I searched the chaos for someone who could help, but Freya's coven members were all busy in varying modes of combat. The coppery scent of blood, and the hum of magic filled the air.

As I searched for a solution, I realized just how outnumbered we truly were. We'd slain a good portion of the golems, vampires, and traitorous witches, but many still fought vehemently. Freya's witches were slowly being overwhelmed. Soon, the tides of the battle would turn, and they wouldn't move in our favor. I looked back at my dad's pale face, and all remnants of hope drained.

A howl pierced the night.

*

Freya

I shot gust after gust of wind at Josephine, but she shielded herself with rocks. I couldn't get close enough to fight her with blades. Gloria, a talented wielder of water, launched her own spells, though she didn't have much better luck than me. I'd never seen the old woman fight so dirty. She conjured water from the air and nearly drowned Josephine with it, but my mentor fought it off with a defense spell and came back even angrier.

A few other witches, all Elders, launched their own spells, but six witches' magic coursed through Josephine's veins. Remnants of my *mother's* magic fueled her.

Vines popped out of the ground and tried to snag my feet, but I danced around them. I kept Arachne's web tucked in my pocket. Though it was tempting to use it as a shield, I knew I needed to save it for when she pulled out the Bloodblade.

Chaos whirled around us, but I couldn't break my attention. One wrong move, and the gash on my shoulder would be the least of my worries. Josephine would not attempt to take me prisoner again.

She would decimate me.

"Behind you!" a dark-haired witch from my coven yelled.

I turned. A boulder sprang from the ground and flew at me. I barely dove out of its path before it crushed me. I felt it *whoosh* past me right as my body hit the ground, but I didn't have time to see what it collided with because vines sprang from the earth. They wrapped around my ankles and legs, then grew thorns that jabbed through my suit and into my flesh.

I cried out in agony, but my mouth was quickly covered by yet another vine. I struggled to think of a spell that could get me out of this mess. Dirt sifted beneath me. If I didn't escape soon, Josephine would bury me alive.

I tried to summon fire, but no flames even sparked from my fingertips.

Think. Think. Think.

When things went wrong, Mom always said the best thing to do was to go back to the basics. I took a calming breath through my nose and dug my fingers into the earth. I let the rich soil fuel my magic and bit down on the vine in my mouth. The second it shriveled away, I muttered a simple unlocking spell. The vines' hold weakened, and I shot to my feet.

No one could make a solid hit, but I had the sinking feeling that my mentor was just letting us tire ourselves out, until she could make the perfect strike.

Time for a change of tactics.

Another vine jutted from the grassy ground, and I moved my foot just a little too slowly. The vine snaked its way up my leg, and Josephine grinned like a madwoman. Meanwhile, I whispered a spell under my breath and launched it at her.

As my stillness spell found its mark, her wild eyes went vacant. She bit her lip in frustration, but my spell left her body paralyzed.

And blind.

It was a little twist to the spell that I'd developed in my

efforts to terrorize Walker. With a few tweaks, the shadows I once made dance now shrouded her vision entirely. I nearly smiled. Mom would've greatly appreciated the irony of it all. The Elders fought off Josephine's minions who dared to intervene.

"Never drop your shields," I recited her own teachings, "not even when you think you've won."

"You little—"

"Ah," I interjected. "Language."

I wrenched the vine off my leg and prowled closer to her. My footsteps crunched over the grass, and Josephine shivered.

"Freya," she crooned. A tear trickled down her cheek. "You wouldn't really hurt me. Would you, dearest?"

I flinched at her endearment, but my steps did not falter. I pulled my last resort—magic-binding titanium cuffs—from the hidden pocket on my suit. They were bone-achingly cold in my hands, and their silver color gleamed under the blood moon's light.

"Freya," Josephine warned. "Don't push me too far!"

Vines continued to chase me, but their movements were sloppy, and I easily avoided their grasp. Without her eyes to see me or her hands to direct them, her attacks were almost pathetic.

"Or what?" I challenged.

I stepped around her and twisted her wrists behind her back. Under my will, her arms were easy to move. I slipped the cuffs over her wrists and whispered a containment spell. As they activated, the runes etched into them glowed. Josephine whimpered.

A howl pierced the air, and the vampires shuddered in fear.

"It's over, *dearest*," I whispered.

While Josephine trembled under my hands, the wolves tore into vampires left and right. I searched the crowd for Walker, but I couldn't find him in the chaos.

It's over, I thought. *Why aren't they retreating?*

Dread pooled in my stomach. The vampires were most

certainly not running. If anything, more seemed to portal into the fray. Seconds ago, their numbers were half of the wolves. Now, they were nearly equally matched. Unless they were killed by the Sol sword, some of the vampires could have bounced back from death, but they didn't bounce back that fast.

"You foolish, arrogant girl," Josephine purred.

She didn't tremble under my grip.

She laughed.

Magic radiated off her in waves, and the runes on the cuffs glowed brighter. The hum of her power hurt my ears so badly, the vibration of it alone was nearly overwhelming. Cursing myself for choosing mercy for a merciless crime, I jumped away from her and reached for the web in my pocket.

"Help!" Cadence called.

Several feet away, she crouched on the ground next to her father, whose face was ghostly pale. Walker stood over them like a forlorn sentry. His eyes searched the crowd for aid, but no one noticed the human family that had been reunited, only to be broken again. No one saw the tears gleaming in his eyes. I yelled Gloria's name, jutted my chin in their direction, and prayed it would be enough.

Snap!

Josephine's cuffs landed in a heap of burning goo. Around us, wolves howled in pain, and my coven fought to keep up with the onslaught of monsters. Blood slicked the ground. One of the wolves took a dagger to chest and landed *hard.* His wide-eyed gaze went vacant. As both armies ripped each other apart with magic and teeth and will, the earth shook.

The pounding under my feet became more violent. It found a steady, three-beat rhythm. Both sides of battle wobbled from its force.

Boom. Boom. Boom.

Rich, bitter magic coated my tongue and raised the hairs on the back of my neck—magic that was usually on a much tighter leash.

Magic that Josephine clearly recognized. Her jaw dropped.

I grinned.

Arion weaved his way through the battle so swiftly, he blurred into a flicker of shadows. Witches and vampires were left nothing more than heaps of flesh and bones under his thundering hooves.

Without wasting another second, I launched myself at Josephine. I grabbed the two throwing daggers strapped to my thighs and aimed for her midsection. The first one landed with a satisfying thud, and she barely avoided the second one. She sneered at the quickly spreading bloodstain that coated her dress. Without so much as a wince, she tore the dagger out her body.

"That," she said and tossed the dagger aside, "was rude."

I answered by summoning winds that battered her left and right, but she shielded herself with thick walls of earth. I tried to swath her mind in shadows, but she was too clever to make the same mistake twice. Her mind was a brick wall, protected in layers of defensive spells.

Josephine cackled. "Really? That's how you want to play this, dearest?"

Her own spell hit me like a landslide. My defenses rattled under the force of her magic. She'd held back before—toyed with me to weaken my magical reserves and hide the raw energy she contained.

The force of six witches shattered my defenses, and my mind splintered.

Lost in anguish, I screamed and dropped to my knees. I braced myself for the impact of the hard ground but instead landed on the plush carpet of my cottage's floors.

CHAPTER TWENTY-NINE

Walker

Death surrounded me. Wolves tore into vampires, and witches tore into each other. Almost all the golems had been eliminated, mostly by the man who lay dying at my feet.

My father.

Clyde's face was clammy and whiter than a sheet. His daggers, slick with blood, lay docile at his sides. Forgotten.

Useless without him.

That's what I had become.

Witches protected our sad excuse of a family, undoubtedly sent by Freya, though I couldn't see her past the chaos. Even among the grunts of pain, the gurgling of blood, and the cackling of witches, I heard my father's rattling breath.

It was so different from his alcohol-induced snores or his occasional breathy bouts of laughter. Just when I finally discovered why he hadn't truly laughed in years, he was going to leave me.

"I-I can get someone," Cadence said. She kneeled at my father's side and wrapped her tiny hand in his, as if she could tether him to us with the sheer force of her will. "One of these witches must know how to heal you."

"No," Dad rasped. Blood stained his pale lips. "No, Cady-Cat, I'm afraid it's too late."

Tears poured down her cheeks. "But there must be

something–"

"The witches do me a great service now," he said. "They give me a chance to say goodbye to my children. They-they let me fight for you, finally."

I fell to my knees beside him and tried to ignore the blood that soaked through my pants. I swallowed the tears and thousands of emotions that scattered my thoughts and said the only thing he'd want to hear.

"Mom would be proud of you, Dad. *We're* proud."

A faint smile graced his face, and blood poured out of his mouth. Cadence poured her own heart out for him, and he found the strength to squeeze her hand even tighter. We had only moments left with him, this father I'd met hours ago, but I noticed the gasp echoed by each of the witches surrounding us.

I found where their gazes landed, and something in my chest cracked. With her face twisted into a mask of pain, Freya lay on the ground. Members of her coven fought to reach her, but Josephine was quick to keep them away. The earth around the wicked witch had become a mess of vines and rocks, ready to attack at her will.

"Go," Dad said. "Don't...don't run from what you are, Walker. Fight for her."

Cadence nodded urgently. I squeezed Dad's shoulder one last time and stood.

It was time to follow my destiny.

It was time to hunt a witch.

*

Freya

I glanced around the cottage in wonder.

No cracks fissured the walls, and no bookcases were toppled over. It was as if the attack had never happened. Soft light flickered from the lamps and the fireplace. Something bubbled in the kitchen.

The kitchen door swung open, and the beckoning scent of spices wafted out. Mom's boots clicked across the floor, and her red dress flowed around her hips. She wore her signature obsidian necklace, and her fiery hair framed her face in loose waves. As her gaze met mine, her eyes crinkled in a smile.

"Dinner's almost ready," my mother announced.

"Mom," I whispered, "you're here?"

She chuckled, and her nose wrinkled.

"Where else would I be?" She put her hands on her hips. "It's me who should be worried about *you*. You've been asleep for eons. I was worried I'd gone too hard on you in training."

"Training?" I asked.

I tried to remember what she was talking about, but my head swam with confusion. Training sounded like something I *should've* been doing, but this past week had been busy and chaotic.

Something horrible had happened, but I couldn't recall what it was.

What is going on?

"Oh, don't cry, darling," she said. "You'll get the hang of fire-magic eventually. You should really be more worried about your healing-abilities. It's much more useful, though not half as flashy."

I touched my damp cheeks.

"I'm crying?" I asked. That wasn't like me. There had to be a reason for the tears, if only I could *think*. "Wait, I *did* heal someone."

She arched an eyebrow. "Oh, really? And this is the first I'm hearing of it?"

"You've been gone," I whispered.

The realization hurt my head, and I tugged at my hair with a hiss. Mom rushed to my side and clasped my hands in hers.

"Don't worry about that, Freya," she crooned. "Can't you see it's hurting you? Come eat with me. We'll talk about magic and the coven and that cute little werewolf you've been seeing."

"But Mom," I said, "why does my head hurt? What's going on?"

"Darling," she crooned and tugged me to her chest. I

leaned into the warmth of her affection. "Don't worry. You can stay with me if you just stop your fretting. That's all you have to do. Let go, Freya."

I closed my eyes, and the pain dissipated. With a smile on my face, I did as my mother asked.

I let go.

*

Walker

Across the bloody battlefield, Freya was crumpled at her goddessmother's feet. She now wore a forced smile that reminded me of the ones clowns painted on their faces. Freya usually smiled like she had a secret.

This wasn't *her* smile at all.

Josephine beamed, and her green eyes shined brighter than the moon. I swallowed the shiver that scurried down my spine and picked up the Sol sword. I tuned out the sound of Dad's ragged breaths and Cadence's desperate cries. I tuned out the cacophony of not-so-mythical creatures. I shut down any and all hope that this was some twisted dream.

This was real.

Witches were real.

Witch *hunters* were real.

Honing into the instincts I'd ignored for most of my life, I stepped out of the witches' circle of protection and into battle. A sixth sense flared to life. I *felt* the vampires lunge at me before I saw them. The second their coldness seeped into my skin, I arched my sword through air. I didn't watch in disbelief as they perished into a pile of ash. I just swung at the next one. And the next.

Locked into my newfound senses, I sensed my bloodline's protective spells shield me from several witches' assaults. The dark witches' spells whispered in my mind, but I ignored the calls to end myself. Rocks and water and fire came at me, but I sidestepped the attacks.

Amid the chaos, I caught glimpses of Freya. She lay still

except for the steady rise and fall of her chest. That tiny motion was enough to propel me forward. To keep blindly cutting, killing, and dodging.

I had to get to her.

Josephine stared at the battle with that same unsettling grin. She wove no spells to help her comrades, though her side was falling behind. Arion charged through the battle like death itself. A few times, he trampled past me.

His hooves shook the earth and crushed those in his path into something unrecognizable. Occasionally, he would leave his victims with a missing throat or an absent head. I didn't want to think about how he accomplished it. I didn't let myself focus on the crushed remains of his kills or worry I might veer into his path.

Keep moving. Keep moving. Keep moving.

Finally, I neared the edge of the chaos, where Freya and Josephine remained in the clearing. Tucked into Freya's jumpsuit was the web. I prayed it offered some inkling of protection for her and gripped my Sol sword tighter. It would have to be enough.

I was ready to charge Josephine, but a dark witch intercepted my path. I only saw a whisper of a grin and glimpse of white-blonde hair before she attacked. She wielded tiny, wickedly sharp blades. It didn't go over my head that I'd been stabbed by a dark witch just earlier this week.

I refused to have a repeat of that experience.

I parried her blows and fought to land one of my own. She was fast—so fast, she must've spelled herself to move with inhuman speed.

Sweat lined my brow and slickened my grip, but I didn't falter. I wouldn't. I attacked the witch with renewed vigor and forced her to back a step. Then another. Closer and closer to Freya, we moved. Clearly frustrated, the witch growled and muttered something under her breath. Magic hummed in the air and rang in my ears. As it pulsed through my body, my head swam. Suddenly, there wasn't one white-haired witch before me, but three.

The triplets leered at me and cackled. One of them flipped her dagger in her hand, while the other swiped for my leg. I danced out of her reach, but barely avoided the next one's strike to my arm.

"Look at the little hunter dance," the witch before me crooned.

I swiped at her with my sword, but she easily evaded the hit. The swing left me vulnerable to the other one, who put me in a headlock.

"Not so sure-footed anymore," she whispered.

Her breath was hot against my neck.

She shoved me into her sister or whatever the hell these things were. Her pale hands gripped my throat tightly enough to make me gasp. Her nails were filed into fine points, and blood leaked from where they dug into my skin. As it trailed down my throat, the witch tracked it with a predatory gaze.

"You Reids," she said and sneered. "Always so damned heroic."

I scrambled out of her hold, but it was no use. The other one caught me in her clutches the next heartbeat. She gripped my arms behind my back in an iron hold and popped my sword out of my hand. It hit the ground with a thud, and its flames fizzled out.

"When will you learn?" she whispered. "We witches don't want your saving."

*

Freya

Mom's stew was exactly like I remembered it—spicy and sweet. We sat at our tiny kitchen table. Just the two of us. Like always.

Except it wasn't.

As if it were fighting to outshine the rest of the cabin, the lamp shone a little too brightly. Its usually warm light swathed the kitchen in a dreamy glow. The windows, however, were a little too dark. Not even moonlight filtered through the panes.

I squinted at the darkness to see the garden that flourished in its view. Despite my efforts, I couldn't see it.

"Freya," Mom chided, "your stew will get cold."

I glanced down at my steaming bowl of food. I waved my hand over the steam but felt no heat. No dampness. Nothing at all.

"Freya." Mom slammed her fork down. It smacked against the table, but nothing vibrated under my hand. Nothing rattled. "Enjoy a meal with your mother."

I recoiled from her harsh tone. Mom wasn't prone to having a bad temper. She always said I got that from my father.

Her frown melted into a smile. "I've missed you, darling."

"Mom," I whispered and leaned closer. "Why have you missed me? Where have you been?"

She frowned. "I'm here *now*. Isn't that enough?"

My heart sank to the floor.

"No," I said and swallowed. "No, it's not."

The dull ache in my head reached a crescendo that traveled to my chest. As reality crashed on the façade Josephine had trapped me in, my heart ached. I squeezed my eyes shut to try to block out the pain.

When I opened them, my mother was gone.

Again.

I no longer sat in my cabin, but in a cell. I ran my fingers along the rough stone beneath my hands and studied the thick iron bars. They surrounded me in every direction. The cage was so small that I couldn't even stand. Endless darkness stretched out beyond its confines. With a cry of fury, I pounded a fist against the cage's ceiling.

"Let me out!" I screamed.

My voice echoed into the darkness, but no one answered me. Panic seized my chest. I was utterly and truly alone. Frantically, I pounded a fist against the ceiling and tried to pry the bars apart. All my effort resulted in was pain.

Think, Freya.

High on power, Josephine had made me a prisoner in my

own mind. Her gilded cage hadn't worked so she'd crammed me into this one. I'd broken free of one of her traps. I could do it again.

But how?

Mom's greatest advice for defending one's mind generally involved not letting things get to this point of severity.

It was time to adlib. It couldn't be that hard—Walker did it all the time.

Walker, who is out there probably dying and in need of my help...Nope.

I wouldn't go down that road. I *would* get out.

"That's it!" I exclaimed.

I was ashamed the idea hadn't hit me earlier. Manifestation wasn't just something humans had added to the long list of their many fads. It was magic in its simplest form—wishing and believing.

I closed my eyes and imagined grass beneath me instead of stone. I recalled the coppery scent of blood and the metallic buzz of magic. I basked in the blood moon's strange heat on my back where I lay in the field. Slowly, the prison melted away.

Cries of pain and grunts of strained effort created a cacophony of nightmares. Somewhere in the distance, a child sobbed.

"Look at the little hunter dance," a witch crooned.

The air stirred as the witch grappled with someone. They were so close, I could reach out and touch them, if only I could lift my arms or even an eyelid. I focused on the blood thrumming through my veins and the earth, strong beneath me. I guided that strength into my body and forced myself to have patience.

"Always so damn stubborn," Josephine purred above me. Her skirt brushed my hand. "Just like your mother."

Her warm hand cupped my forehead, as gently as a mother would to her child to check for a fever. The sensation only lasted a single breath.

Josephine attacked.

Magic—pure and violent and heavy like death—rattled my head. I screamed, but no sound passed through my lips. My very brain *ached.* I fought her spell, but I couldn't stop it from spreading. She was done trapping me in cages and putting me to sleep.

"I won't simply kill you, dearest," she promised. I could barely hear her over the roar in my ears. "I'm only going to keep you with me another way."

The aching spread through my limbs, into my heart, and, beyond that, to my well of magic. To the one sacred place I could always tap into in time of trouble—to the one place most witches would never dare trespass, even when faced with their greatest enemy.

Her spell pulled me apart from the inside and ripped my magic, my energy, my *everything* into her.

She Embraced me.

She whisked all the power I'd gathered from the earth away from me. Her hand—so horrifically gentle—sucked it through my body and into hers. I quickly grew cold, but I was too separated from myself to even shiver.

It was like a brain-freeze on steroids that seized my whole body. I scrambled and screamed and fought, but I didn't twitch a muscle. I tried to conjure a defense spell, but I couldn't grasp my magic. It slipped through my control like sand.

"Shh," Josephine crooned. "Don't fight it—it'll only hurt worse."

Distantly, I knew she was right. She was fighting with the strength of six witches. I was no match for her. It was far too late for a defensive spell, even if I could access my powers. My thoughts raced, too quickly for me to launch any of them into action, and the aching lessened.

This was it.

I was dying.

CHAPTER THIRTY

Walker

The dark witch crept closer, while her duplicate held me in a headlock. The witch's stare was icy as it bore into mine. Her mouth was set in a smug line. The other triplet put a hand on her shoulder, urging the witch to finish me off.

Out of the corner of my eye, I saw Josephine reach down to Freya. The blonde witch's lips curled back in disgust, and her gaze shot to Josephine. Her duplicates' concentration was broken too.

I slammed my foot down on the top of my captor's foot, and she hissed in pain. Her grip loosened enough for me to slip free. I grabbed my sword, and its flames whooshed back to life. One of the witches clawed at my back, but she was too late. My sword swung for her head and thoroughly separated it from her shoulders.

That's an image for future nightmares.

I swung at her sisters, but they dissipated into puddles of water.

And that's going to be a question for Freya.

I looked up, and my eyes locked on her still form. Her skin's usual creamy glow had become a sickly yellow. Her hair had lost its fire and framed her blank face in limp sheets. Arion whinnied like a maniac, but electrical currents, summoned by a small troupe of frantically chanting witches, corralled him.

All around us, her coven was blockaded from coming to her aid, but there were less witches fighting for the opposing team than there had been. Confusion and dread warred inside me.

Power, stronger than ever, hummed in the air. It rattled the breath in my lungs and the blood in my veins. And weirder, it felt *familiar.*

Horror annihilated my courage.

Josephine Embraced Freya.

Seeing a witch Embraced, rather than just hearing about it, was anough to make even devil-worshippers pause.

"No," I whispered to myself, then my voice became a command. "Stop!"

I raced toward Josephine, and her bright eyes met mine. She laughed, but it sounded more like the screech of metal against metal.

"Stop?" she mocked, "you think asking nicely will do the trick?"

"I know you don't want to do this." I paused, only a few feet from her. Only a few feet from Freya. "You don't want to kill her."

Josephine frowned. "I'm *not* killing her. I'm keeping her."

"Not how you planned to," I argued.

"Plans change," she snapped.

I held my hands up. "They don't have to. I have a proposition for you, but you have to stop."

Josephine hesitated, and I feared she wouldn't listen to me after all. Then, the magic in the air stilled.

"Okay, hunter," she purred. "Let's hear it."

"Fight me," I challenged.

Josephine cackled.

"Dual me," I continued, "and if I win, your whole army backs down. This is *over*. If you win, Freya's allies will bow down, and I'll be out of the picture. My sister will remain intact, but Freya will too. With you."

She crossed her arms and sighed.

"Really? That was all you came up with–"

"Think about it," I interjected. "Without me or her coven

to back her, or even her familiar, Freya will be yours. She'll have no one else to turn to."

Arion's powerful hooves pounded the ground in denial, but Josephine didn't notice. She was too high on power and too enthralled with the idea of destroying me.

"You don't really need Cadence, do you?" I pushed. "Not when you have her by your side."

She searched the crowd for my sister with ravenous eyes. When she found Cadence—staring Josephine down with all the bravery of a warrior—her expression pained. I was asking her to give up on the thing she killed her dearest friend for, but that was also why I had a shot of convincing her. Sparing Freya was her chance of redemption. It was her chance to do something right.

Even if her version of *right* involved killing me.

Josephine swiveled her gaze back to mine. Her moods shifted every second, as if her body couldn't manage its emotions on top of all the magic rushing through it.

"How do you know she'll come back to me?" she asked fervently, "that getting you out of the picture will change her mind?"

I swallowed. "Because we're in love."

Gasps flooded the crowd, which I hadn't even realized had stopped battling. They stared at us in confusion. I cleared my throat and hid my shaking hands behind my back. I couldn't give her any reason to doubt my lies.

Are they really lies? my mind taunted. *You're about to die for her.*

I shut out the thoughts. I didn't have time for a crisis of heart.

"Losing her mom and me in such a short time?" I said and clutched my hand to my chest. "It'll destroy her, but *you* will be there for her. Seeing how much you love her will prove to her what a sacrifice it was for you to cause her all this pain. And losing me, well, she'll finally understand your grief and why your mission is so important. She'll forgive you, and you won't have to conquer the High Witch alone. You won't have to *be* alone."

Slowly, the story I weaved settled in. Josephine's hand clutched her chest, and her jaw set in determination. She opened her mouth to agree to my terms, but another voice chimed in.

"The rules shall bind both of you in blood," Gloria said. "You and the hunter will fight alone. No interferences."

My heart skipped a beat. I didn't *actually* want to give Freya over to Josephine.

But that's not what I agreed to.

Josephine believed Freya would go willingly with her.

That would be her downfall. Even if I failed, I would at least buy Freya enough time to put an end to her mother's killer. I would help put an end to the witch who wanted to destroy my sister and avenge the witch who'd died protecting her.

"You don't trust me, old friend?" Josephine asked Gloria.

Josephine feigned nonchalance, but, as she peered down at the silver-haired witch, her neck was tense. Gloria didn't blink an eye. The old woman held Josephine's stare like a matador facing a bull.

"No," Gloria answered flatly.

Josephine cackled, and her face stretched in an unnaturally wide grin. The magic that roared in her veins was having ill effects. The higher the Blood Moon rose in the sky, the more humanity left her. Reddish light flickered under her tan skin that now glistened with sweat. Dark veins crowded around her eyes, which burned so brightly they were more yellow than green.

Her laughing-fit finally ended.

"I always knew you were smarter than the rest," she said.

Her gaze homed in on me. "If it's blood you want, it's blood you'll get."

Without warning, a thorny vine sprouted from the ground and nicked a small cut into my forearm. A single drop dripped onto the soil. Too much adrenaline pumped through my veins for me to even feel the sting.

With one of her long fingernails, Josephine cut a similar gash into her own arm. I gulped. She'd sharpened her nails into *talons.* In the grand scheme of things, it was a small reminder that what I faced was far from human or even witch.

I faced power itself.

Dark and angry and ancient power. Though I couldn't see the Bloodblade's dark magic, it electrified the space between Josephine and me. The stolen magic coursing through Josephine's veins only amplified its song. With my hunter's senses unlocked, I could hear it.

More, more, more, the Bloodblade's magic purred. It wanted to snuff me out and take my soul to add to its wicked collection.

Josephine prowled closer. Only a couple feet separated us. I didn't feel frightened or disturbed. I didn't feel anything at all, but bleak determination.

"By blood and by honor," Gloria chanted. "By the power of Hecate herself…"

Heat flared through the wound on my forearm and glowed bright red. The light transferred to the drop of blood that had fallen to the ground. As it glowed like a ruby and coagulated, so did Josephine's. Like slugs, the drops moved toward each other. My stomach churned at the sight.

Josephine noticed my grimace and bared her teeth in a smile. I steeled myself and focused on Gloria's words. She recited the terms we agreed to, exactly as we had agreed to them. Still, the Bloodblade hummed.

Instead of letting it deter me, I welcomed the sound. With a start, I realized magic no longer frightened me—not when magic needed to be wielded by someone strong enough to manage it and not when it knew nothing of fighting for something other than its own mindless greed.

As Gloria finished her speech, the droplets of blood became one and burned even brighter. Heat burned my wound, then the small cut healed altogether. A serpent-shaped scar took its place.

"Ready, hunter?" Josephine taunted.

She launched her attack.

I dodged the first swipe of Josephine's dagger, only for my foot to be snagged by a vine. I barely caught my balance, then hacked the thing off with the Sol Sword. Josephine launched spells at me, but the charms from my bloodline held strong. Magic buzzed against my skin and hummed in the air, but my frantically beating heart drowned out almost everything else.

"Your blood saves you now," Josephine taunted. "It won't save you forever."

I barely stepped out of the way of another vine, but yet another one after that snagged my wrist. I chopped it down, but not quickly enough. Josephine swiped her dagger across my arm that held the sword. Adrenaline kept me from fully recognizing the pain and my grip did not slacken, but I knew I couldn't go on like this for much longer.

An idea struck me. I jutted my sword forward, as if I meant to strike the witch. She easily dodged it, which gave me the space and time to spread my flaming sword across the grass we stood on. Its unnatural flames lit the blades of grass instantly and kept them burning, as if the sword could read my mind.

Hell, I thought, *maybe it can.*

Josephine snarled. "Think that will stop me?"

I didn't bother answering her. I knew she only meant to distract me, and distractions could be lethal. Besides, my idea had worked. No more vines reached from the ground for my ankles.

Josephine lunged for my hamstring with a swipe of her dagger, but I blocked it with the Sol sword, then surprised her with an offensive strike to her leg. Its flames and steel bounced off her like they were made of rubber.

"I remember your family, hunter," she said and sneered. "I knew to protect myself with a few carefully crafted spells from the Reids' prized Sol Sword."

I tried to shut down my panic. There was no time to dwell. Josephine came at me harder with vicious swipes of her dagger.

She reached for a matching silver blade strapped to her thigh, but not before I caught a glimpse of what else she hid under there.

The Bloodblade.

It couldn't have been anything else. It glimmered ruby red and radiated with power that hummed a deep, bone-rattling song. Laying eyes on the infamous instrument of death was more jarring than I could've anticipated. Josephine nicked my arm with one of her blades. I shook off my fear once more and focused.

I recalled Dad's brief lesson on daggers. Only the most skilled warriors fought with them, and those who did put their opponents, should they be less skilled at close combat, at a huge disadvantage. I wouldn't count a few fistfights as close-combat, but I was born to fight witches.

I faced witch-clones for crying out loud.

I could do this.

Josephine suddenly lunged from my left, with a quick back-handed swipe at my throat. I narrowly avoided it, then skirted out of her other knife's path as it came for my hamstring. I let instinct take over and dodged all of her quick attacks.

For the first time since discovering the supernatural world, I became a part of it.

"You have to accept your ancestry."

My father had been right for once. So had Freya. Even Cadence had done her part to convince me that maybe different wasn't *worse.* Maybe I'd only felt so out of place in all of this because I hadn't wanted to give up safety, for myself or my family.

Life had other plans.

It was time I got with them.

Frustration lined Josephine's face. She was toying with me, but I still wasn't as easy of prey as she'd expected. She increased the speed of her knives, and sweat slickened my brow. I struggled to keep up with the pace of her blows, and she smiled once more.

Something flew at me from my right and knocked me to the ground. My sword flew out of my grip, and pain raced up my arm. Cadence screamed, which pierced the silence I hadn't even realized had descended over the battlefield. Driven by fear I'd never known, I struggled to my feet and stomped on a vine that tried to trap me.

"You're quicker than I expected," Josephine crooned, "but you're still human. How long will it take you to tire?"

I raced for my sword and my only defense from her attacks, but I couldn't make it a step without a vine or rock or dagger snagging my progress. Leaning into my instincts, I avoided all the obstacles, but I knew that was only because Josephine allowed me to. She wanted to draw out the death of the human who dared challenge her. She wanted to savor killing the man she believed was the reason for Freya's *betrayal.*

My sword was too far away, and I would never reach it. It couldn't kill her anyway. It was time to face the facts—there was only one weapon that could kill Josephine.

The Bloodblade.

I had to get back to it.

It was my only hope of winning the dual.

Even if wielding it killed me.

Another bolder knocked me to the ground, but this time it hit me square on my chest. It knocked all the breath from my lungs. I couldn't orient myself as to which way was down or which way was up. My arms were weightless and out of reach. My chest heaved for breaths that only brought more pain.

This is it, I thought, *I'm going to die.*

CHAPTER THIRTY-ONE

Freya

The world rushed away from me. Colors blurred past, and the wind's hollow screams echoed in my ears. I flailed wildly, but it did nothing to control my fall. Just as abruptly as it had begun, it was over.

I fell back inside my own body. Magic roared in my veins and kept me connected to something—*someone*—else. I grappled with my thoughts and tried with all my might to shake the disorientation that engulfed me.

A scream pierced the roar of magic.

It was so agonized, I thought it might be from an animal, but I recognized its tinny ring and the magic that made it even louder.

Cadence.

I tried and failed to jerk upright then wondered how I was able to hear at all. Josephine had Embraced me. It wasn't something, not even Redferns, came back from.

Then I felt it.

What kept me to tethered to existence.

Josephine's magic tangled with mine and slowly pulled energy from me. The onslaught of power had been reduced to a small tug that jerked violently on occasion.

She's using me to cast spells.

I held on tight to that tether and used it to ground me, so I could access my other senses. I let the tether pull me back to life.

"You're quicker than I expected," a woman crooned, "but you're still human. How long will it take you to tire?"

I would recognize Josephine's voice from anywhere, but it held a strange ring to it. Her words reverbed, as if multiple people spoke through her mouth. Magic pulsed through the air and shook the earth.

If only I could access it.

Someone grunted, and I was shocked I could single out the sound. The craze of battle had ended. I spread my senses wider across the earth's floor and confirmed that everything had gone still.

You're still human.

Panic gripped my heart.

Walker fought Josephine *alone.*

It was no wonder Cadence screamed. If I could've opened my godsdamned mouth, I would've screamed. Horror and pride warred in my chest. Walker—goofy, clueless Walker—faced off a power-crazed witch. A witch who dared to use *my* power against him.

Even worse, the Bloodblade's magic hummed in the air like a death march. Surely, Josephine didn't plan to wield it against him.

Unless the cowboy had proven to be stronger than she'd thought.

Unless she wanted to decimate him so completely, he'd be nothing but a meager bone. Walker would just be another thing taken from me, her goddessdaughter who *didn't understand.*

Josephine had taken my mother and nearly taken my own coven's loyalty. She wouldn't take anything from me again.

I tuned out Walker's grunts of struggle and Josephine's maniacal laughter. I drowned out the heady thrum of magic and the stillness that had descended upon the battlefield. All my focus went to the tether between Josephine and me. It operated like a tunnel. A current tugged my magic through it and into Josephine.

Air had always been my most natural element.

Reverse, I told the spell.

As if it were confused, the current of magic stalled. With one last ounce of energy, I tugged harder.

Reverse. Reverse. Reverse.

There was one more heartbeat of stillness, then chaos erupted. The channel of magic reversed and power unlike anything I'd ever experienced rushed into me. It seized my limbs and stole my breath. Some of it was my own, which I recognized like a missing limb returned. Some of it was richer, or slicker, or brighter. It heated my veins and sped my heart.

It was the magic of my fallen sisters.

I opened my eyes and jerked upright. Magic rolled through me like a tidal wave and begged to be set free.

Wild green eyes met mine. Josephine's face was slack with shock, and I couldn't stop my grin. In the edges of my vision, Walker scrambled to his feet.

The whirlwind of power threatened to loosen my resolve, but I remembered all she'd taken from me and pulled harder.

More and more and more, I took.

Josephine shook like a brittle leaf on a windy day. Rage marred her face, and, with painful cry, she broke free from my spell. A pop rang in my ears, and the sudden disconnection knocked me off my feet. I quickly stood and fought to ignore the burning of my blood. My skin.

Too much magic roared inside me.

I took too much.

"You foolish girl," she growled. "This is on you."

Josephine reached under the slit of her dress and pulled out what could only be the Bloodblade. As she hefted it to the sky with a roar, it glowed crimson. Dark magic, thicker and more suffocating than ever before, descended over the battlefield.

Walker was going to die.

Josephine pointed the Bloodblade. I screamed, but an unnatural silence muffled the air. Heartbeats turned into years.

No, I realized. *She's aiming for Cadence.*

Arachne's web burned where it lay against thigh. I reached for it with blessedly nimble fingers and threw it with all my might.

Crimson lightning stretched across the battlefield. It was so bright, it hurt to look at. Every hair on my skin rose. Where the Bloodblade's lightning trekked, charred earth was left in its path. Witches and vampires jumped out of its way, but one vampire wasn't fast enough. The Bloodblade's power grazed his foot and he crumbled into a pile of ashes.

As it soared through the air, Arachne's web shimmered under the blood moon's light. There was no way to tell which would reach Cadence first—the crimson streak of death or the iridescent shield.

Please, I begged the goddesses. *Please save her.*

The web wrapped Cadence in a cocoon of safety, and the Bloodblade's magic plummeted against it. As red lightning raged around the web, I held my breath.

Brilliant streams of light erupted from the web. They shone in every color and destroyed the Bloodblade's electric veins of magic. The silence lifted, and relief bloomed in my chest. The web fell to the ground and revealed a perfectly whole and healthy Cadence. She stared down Josephine with bravery even my mother would've been impressed by.

This is on you.

Josephine would've killed and Embraced the girl just to earn back a scrap of the power I'd stolen from her.

But, I thought, *why didn't she just use the Bloodblade against me?*

"Mercy, dearest," Josephine said and clenched her teeth. "I wanted to show you mercy, but you've left me no choice."

I hadn't realized I'd asked the question out loud, but it was hard to think over the magic roaring in my ears. It was no wonder bleeding me dry of my magic and killing a child with a vile weapon had become *merciful* to her. No one could carry all this power without going mad.

"Mercy?" Walker shouted. "This is between us—you were

supposed to leave my damn sister out of it!"

"You should've used more careful wording," Josephine chided. "The rules stated no interference, meaning no one could intervene between our fight. Dear old Gloria never said we couldn't intervene with the rest of the battle as long as we're both alive. Don't worry, let me handle dearest Freya, and your death will be arranged."

I tried to understand their words, but my thoughts were consumed by the magic wreaking havoc on my body. I studied the black, swollen veins on my hands and the flush of my skin. Josephine had taken months to acquire the magic I'd stolen in mere seconds. If I didn't get rid of all this power soon, it would kill me, but I couldn't. If I loosened my grip on it just a hair, it would overwhelm me. I could kill everyone in the five-mile radius. I could kill everyone in Hol Creek.

Panic clogged my throat.

Walker stood only a couple feet from Josephine and stared at me in wide-eyed horror. I glanced down at my hands and grimaced. Light *moved* beneath my skin. Josephine snickered.

"It's too much, isn't it?" Josephine taunted. "You Embraced magic I've taken months to consume. You signed your own death warrant, dearest."

I had to be able to control it. I *would* control it. One easy kill shot, and Josephine would be gone. Screw her mercy. I took a deep breath and prepared a spell. If I could contain the magic in a spell rather than using raw elemental magic, I had a chance at saving everyone.

Just not myself.

Binding this magic into a spell would take everything I had. I knew it, but the realization didn't fill me with trepidation. An odd sense of peace settled in my bones. My mother had died in the most noble of sacrifices. I could follow her into Summerland doing the same.

"Kill me and you kill him!" Josephine shouted. Her harsh words were enough to grab my attention. "He's blood-bound to a dual, remember? Can you hear me past the magic's roar? No interference."

My heart dropped.

Cowboy, I thought. *What have you done?*

CHAPTER THIRTY-TWO

Walker

"He's blood-bound to a dual. No interference."

Freya stared at me in horror.

Her skin glowed from the power writhing inside her, and her dark veins grew more and more swollen. Light completely swallowed her irises, and her hands shook. I didn't doubt Josephine's claims—if Freya didn't release that magic soon, she'd die.

And she wouldn't release it until my blood pact was complete, not if it meant taking out Josephine in the process.

And killing me.

Josephine still faced Freya. The Bloodblade was loose in her grip, and breathlessness had slipped into her speech. Using the Bloodblade—*trying to kill my sister*—had tired her. Even more to my advantage, a witch had once again underestimated me.

For the *last* time, a witch underestimated me.

Hesitation no longer existed for me. It had ceased the moment Josephine wielded the Bloodblade against Cadence. Hell, it had ceased the moment I'd seen Freya crumpled on the ground. With a true witch hunter's speed, I slipped around Josephine, wrenched the Bloodblade from her grip, and drove it into her stomach.

Its jet-black hilt burned my palms, and molten heat moved through my whole body. Its magic rattled my chest and shook my bones. Red light streaked from the blade and into Josephine's prone body.

For the first time, Josephine faced me with fear in her eyes. Red lightning snaked under her skin, but she found the strength to look over my shoulder.

"You'll understand now, dearest," she whispered.

Freya screamed.

I finally grasped the Bloodblade's true power. It raged through me like a lightning rod. The heat before was nothing. It had been a hot summer day or a warm bath.

This was an inferno.

My vision darkened around the edges, but the blade glowed brighter and brighter. I closed my eyes against its blinding heat, but it still burned the backs of my eyelids. Its deep, bellowing power filled my ears. Every inch of my skin was on fire from the pain of holding it, but I couldn't let go if I wanted to. My hand was no longer my own to control. I opened my mouth to scream, but my throat felt like ash itself.

My lungs gave up on breathing, and the familiar beat of my heart stuttered to an end. Calm darkness settled over me.

I was done.

I'd saved them.

*

Freya

You'll understand now, dearest.

As red lightning moved through Walker, the Bloodblade, and into Josephine herself, the echo of those words drowned out Josephine's dying screams. The power killed her in what felt like an instant, though it must have been more like a century to her, judging by the torment on her face. One heartbeat, she stood shrieking. The next, she was nothing but a dry bone on the forest floor.

When Walker fell to the ground, I did understand.

Humans were so very, very fragile.

Josephine had learned the hard way. Now, so had I.

I rushed to his side, only to be met by the Master. He

grinned and revealed his blood-stained fangs.

"Pity, little witch," he teased. "He would've been *so* delicious."

Cadence sobbed at his words, but one of the Elders kept her from trying to bypass the vampire before us. I simmered in my own stillness, even as magic roiled and raged in my veins.

Walker could not be gone.

"You must leave here now," Gloria said from behind me. "You too are bound by the rules of the blood bond."

"*Tsk, tsk, tsk,*" he said and shook his pointer finger. "They technically died at the same time. Josephine was not the only one tired of living in darkness, stuck under the thumb of the Leaders' rule. Our fight is not over."

The Master's followers and the dark witches stirred behind him. All the golems had promptly turned back into sand upon Josephine's death. My grip on the magic raging inside me loosened a fraction, and my skin glowed even brighter.

I shook with disbelief.

Walker had saved us.

A human boy who hadn't even thought himself capable of fitting into this world had *saved* it, yet these monsters were still hungry for blood. They would make nothing of his bravery because he was nothing to them.

As I realized just how much he was to me, my heart cracked open and, with it, power that was distinctly mine unleashed itself, mingling with the magic of my fallen sisters.

It *burned.*

"Get out of here," I whispered to my remaining allies.

I only held back a second longer. It was the last saving grace I had left for them.

With one shuddering breath, I erupted.

Flames as red as my hair flew across the field and assaulted my enemies. Sweat beaded down my skin, and power roared in my ears. Vampires and witches portaled away, but many were not quick enough. I didn't care one way or another. All I knew was that this had to end.

No one else would get in my way.

I had to save him.

My flames burned for a few heartbeats after the last dark witch had escaped. My fire burned the blood from the ground and the dark magic from the soil. I stopped the flames before all the power I contained could slip away. For a moment, there was only my ragged breaths, the dim hum of magic, and Walker's too-still form on the only unburned patch of ground left.

"They're all gone, Freya," Cadence said behind me. "It's over."

Her small, broken voice brought me back to reality. I turned and saw that all of my coven had returned. They must've portaled back to me as soon as they felt my flames run their course. Each witch stood like statues, unsure of how to mourn the witch hunter who'd saved us all.

Cadence ran to her brother, but I took careful steps in his direction. Now that the rage had burned its way across the whole battlefield, I was filled with dread.

"The wolves?" I said. "Arion?"

"They made it out," Gloria answered. "We'd already begun portaling them away when we saw the magic fighting to be unleashed."

I nodded, but I didn't have it in my heart to feel relief.

You'll understand now, darling.

As the blood moon gave way to sunrise, Walker's sun-kissed skin remained pale. His curls were crusted with blood and dirt. The Bloodblade lay dormant at his side. Its power was nothing more than a whisper on the wind. Even his godsdamned hat had fallen off. Everything was so terribly still.

Except for Cadence.

She sobbed and fell to the ground from the force of her pain. She really was a witch—she'd waited to truly lose it until our enemy was defeated once and for all. An Elder, Rhea, tried to comfort her. I couldn't bring myself to do the same, though I knew it was what he would've wanted.

He'd gotten enough of what he wanted when he died for

me.

I knelt by his side and wondered how I'd ever get up. There would be no vengeance for me to chase, and no kind-eyed boy to raise my spirits. Staring at his ghastly face, a part of me shattered. That part of me screamed and cried and raged at the world for taking something so precious from her. So *vital.*

I didn't name the feeling that welled in my chest. Staring at his corpse, I couldn't bear to.

Physically, I was as still as Walker. Drained of energy, my body felt disconnected from the emotions that clenched my heart. It was as if it had broken so terribly, my body knew the organ would never be righted. My body would have to learn to make do without it.

With shaking hands, I brushed his hair out of his eyes, which remained closed under my touch. Slowly, my hand traveled over the smooth planes of his face to his throat.

"You stupid boy," I whispered.

It was still warm, but nothing fluttered under my touch.

Then, I felt it.

A flicker of life emanated from him. As I pushed magic into his veins to be sure of what I sensed, my heart sprang back to life. It wasn't just warmth that his body still held.

His spirit hadn't gone to the Beyond yet.

I gasped.

My mother always said that everything left its print on the world. It was why powerful spells left behind reverberations. Nothing could come into and out of existence without leaving a print, unless its spirit or life force was truly gone.

Life was the one element of the world witches were taught to leave be.

For the first time, it felt like such a terrible, silly rule. Faced with Walker's death, my kind's most sacred law was whittled down to a brittle obstacle.

What good does a rule do the world if Walker isn't in that world?

And besides that, he *wanted* to live. His spirit still clung to this realm. This was what had driven me to cling to the remnants of magic. I couldn't save my mother or the other fallen witches, but I could save him.

"Freya," Gloria chided. "Let him go, child. His time here is done."

I glanced back at her. Her brows were furrowed in worry.

Stupid, senseless hope swelled in my chest.

"You feel it too," I said. "He's not gone—not yet."

The rest of my coven gathered closer and shifted uncomfortably. The wolves—possible witnesses—remained absent.

"What do you mean?" Cadence whispered.

She lifted her head and her bloodshot eyes met mine. Desperation lined her face, and she crawled to where I knelt.

"If he's not gone," she said and swallowed tears, "then *save* him!"

His heart no longer beat in his chest. Every second wasted was a step further from bringing him back. It was likely already too late.

Even if it does work, he might kill me for doing it.

"Freya," Gloria snapped. "You *can't.*"

Cadence refused to tear her gaze from mine, but I couldn't stand its weight. I looked at Walker, who lay so, so still. He didn't crack a smile or nervously run a hand through his hair. He didn't offer any goofy compliments or trade insults. He couldn't even open his eyes, which I'd grown to find beautiful. Not just because of their sky blue color, but because they looked at me like I was the most captivating thing they'd ever seen.

Walker, who was so painfully human, yet more *alive* than any immortal who'd crossed my path.

Walker, who'd died for me.

"He's the only reason we still stand here." I rose to my feet. "His fate was sealed by a member of *our* coven. *Our* responsibility. A life-debt is owed."

I met the gazes of the Elders with unflinching certainty. This was the right thing to do. It was the *only* thing to do.

Walker could not be gone. And not because of a debt, but because, without him, I might choke on all the things I didn't get to say.

"He can't die," I whispered.

"Your mother died for his sister," one of the Elders, Lyra, argued. "It's already been paid."

I ran my eyes over her fine robes, grim face, and silky hair. Of course, she couldn't understand the weight of death. She was over three hundred years old.

"He saved countless lives today," I argued. "My mother, brave as she was, technically saved a witch—a member of our coven at that."

"You'll get us all killed," Gloria accused.

My resolve wavered, but only for a second. Saving Walker, no matter how it had to happen, could not be a bad thing. There was no world that would be better without him. He was so godsdamned *good*.

I only hoped I didn't get my coven killed to save him.

"What about him, Freya?" Rhea challenged. "You know the risks."

"He's not a normal human," I argued. "He's different—his spirit still fights even after wielding the Bloodblade."

Cadence wiped the tears from her face. "Whatever it is, my brother can handle it. Walker handles everything."

They still stared at us in uncertainty.

"No one's ever tried to turn a hunter," I reminded them, "or a man with witch blood."

Gloria scoffed. "That's for certain."

"The High Witch won't be happy," Lyra added.

"The High Witch failed to lift a damn finger throughout Josephine's entire crusade," I shot back and took a deep breath. "I'm doing this, with or without you, but I'd very much prefer your help. The more power thrown into this, the better chance of it working. You all know that."

Like lost lambs, they stared at me. Unsure of how else to convince them, I faced Walker and once again knelt by his side. I took his hand in mine. Already, it had cooled, but his soul fought.

    Keep fighting, cowboy, I thought. *You'll need that spirit if you're to become a witch.*

EPILOGUE

Walker

Cold darkness surrounded me. No stars twinkled in the sky, and no trees swayed on the horizon. I couldn't even discern my own body in the endless sea of nothing. I only felt the absence of heat in my limbs and the lack of air in my lungs.

Is this death?

At least flames no longer burned through my veins. I didn't have to dodge any mythical creatures' attacks. I didn't have to fear I might not see tomorrow. The fight was over. I'd made sure of it.

I could sleep.

A close-lipped smile stretched across my face.

"I know how you feel," a warm, feminine voice said. "Peace is a wondrous thing."

I opened my eyes and surged upright. Her green eyes shone like gems in the night, and her warm brown skin glowed. She sat cross-legged on a floor of nothing at all, though her shimmery white dress pooled by her feet.

Peace you just ruined.

"Who are you?" I asked.

"I don't like to list all the necessary greats," she said and cast her dark brown hair over her shoulder. "But I'm essentially your grandmother, Gwendolyn Moonflower."

I swallowed.

"You're the witch," I whispered. "The one who left her coven."

She smiled, then sighed. "The one and only."

I floundered with this information. As if I shouldn't be thinking at all, my thoughts moved sluggishly.

"Am I dead?" I asked.

She shrugged. "That's up to you."

I ran a hand through my hair. Though I couldn't see myself, I still sensed all my body parts. The longer I spoke to my ancestor, the more awake I became.

"You really are a witch," I muttered. "You speak in riddles."

She laughed, and it echoed into the void that surrounded us.

"I can help you get back, child," she promised. "Even in death, I'm not completely without power, though it has to be your choice."

I stared into the darkness until images formed in their depths. The arc of a flaming sword. Dad's strong embrace. The fluid gait of my horse. The sun as it set on the skyline, and the world flared with color. Trees as green as Cadence's eyes. The lift of my fearless sister's chin when anyone dared challenge her.

Sunshine that burned as vibrantly as Freya's hair. The curve of her smile she reluctantly let take shape on her face when she thought no one was looking. Little did she know, I was always looking at her.

I couldn't help myself.

"Can I see them?" I asked.

Gwendolyn shook her head. "Not like this. You can rest and dream, or you can return and be among them."

Her voice was free of judgement. I deserved rest after all. All my life, I worked and worked and fought just for the next day. Cadence wouldn't judge me for wanting some damn sleep.

Freya would.

A smile tugged on my lips.

"I want to go back," I said, then added, "please."

"Know your life will not be without great pain," she warned. "I can't even promise I won't see you again here soon."

A real optimist, I thought.

"Better then than now," I said.

She peered at me for a moment longer, then grinned.

"Have a safe trip back."

Into the fire, I returned.

ACKNOWLEDGEMENT

First and foremost, I'd like to thank my big sister because if I don't, she might kill me. For real, thank you Riley for always pushing me to be my best, making me laugh when I'm down, and reading everything I throw at you, good or bad. Thank you to my parents again for providing me with everything I could ever need, including my education. I'd like to give a special shoutout to my mom for driving me to the bookstore day or night, rain or shine, to foster my love of literature. I'm also forever grateful to the professor who made me believe I could do this, Mel Odom. I'll never forget your dedication to storytelling, your devotion to teaching, nor your hatred of -ing verbs.

Thank you to all my Gaylord College peers for creating such a warm and welcoming community that allowed my writing skills to prosper in a way I never imagined they could. I'd like to specifically thank my classmate and friend Robbie Wood for creating such a beautiful cover. Thank you to all my friends and family from other facets of life who have offered me nothing but support. My horse show community, my choir buddies, and my wonderful extended family, thank you. I am lucky to have such a wonderful and diverse group of people in my corner.

ABOUT THE AUTHOR

Ryen Rowe is a Norman, Oklahoma native and proud student at the University of Oklahoma. She is currently pursuing degrees in both Professional Writing and Music, with a Minor in Sociology. Ryen is an animal lover and a multi-world champion equestrian. When she's not reading, writing, or singing, she is probably at the barn, caring for her family's many Morgan horses. She loves stretching the limits of her imagination with her fantastical stories, but also writing about love in all its forms —familial, platonic, and romantic. For more information and to stay up to date with her future publications, follow her Instagram, and check out her website.

Instagram: @ryen_the_writer

Website: ryenthewriter.com

Made in the USA
Las Vegas, NV
01 December 2024

13041487R00138